RETRIBUTION

RETRIBUTION

WILBUR MCKESSON

*In memory of my aunt Riley Rose McKesson.
I wouldn't have made it this far without you.*

CHARACTERS

THE BERING GROUP

Jack Knowles – Leader in charge of the Bering Group

Max Fontaine – Senior Clandestine Operator

Courtney Dixon – Clandestine Operator

Kwame Gbeho – Clandestine Operator

Alex Fuentes – Clandestine Operator

Nate Ridley – Clandestine Operator

Antonio Diaz – Clandestine Operator

CIA "THE AGENCY"

Alexis Moore – Director of National Intelligence

Janet Carrera – Chief of Clandestine Operations, CIA

David Carter – Director, CIA

Lakshani Dissayanke – Directorate of Operations Language
Officer in Sri Lanka

Aydin Aksoy — Directorate of Operations in Turkey

WHITE HOUSE STAFF

Harrison Abner – President of the United States

Ethan Cox – Secretary of Defense

Jake Bower – Department of Justice

General Godwin – General and Commander, USSOCOM

EXTRA CHARACTERS

Josh Quinn – Commander, HRT

Bryce Holden – Second-in-Command, HRT

Dennis Baker – Drone pilot

Khaled Ahmadi – ISIS member

Matthew Siff – Employee of Khaled Ahmadi

PROLOGUE

The southwest monsoon rains during the month of September typically plagued Sri Lanka at any time of the day or night, but Mother Nature had a different schedule for when the terrorists entered the country.

Landing in Colombo at ten o' clock in the morning, short sleeves and sunglasses were the weapons of choice for the bright sun reflecting off the mirrored skyscrapers in the city. The three-and-a-half-hour drive to Minneriya should have been an easy one. Cracked streets, herds of elephants, and brightly colored, open-air, three-wheeled vehicles mimicking the sound of a small engine, also known as a *tuk-tuk*, added an additional two and a half hours to the rendezvous point. The heat, coupled with the humidity, was unbearable. Rumor had it you could fry an egg on whatever slab of intact concrete you could find.

The beat-up minivan navigated the maze of obstructions, and Khaled Ahmadi, sitting in the back of the vehicle, closed his eyes and prayed the destination would arrive soon. Suffering from fatigue, dizziness, and slight vomiting in his mouth, he cursed every time the driver ran over a pothole or swerved to avoid one. He'd purchased a sickness patch for the long drive, which he'd placed behind his right ear, however, it didn't seem to be working.

The group of four flew with no checked bags, only carry-ons. Staying any longer than their plan of one night would be a problem. The contact they were meeting came highly recommended. If this was not the case Khaled would have asked—no insisted—that their contact meet them in Syria. The terrorist hated traveling.

People were disgusting, nobody respected personal space, and the constant staring at him and his entourage like he had a bomb strapped to his chest was infuriating. Especially the Americans, the infidels, they always thought—no, expected—something to happen when he passed by them.

He didn't just hate traveling, he despised it with a passion.

Khaled was a part of the Islamic State of Iraq and Syria, also known as ISIS. He was a deputy, one of the highest positions bestowed on someone in his organization. The only position above him was the Baghdadi, the supreme political and religious leader in a territory. When he was younger, he dreamed of one day becoming a Baghdadi, but that flame was extinguished a long time ago.

Khaled oversaw a portion of the northern territory in Syria, each part of the country divided to their own deputies. Decades passed as Khaled gnawed and climbed his way to his current position. He did this by working hard, fighting harder, and losing loyal men. His ambitious efforts over the course of his tenure yielded a substantial leg injury, but it was worth it.

Khaled just had to convince the Baghdadi and his council of appointees, called the Shura, to approve his request. With a mission as important as this—his last, and leading to his version of retirement—his orders were to meet the contact himself in person and immediately report back. The council would then decide whether or not the plan Khaled wanted to implement could come to fruition, and if the endgame was worth the risk.

The driver swerved into oncoming traffic, overtaking a blue tuk-tuk. Instincts kicked in as Khaled gripped the bar on the ceiling, scolding his driver. After hours of endless praying, swerving, and praying some more, they pulled off the road into the dirt. The driver shifted into neutral and turned off the engine.

The three other men, wearing shorts, short sleeve shirts, and tennis shoes, not typically the uniform of choice, but trying to not stand out too much, jumped out of the van and headed into the small restaurant to ensure it was safe. Jalal, the driver and youngest member of the group, opened the door as yet another tuk-tuk passed him by at arm's length. Quickly reaching into the door panel, Jalal snatched the old-school Colt .45 pistol and brought it to eye level, bringing the front sight to the back of the tuk-tuk gaining distance.

"Fuck this place!" Jalal exclaimed, taking his finger off the trigger and shoving the pistol into the small of his back. He closed the door and walked around the van and waited for the other guards to give the all clear inside the restaurant. After the group landed in Colombo, making their way out of the airport and to the van, they found the keys in the tailpipe and the pistols in a cutout underneath the carpet in the cargo area.

Sitting inside the van, Khaled put the sunglasses over his eyes and witnessed life around him. Nothing but luscious Mee, Batadomba, Kenda, and Kos Del trees as far as the eye could see, engulfing the sides of the streets for miles. The scenery was better than the barren desert he was used to. Two cement houses with tin roofs sat quietly across the street. Children played in the dirt front yards while the occasional Sri-Lankan man or woman walked past them, wearing ragged shirts and pants. All else was quiet except for the vehicles passing by.

Three hours outside of Colombo reminded Khaled how far removed from civilization they actually were. Leaning back on the weathered seat, the springs underneath screamed in agony. One of his security guards exited the establishment and waved them forward. *Here we go*, he thought.

Jalal slid the passenger-side door open for Khaled, reached underneath the seat, and grabbed his boss's cane, noting the unusual black shaft with a golden circle at the top. He handed it to Khaled, who gripped it and drove it carefully onto the soft dirt below. The shaft sank into the dirt while he willed his injured right leg forward. Leaning on it hurt like hell every now and then, but it was possible. Before the surgery, resulting in the cane, painkillers, and muscle relaxers had helped numb the pain.

A herniated disc was the diagnosis, and every now and then the muscles surrounding the disc became inflamed, causing tightness and excruciating pain to shoot down the leg. He had talked to numerous doctors who'd informed him that a potential back surgery to remove the disc to relieve the pain was a last resort. This was because once you started, while the immediate pain might go away, the back developed more problems as a result of the surgery. Regardless, the surgery had been completed, and two years later he was walking almost pain-free and with a massive limp. That's what happens when you go to the best black market doctor who does surgeries in his guest bedroom.

And yet, Allah wanted him stable.

Following up with his left leg, he stood tall and arched his back, stretching the tensed muscles. Sitting for long rides never helped the situation. Breathing in the humid air, a sigh of relief swept over his body. Sure, it was hot, but at least he was out of that fucking van. Walking forward, he finally started his journey to the entrance of the restaurant. Jalal following close behind.

Moving past his first security guard, who was standing outside, monitoring the street, and watching the van, Khaled awarded the guard an appreciative nod. Thrusting his cane first, left leg, then right, he moved down the dilapidated path through the front of the outdoor restaurant and into the back. He had never met this person before, but the amount of conversation with him over the previous months on the phone had put his mind at ease, although, in his line of work, he was never truly *at ease*.

His other two security guards were waiting for him further along the short path, guiding him with their hands in the proper direction. Khaled tried his best, using his cane and feet with the numerous two-foot by two-foot concrete squares that were evenly spaced between dirt and grass and led deeper into the canopy-laden restaurant. Step by step, he moved past a young American couple enjoying their drinks and gazing into each other's eyes, *Infidels*, he thought. The path ended, exposing a group of tables tightly inter-twined together. Moving toward his target, the soft *thump, thump* of his cane caused the man to turn.

"I imagined you would be shorter," said the man, sipping his Lion beer.

Ignoring the comment, Khaled pulled a chair across from the blond-haired man and sat down. The man was built like a wres-tler, with all the confidence in the world that if someone were to sneak up on him, he would hip toss him into oblivion. He wore a bright blue Hawaiian button-up shirt with orange-red flowers, the top two buttons undone, and tan cargo pants. Lifting his arm to take another swig, Khaled noticed his watch sported a crown logo on the dial and a half-blue, half-red bezel resembling the colors of a Pepsi can. He knew a Rolex when he saw one. *Americans are always flaunting their money*, he thought.

"Tell me, Matthew, do all you Americans purposely dress like they do in the movies or do some of you actually try to look like you're blending into the surroundings?" asked Khaled. Looking past Matthew, Khaled witnessed Jalal and the two other guards flag a waiter down to order drinks.

"Depends on my mood," said Matthew, smiling and taking another sip of his beer. Grabbing a plastic water bottle that was covered in duct tape, Matthew put it to his mouth and spat a brown liquid into it. "Do you always travel with security to show the world that you're someone of importance? It's not very subtle if you ask me."

"I thought you were supposed to be from Georgia or some-place like that; you don't sound like it," said Khaled.

"It'll come out when I get excited," Matthew answered.

Leaning back in his rickety chair and feeling the wood bend, Khaled said, "I don't want to be here any longer than I have to and I have a long drive back. Show me the documents."

"Straight to the point. I knew there was a reason I liked you," Matthew said, reaching into the backpack sitting underneath the table. Producing a five-part folder and sliding it to Khaled, he tilted his head back, finishing the last of the Lion. Setting the empty bottle back onto the table and waving to the waiter, he ordered a second beer. "Khaled, what do you want to drink? My treat."

"Water," he said, without looking up from opening the folder. The waiter left as Khaled pulled the individual files from inside the black folder, studying every inch of paper laid out in front of him as if it was a study guide to the bar exam. "It's been a long time coming, but finally."

"Out of curiosity," said Matthew, "what did these people do that caused you to shell out so much money? I've been in this business a long time and you are by far my highest paying client."

Ignoring Matthew, Khaled flipped through the four files and reached yet again through the folder as if to look for one more. "Where is the fifth file?" he asked.

"I couldn't get it," Matthew answered.

"I paid you top dollar for all five files and that's exactly what I expected," said Khaled, his blood pressure starting to rise.

Matthew said, "Listen, the last guy is CIA, that's all I know. I'm good at what I do and am confident..." He paused as the waiter came back, delivered their drinks with a polite nod, and walked back to Jalal's table. "...Confident in my abilities, but I couldn't get it. My contact in the CIA who I used to go through was pronounced dead a couple of months ago in Key West. She was good, but unfortunately that was the closest link I had. I had to start from scratch finding someone to fill your order," he said.

"Do you have any idea how far I've flown and how tired I am?" asked Khaled, slamming his fists on the files in front of him. His guards, noticing, started to rise as Khaled raised his left hand slightly off the table, causing the guards to sit back down. "I have to go back and ask the council if I can proceed as planned even though I only have four of the five people I requested."

Taking a long sip of his beer, Matthew said, "Look, I tried and unfortunately it wasn't in the cards. You should be lucky I got you the files that I did. Those weren't easy to come by."

Leaning back in his seat once more, closing his eyes and letting out a short prayer to Allah, he breathed deeply and exhaled. "Fine," he said, "I'll take these, but you're only getting half the money we agreed to."

"Excuse me?" asked Matthew, "We had a deal and it's not my fault—"

"It's not your fault my flight was delayed for an hour on the way here, it's not your fault a woman gets raped because some guy is too horny and incompetent to just ask for a date, but it *is* your fault that you promised to deliver on a product you couldn't. I'm old and my body has no time for excuses anymore. Especially from Americans. You people are full of it, never accepting responsibility and always blaming everyone else."

Sighing, reaching for his beer and spilling some of it in the process, Matthew brought it to his mouth and paused. "Alright, calm down, calm down. I tried, and if you can't appreciate it then so be it. I'll get paid from whatever project comes up next."

Giving the nod, which signaled to his men that it was time to go, Khaled took a couple of long sips from his water glass. "Don't worry," he said, "I've already got an idea how to clean up your mess."

"Oh really? And what's that?"

"You mentioned once over the phone that you're a pilot, correct?"

"Sure am, get me anything with wings and I'll get you to your destination," Matthew said. "Where you tryin' to go?"

Khaled reached for his cane, "Just keep your phone on. I may have a way for you to earn that last half of your money back."

CHAPTER 1

Dennis Baker walked into the two-story building, through the metal detector, and down the hall. Walking up to the door at the end of the hall with the encrypted keypad, he entered the five-digit numerical code and listened to the lock as it slid to the left. Pulling the heavy door open, he entered the room precisely ten minutes before his shift.

The room was dark, cold, and illuminated by the assortment of screens on the two desks next to the wall directly in front of Dennis. Each desk contained a nice, big, black leather chair for each pilot, and four large monitors each portraying a different scene. The images ranged from the camera on the actual drone to a simple desktop background with Microsoft Outlook for emails. It had to be as comfortable as possible if the pilots were going to be sitting in the chairs for hours on end.

Dennis was one of few unmanned aerial vehicle pilots for the new Border Patrol UAV assaulter program, a position he didn't think he would get. With only a handful of years working with Border Patrol, he was sure one of his senior officers would snag the position, but no one in his division applied for it.

The black coffee he sipped scalded the inside of his mouth. Jerking his head back, he set the cup back on the desk. Rubbing his eyes, he checked his watch. The orange minute hand rested over the twelve o'clock position, while the hour hand sat above the nine on his Caribbean Doxa Sub 300T. He had wanted the well-known orange dial on the dive watch, but settled on the blue. It would go better with the suits he imagined himself wearing on dates, however, he was so caught up with work that he hadn't been on any for over a year.

Pushing his loser status out of his mind, Dennis plugged his personal identification card into the slot on his computer, and the screen changed colors, pulling his profile information from the chip embedded within the card.

Up until now, all the UAVs acquired by Border Patrol were used strictly for surveillance, ensuring their agents working downrange had some sort of oversight. It wasn't until agents started getting killed at the border by cartel members, that Border Patrol decided to attach a modified lightweight M230 chain gun. Similar to the ones used on Apaches, the machine gun fired the same 30mm rounds to a target, and was attached to the bottom center of the drone.

The chain gun weighed approximately one-hundred thirty pounds, so modifications were done to the rear of the aircraft to ensure it was perfectly balanced. The idea of missiles was considered, then disbanded just as quickly. Missiles were associated with the military, which in turn was associated with war. Even though the United States versus the cartels in Mexico was a war that had been raging for decades, American citizens didn't need to see it as such and the Border Patrol didn't need any bad press of its new program.

The drones were scheduled to fly several miles into the desert and shoot the targets that had been set up the day before. Dennis and Jessica were based out of Nogales, Arizona, and their drones sat inside the safety of a hangar on Nellis Air Force Base, in Las Vegas, Nevada. Using satellites, GPS, and a wide array of computers, the pilots were able to fly the drones virtually anywhere in the world from the safety of their desks inside an air-conditioned building.

Taking another sip of his coffee, this one a tad cooler, he heard the lock disengage and he turned his head, catching a quick a glimpse of his boss and the man's entourage entering the room. Closing his eyes only for a brief moment, he relaxed and mentally prepared for the drone's final test run before being implemented into full service. Moving the lever below his seat, the chair dropped as he turned to make small talk with his coworker and office mate, Jessica.

She was a hair shorter than him at five feet six inches and she had light brown eyes matching her short hair that fell just below her chin. A physique competitor in her college days, Jessica was considered the most fit person in the entire building and was the only person, on the team of eight rotating pilots, who showed up to their shift earlier than Dennis.

"First things first, happy Veterans Day," he said.

"Happy Veterans Day to you as well, Dennis," responded Jessica.

"Second, how are we looking?" he asked. Dennis already knew the answer, having double and triple-checked the weather and radar on his personal tablet before leaving his apartment.

"We're fine, Dennis," she said. "The same answer I gave you right when you texted me as you pulled in, and it'll be the same answer I will give you when you ask five minutes from now." She loved working with Dennis and knew he was a stickler about everything involving the drones. Her, not so much, but he knew she enjoyed the playful banter and friendly relationship the pair had developed.

Dennis gave her a thumbs-up and slid his headset on. "I can't wait to show these guys what this bad boy can do."

"Yeah, it should be exciting," she replied. "I was up all night dreaming of this moment, sitting in this chair, and answering all your crazy-ass questions."

"Really?" asked Dennis, conducting his preflight checks.

"No," said Jessica, her blank expression with one raised eyebrow conveying everything. "I have two kids who had homework to do last night and a husband who got home late from work. I was dreaming I was getting chased by long division all damn night," she finished. Rolling her eyes, she looked back at the satellite imagery depicting their test field.

"Ugh, kids," was all Dennis could muster, turning back to continue with his preflight checks.

Fifteen minutes later, after answering questions from his boss and associates, Dennis received the all clear to launch the drone and begin the flight to the testing zone. He was beyond excited. Barely being able to contain himself, his hands shook keying the codes into the computer. The massive touchscreen and joystick combination sitting in front of him, in addition to the four, twenty-inch monitors sitting two by two on top of one another, was every hacker's dream.

Looking at Jessica, he reached over and held his arm out with a clenched fist. She bumped it twice, and immediately after the second fist bump they widened their fingers, imitating an explosion. It was their preflight ritual. The pair never encountered any accidents or technical issues, attributing some of the luck to the ritual. Neither one was superstitions, but when you were in control of a multimillion-dollar aircraft, you were better safe than sorry.

"Taxiing on the runway," said Dennis through his headset. The MQ-9 Reaper rolled out to the edge of the runway, and stopped, waiting for the next command.

"Reaper, six-eight-niner decimal one-five, you are clear for take-off," came the response from the control tower on the air force base.

"Weather is good...radar is good...you're clear to me," said Jessica, monitoring her quad screens. She was Dennis's eyes and ears to everything besides flying the drone.

"Roger," replied Dennis. "Initiating takeoff in three...two...one...rolling!"

Dennis eased the joystick forward, his other fingers resting on the respective buttons on the keyboard. Five seconds later the drone was soaring through the clear morning sky.

"Successful takeoff, sir," said Dennis, loud enough so the people standing behind him could hear.

"Thanks, Dennis," said Mark his boss, who gave him a pat on the shoulder. "Now fly us to our target and show us what that new cannon of hers can do."

"You got it, sir," he responded.

Dennis flew the drone over the next hour to their target destination and then, once he got closer to the target, he tilted the joystick ever so slightly to the left, but the drone didn't respond. Instead, it glided to the right.

"Dennis, I have your track line going left not right knucklehead," whispered Jessica. She was trying not to make a scene in front of Mark, who had gone back to talking amongst the rest of the group.

"Jess, I'm trying, but it won't budge."

"What do you mean it won't budge?" she asked, looking at his monitor. The camera on Dennis's screen, attached to the front of the drone, gave a crystal-clear view of the city below.

"Jess, something is wrong. I don't have the stick anymore," he said, meaning he had lost control of his aircraft. The slight resistance that was there when he moved the joystick just seconds prior was gone. It was as if the joystick was suddenly turned "off." Moving his right hand from the top of the joystick to the base, he tilted the stick as far left as it could go until it sat at a forty-five-degree angle. Nothing happened. Doing the same thing to the right, then forward and backward. Nothing. His blood pressure rising and getting the better of him, he angrily tapped the joystick with an open palm to the left and watched it spring back into the neutral position. "Oh, fuck me," he said under his breath.

"Wha—," Jessica stopped mid-sentence and wasn't ready for what happened next. The top left monitor, showing the image from the camera underneath the drone, showed the drone banking hard to the right and adjusting its path of flight. Jessica looked at the track line on the monitor sitting on the top right. A solid yellow line placed on a light blue background showed the track the drone was *supposed* to fly. The second the drone banked to the right, a red line appeared and branched off from the yellow one. The red line increased in length the further the drone flew from its main course.

"Dennis, radio it in," she whispered.

"Shit," he cursed under his breath. The last thing he wanted to do was radio in a rogue UAV, but there was nothing he could do.

"Sir," said Dennis, just loud enough to get Mark's attention. His boss walked over and stared at the screen, which showed the aircraft flying south over the I-10 Freeway. "We have a problem, sir."

"What do you mean, son?"

"Sir, I no longer have the sticks," he said in a low tone of voice, trying not to cause a commotion.

The amount of paperwork it took to acquire just one drone for the Border Patrol killed a small forest. Over the course of a year, everything from worst-case scenario to best-case scenario had to be written into a million and one different memos, routed up the chain of command, and sent back down when certain things were not listed. Once the program was given a green light, then came the test flights.

Day in and day out for six months, Dennis, Jessica, and the rest of the pilots were rotating around the clock. Preparing for every possible scenario from inclement weather to shooting specific targets with fake civilian targets close by. The commissioner of Border Patrol, who was causing the headache for the entire program despite the fact everyone below her wanted it to succeed, wanted something to go wrong, but it never happened. The culmination would be that day and Dennis wanted to be known as the guy who kickstarted the program, not the one who ended it.

There was a slight pause. "Are you sure?" Mark asked.

"Yes, sir, positive," he said, then demonstrated this by smacking the joystick to the left, to which the aircraft did not respond.

Sighing, Mark said, "Okay, stand by." Turning around, Mark made up some technical difficulties to clear out the space. Everyone exited except Mark and Mark's boss. Both men walked back to look at the screen.

"What should I do, sir?" asked Dennis. All four individuals in the space were in shock and awe, monitoring the drone that was now pulling off the freeway and showing desert mixed with suburban neighborhoods.

"Sir, it looks like the drone has picked a target," said Jessica, as a bright red, box notification appeared across the huge touchscreen on the desk.

"What? Who's calling the shots if it's not you two?" asked Mark, leaning over Jessica's right shoulder at the address now appearing on her screen.

"Sir!" screamed Dennis, pointing at the red warning indication blinking on the bottom of his monitor.

"It's armed itself!" he screamed.

"Dennis, call it in, now!" said Mark.

Dennis clicked a switch on the base of the joystick then cleared his throat. "Control tower, this is Border Patrol Reaper six-eight-niner decimal one-five, over."

After a brief couple of seconds they responded, "Reaper, this is the control tower, you have us, go ahead."

"Control tower, reaper...ugh...I have lost control of our drone and it has acquired a target—." Looking at Jessica, he watched her slide her right index finger up on the touchscreen on the desk as the address and approximate distance from Pheonix, the closest city, slid onto one of the monitors "—approximately ten minutes outside of the city, over."

With the amount of sweat dripping from his forehead, Dennis was surprised he could still grip the joystick. Anxiety caused his hands to shake every time he tried to touch it.

"Roger, Reaper, authenticate distress code," came the response through the external speaker. Mark reached over, turning up the volume loud enough to reverberate across the entire room.

"Control tower, Roger...stand by," said Dennis. Leaning over to his right he ripped open the desk drawer looking for the list of codes for certain situations.

"Shit, where is it?!" he said, now leaning over completely to rummage through the drawer.

"Dennis!" shouted Jessica. "I got it," she said. When she finished reading the codes, all she heard was, "Roger, Reaper, we're scrambling the quick reaction alert team out of Luke Air Force Base in Phoenix. We have the drone's position and are tracking it via satellite feeds."

"Roger," Jessica responded. The red distance to target indicator in the top right corner of the screen calculated eight and a half minutes to target. Deep down all four members knew by the time the pilots scrambled to their jets, taxied to the runway, took off and intercepted the drone it would be close.

Everyone watched Jessica's monitor as the drone flew over small towns, miles of dirt and desert seeming like an endless wasteland, and small rock formations as it neared its target. Time ticked away as it lowered altitude and was now five hundred feet above a one-story house, circling it. Just then, the clear imagery was replaced by thermal imaging. On the monitor were two orange and reddish colored heat signatures moving around inside of the house.

"Reaper, control tower, our jets are scrambled and are three minutes out from the target. The pilots are requesting any amplifying information about the drone."

"We have nothing! And tell them they don't have three minutes!" barked Mark, but by the time Dennis relayed what they were witnessing, it was too late.

The room was silent as everyone watched in horror as a short burst of gunfire erupted from the turret. In the blink of an eye the two thermal figures moving around were immobile, and the nice roof of the house had been replaced by a gaping hole. A plume of smoke appeared, and then as quickly as the chain of events started, the thermal imaging returned to normal, and Dennis resumed control of the aircraft.

"Reaper, Luke Air Force Base...I...I have control again of the drone."

"Roger, understand, you have control of the drone, confirmed?"

"Yes," replied Dennis.

"Roger, the jets are approaching the target and you are required to fly the drone immediately to Luke Air Force Base. Be advised, the pilots have full authorization to shoot it down if you lose control again."

"Roger control, good copy on all," said Dennis. Mark's boss cursed, walked over to one of the barren walls, and slammed his open palm against it at full strength. Taking a second or two he said, "Listen, whatever happens after this, being in charge of this program and working with you guys day in and day out was some of the most fun I've had my whole career." And with that, Dennis, Jessica, and Mark watched their boss leave the room. The door closed on its own.

CHAPTER 2

"That traffic was insane," said Brandon Clark. "I knew we shouldn't have gone to the Mexican restaurant in Virginia Beach."

His wife, Peggy, ignored the comment and continued staring at her phone. It was just after one o'clock in the afternoon as the couple passed the last exit before diving through the Hampton Bridge Road Tunnel underneath the James River. Brandon and Peggy had made plans with their daughter to watch her two children while she and her husband enjoyed a long, three- day weekend in Asheville, North Carolina.

Both of them loved seeing their grandchildren, especially Brandon. Best of all, listening to his daughter lecturing him on how her children didn't need any more toys brought a smile to his face. *If only she knew how she was as a child*, Brandon always thought. He never said a word though, just smiled and nodded.

Together Brandon and Peggy had raised two children, Margaret and Leon, or at least that's what Brandon liked to think. Brandon joined the Navy at the young age of eighteen. After watching Navy SEAL documentaries and movies and television shows based on the elite Special Forces group, he knew he found his calling. Nothing would get in his way of becoming what most people in his situation only dreamt about. Shortly after completing basic underwater demolition training, better known as BUDs, he met Peggy and the world as he knew it was flipped on its axis. Years passed and as time moved on Peggy began to understand what it meant to be married to a military husband.

Each time Brandon prepped to take his wife to the hospital his burner phone connected to the operations center for the SEAL team he was attached to would ring. Then he would be off to save the world, leaving Peggy to give birth to both of their children alone. On the surface, she was appalled, and words couldn't describe the level of anger she expelled at him in rage and frustration, but on the inside she knew what came with the territory of marrying a SEAL. As the children grew up, whenever Brandon mentioned to either one of his children how much energy it took from him to raise them, his wife raised an eyebrow in his direction. He would quickly correct his statement to, "I mean your mother." This always got laughs from their kids and sent their dad into another room like a dog with his tail between his legs. But that was then. Now he had grandchildren of his own and he vowed to give them all the time he had never given his children.

After passing the last exit, traffic started to move again. Serving a majority of his military time in Virginia and living in Chesapeake, he had made a pact with Peggy to live on the opposite side of the tunnel. The Chesapeake-Norfolk side was always a mess.

The tunnel in question stretched three and a half miles, crossing from Hampton Roads into the southeastern portion of Virginia. There was another way to get to the southeastern portion, however, it often added time to the drive. The majority of people in the area found their route to Virginia Beach, Norfolk, and Suffolk through the Hampton Roads Bridge Tunnel (HBRT). This was comprised of a four-lane system, two-lanes on each side, going over manmade islands and taking the driver underneath the James River. Traffic was known all throughout the state as horrendous and to be avoided at all costs during rush hours. However, sometimes it would stop randomly throughout the day for whatever reason, causing traffic jams in all hours of the day. Moving closer to the bridge entrance, Brandon spotted red taillights and traffic was back at a standstill.

"There has to be something going on," said Peggy, straining to try and see over the cars in front of their truck. She brushed her red hair behind her left ear, and Brandon took a second, admiring her beauty, before turning back to the road and seeing red-and-blue lights in his rear- view mirror.

Being next to the turn off, where tunnel workers and operators sat right before the tunnel sloped underneath the bay, he had the space and turned the steering wheel slightly to the left, allowing the police SUV to pass through.

Honking behind him with their klaxon blaring, he said, "That's weird, I think they want us to pull over."

"Well, pull over then," Peggy said, telling their grandchildren in the back of the truck to settle down. Pulling further into the vacant parking lot full of random construction vehicles, concrete pipes, and slabs, Brandon threw the shifter into park and turned off the engine. Watching the police cruiser pull up and park behind him, lights still on, he watched as two police officers opened their doors, slowly approaching his truck on each side.

"I wonder what they want," said Peggy. "You paid the registration, right?"

"I'm pretty sure I did. Oh, no," said Brandon, "I did pay it but I forgot to put the sticker on the license plate."

"Jesus, Brandon, well, let's hope that's all it is."

"Yeah, no kidding, it should be fine though. The sticker is sitting at the house in the envelope on the counter," responded Brandon. "I'll put it on the license plate the second we get home."

Brandon rolled down both passenger and driver side windows as the police approached. "Officer, I apologize," he said, trying to get ahead of the way he thought the conversation was going to go.

"If it's about the sticker its literally sitting on the counter at the house. I'll put it on the second I get home."

There was a pregnant pause as both officers, of Middle Eastern descent, looked around at the deserted parking lot—empty for Veterans Day—and turned back to stare at Brandon and Peggy from their respective sides of the vehicle. "Sir, are you Brandon Clark?" The officer asked, his right hand on his firearm, holster unstrapped. Both officers were extremely close to the vehicle, but no closer than other times that Brandon had been pulled over.

"Yes, that's me. But how did you know my first name? This car is registered in my wife's name," he said, but it was too late. In light-ning speed, the officer on his side drew his taser and shot Brandon square in the chest at point-blank range. His wife screamed, while the other police officer unholstered his pistol, quickly screwed on a silencer, rested it gently on the windowsill, and told her to cover her mouth. She did.

Brandon "rode the lightning" as fifty-thousand volts moved effortlessly through his body. The plan was to pull Brandon over and get him completely off the bridge way before the tunnel, but due to traffic, this was the next best thing. While Brandon was immobilized, feeling every jolt of electricity flow through his body, the officer unsheathed a four-inch knife from his belt and simulta-neously released the trigger of the taser, ending the wave of volt-age. In a matter of seconds, the police officer had pressed the but-ton on the blade, releasing the safety and exposing the blade. In a quick motion, he slashed Brandon's throat.

A gunshot to the head would be easy, but there were too many cars passing by, and with the traffic jam, the method had to be adjusted. The police officers calmly walked back to their cars, killed the lights, pulled out, and merged back into the now moving traffic. The screams of Peggy and the cries of the chil-dren in the backseat echoed in the distance.

Daniel Lazar and Clarence Smith, along with their wives, checked into the Courtyard Marriott in Oahu. Between the two of them they had served forty years plus in the military, specifically on the SEAL teams. Daniel and Clarence were stationed on the West Coast the majority of their careers, constantly training in the Hawaiian Islands and making the islands their second home after San Diego.

The constant traveling to the islands was great and every time they traveled there they grew more fond of the island, its people, and the food, but there was one problem. Neither of their wives were ever able to fly out with them; they were always stuck at the house. Both Clarence and Daniel made promises to take them, but between the constant training and operations in the Special Forces community, they somehow never found the time. Now both men were retired and living in San Diego, one working at a local golf course, the other at a dive shop. The world was their oyster.

Landing around six in the early evening after a turbulent flight, the only thing on the minds of both couples was food and sleep. After checking in, a scrawny bellhop by the name of Adil greeted them, sporting a warm smile. He asked for their room numbers to take the luggage. Daniel and Clarence gave him their room numbers, left their luggage with him, and guided their beautiful wives to the rooms.

After the Americans were inside of the elevator and the door closed, Adil's smile went away and he walked into the employee break room. Entering, he looked around, and then realizing no one was in the room, he closed the door behind him. Reaching into his pocket while walking to his locker, he pulled out his burner phone to make a call. Flipping through the contacts he found the name he was looking for and dialed.

"Have you done it yet?" came the question.

"No, they just got here. Listening to them, it seems like they're going out to get food, then going to come back for the night," answered Adil, looking behind him.

"Good, call me when it's done."

Hanging up, he reached into the bottom of his locker and pulled out a small fanny pack. Unzipping it and reaching inside, he felt around until his hand wrapped around the handle of his Springfield XD RSP 9mm pistol. There was also a small silencer and an extra magazine. Perfect.

He was smiling, as this would be his first real assignment, given to him by his handler. He zipped the fanny pack, shoved it into the bowels of the locker, and shut the door and the lock. Leaving the room, he went back to grab the luggage cart to finish delivering it to their rooms.

A couple of hours later, as if on cue, while he was flirting with his blond co-worker, he noticed his targets walking back through the lobby and to the elevators. Adil ended the conversation. He had only been working there a short while and told people he was using the money to, "help him get through college." In reality, the money he received from providing valuable information to his handler about various military training sites, facilities, and people on the island helped to fund his way through the University of Hawaii. He was a straight A student studying businesses administration and while the material came easily to him, putting thoughts of starting some sort of lucrative business in the United States into his head, he couldn't fathom it. He would be letting the caliphate down, but more importantly he would be letting Allah down.

He was just one member of what was known as a "sleeper cell"—a secretive group of terrorist agents that remained inactive within a target population until they were ordered to act. It's what he was paid to do and when the phone call came it didn't matter what he was currently engaged in. He did as he was told.

Entering the break room once again, after the afternoon shift had gone home, he unlocked his locker and reached for his bag. Quickly pulling out his pistol, threading on the silencer, and grabbing the extra magazine, he tucked it into the small of his back, covering it with his red Hawaiian shirt. Stepping back outside, he shut the door and waved to the attractive blond, but she didn't see him. She was busy with a new customer checking in. He didn't worry. He was promised money, a promotion in the terrorist ranks, and multiple women after three years of dedication and hard work reporting to his handler. This was it. After he completed this simple task he could finally go back to Syria and begin his training to become a soldier in ISIS.

Walking to the elevator, he pressed the button to go up, and the door automatically chimed open as he stepped inside. Turning to the right, he pressed the button for the tenth floor as the doors shut. He was a little nervous, but his excitement to prove to his handlers he could execute orders outweighed any other feelings he had. Adil took a couple of long breaths and with his eyes closed, tried to remember what his handler had told him. *Don't keep thinking about it or you will overthink and mess something up.* The elevator kept climbing and the higher it went the easier his breathing techniques became. It took some time, but eventually his heart rate slowed.

The two couples had booked rooms on the same floor. *This would be easy,* Adil thought. Although he had never killed anyone, the fact he could kill both of them without having to run to another side of the hotel was a plus. The elevator stopped and as he exited, he paused, letting the door close behind him. Feeling around and double-checking, no, triple-checking that the pistol was still there, he paused again. No noise anywhere in the hallway. Easy day.

Continuing to the first door on the right, he took a long breath and pressed the doorbell outside of the room. Moving his arms behind his back he practiced his smile. *That will throw them off for sure,* he thought.

As Clarence's wife opened the door, she was confused. A towel wrapped around her body, another around her hair, she leaned on the open door. "Oh, I remember you, did we forget something?" she asked.

Adil exposed his brown teeth with a gigantic smile. "No ma'am, not at all, I was just making sure all of your amenities were what you expected," Adil said.

"Oh, yes! My husband is in the shower but I think we both agree we couldn't have asked for a better hotel. It's amazing," she said. But with that, she had already provided more than enough information and Adil had heard enough. Gripping the butt of his pistol, he whipped his right arm around quickly, slamming the slide of the gun against her left temple. The force from the pistol, in conjunction with her head connecting with the side of the door-frame, knocked her out cold. Blood trickled from her ear.

Moving fast and stepping inside, he brought his gun up to eye level. Conducting a quick scan of the room, and after hearing the shower and a radio playing with some sort of country song in the background, he stashed the pistol in the small of his back again. Grabbing the unconscious victim's legs, he pulled her body into the room so the door could close.

Reacquiring his pistol, he turned the knob to the bathroom. Slowly opening the door, he saw the steam-filled mirror in front of him and the shower off to his left. Reaching for the hand towel sitting on the counter and wrapping it around his silencer, he knew better than to think the sound from the silenced pistol would render it as quiet as that of a pistol in a Hollywood movie.

"Hey baby, can you hand me a towel?" said the voice, as the

shower water stopped and the curtain was pulled back. Adil wasted no time, letting his pistol respond to the shocked man.

Adil pulled the trigger sending three muffled rounds point-blank into the man's chest, causing him to drop. Immobilized. Stepping into the shower, he admired his handiwork. He then stepped back outside the bathroom and into the hallway to start on the second SEAL down the hall. The wives weren't the targets, and he had specific instructions to only kill them if they posed a threat. A clear and concise message needed to be sent. Walking back to the unconscious wife lying on the floor, he reached down and felt a pulse on her neck.

"Good enough," he spoke to himself softly. "Time for the next one."

CHAPTER 3

"Everything looks good on my end," whispered Nate Ridley, the first of the Bering Group members. Nate had pale skin with black hair, and his thin, swimmer-cut frame made it easier to hide in the shadows and match his surroundings behind his M24 sniper rifle. The M24 was adopted by the United States Army in 1988 and was their equivalent to the Remington Model 700. Coincidentally, the Remington Model 700 was Nate's weapon of choice growing up and hunting elk in Montana with his brother and father. Being the precision marksman, Nate had an assortment of rifles at his disposal, so naturally the M24 was his soulmate.

Adjusting the expensive Leupold scope, Nate said, "I just watched the target enter the house."

"Copy," answered Antonio Diaz, the second member. He was only an inch taller than Nate but was ex-Colombian Special Forces. At forty-five years old, he still maintained his lean muscular frame due to earlier years of chasing cartels every week. Antonio had black hair, brown eyes, and grew his beard to its full potential, which helped to hide the wrinkles and small scars from the knife fights with the occasional *sicario*.

Antonio swept his binoculars from left to right, scanning for other threats on the property. If Nate was busy behind the scope of his rifle, he needed overwatch ensuring no one surprised him from behind.

Over the past couple of days, the team tracked their target to a cabin in the Blue Ridge Mountains. It was November, the leaves on the trees were long gone, and the temperature only continued to decrease. It wasn't freezing, but none of the Bering Group members favored the cold. Always looking toward the positives, it wasn't cold enough for snow on the ground. Yet. It could always be worse.

"I don't see anything on my end; you guys are in the clear," said Courtney Dixon, monitoring everything from a small computer screen connected to a drone overhead. She was the next member and was seated inside of a blacked-out van two miles down the heavily wooded hill across the street in a strip mall parking lot. At five feet six, she had blond hair and a CrossFit build. Her rigorous dedication to her workouts, in conjunction with her Brazilian jujitsu classes, made her a force to be reckoned with.

"I can't wait to have Ben back," she said to herself.

Ben Williamson was the only person on the team who was hired specifically for technological assistance. He deployed with the rest of the team but was behind the scenes hacking into computers and databases to give the team access where they couldn't go. He was invaluable. Unfortunately, because he worked behind the scenes, he often didn't train as hard or as much as the rest of the group, making him an easy target for his enemies.

A couple of months prior, Ben had been kidnapped by the Saint Bertrand Cartel then subsequently rescued soon after by the Bering Group. Ben was given a two-month sabbatical after the incident, and was currently going through a psychological evaluation before he could be cleared to work with the team again. Until he was cleared, it left the team at a significant disadvantage if they were called to action.

"Kwame, Alex, you ready to push?" asked Antonio.

"Yes, just give us the word," replied Alex Fuentes. Alex had been raised in Texas by his grandmother and grandfather after both of his parents had passed away in a car crash when he was only two years old. His grandmother spoke no English and his grandfather could barely get by, causing him to quickly learn English and inter-pret for the household. Even with all the translating as he grew up, he never could drop the heavy Hispanic accent. So, he just embraced it. But he really didn't care. He was built similarly to Antonio, but was just a tad bit leaner. Same black hair and brown eye color, but he was clean-shaven. Kwame Gbeho, on the other hand, was the exact opposite of all of them.

Kwame was gargantuan. Standing at six feet five, his medi-um-dark-skinned build intimidated even the hardest of people. He was an avid power lifter, ex-Ghanaian Special Forces operator, had black eyes, and was bald. Although his stature often scared people upon first glance, the second he opened his mouth to speak he was one of the sweetest people any of the other members knew. Their ages all ranged from twenty-four to forty-five, with Antonio being the eldest and the only person in their forties.

"Roger. Stand by," said Antonio. Taking one more look at the front of the house and not seeing anything moving, he said, "Execute."

Alex and Kwame, camouflaged in various woodland patterns matching their surroundings, began moving at a snail's pace to the back of the house. As long as the pair stayed in the tree line, they would be fine.

As the pair rotated around back, Kwame kept a solid number of paces behind Alex. "All clear," said Alex, who was the first to round the back portion of the cabin, the orange, red, and brown leaves crunching underneath his Merrills.

"I'm getting a bad feeling about this," said Kwame. His English was great, but when he was nervous or scared, which was rare, his Ghanaian accent stood out.

"What do you mean?"

Just then Courtney's voice was heard cackling through their earpieces, "Guys my screen just went black."

"What?—" asked Nate, stopping mid-sentence after catching movement in his peripherals. His eyes, darting up from his scope, narrowed in on a black widow just two feet beyond his left arm. Spiders were his worst nightmare.

"Bro! Do you not see that!" said Nate to Antonio, using his head to motion toward the arachnid.

Antonio pulled away from the binoculars and looked at the spider, now one foot away and between the both of them. "Relax, *compadre*, he's more scared of you than you are of him."

"I hate spiders, bro."

"Then pretend like he's not even there."

Nate raised his eyebrows at his partner and watched Antonio bury his eyes back into his binoculars. Moving his rifle to the left, just above the spider, he brought it down hard, killing it instantly. "Okay, now I'm good," Nate said. Antonio just shook his head.

"Courtney, we're almost set," said Alex from the back of the cabin. He and Kwame managed to nestle themselves behind a handful of thick trees right before the twenty-yard clearing to the back door. "You ready?" he asked Kwame.

"Courtney's drone had a perfect feed; there's not one cloud in the sky, and the feed goes down? Not a coincidence."

"You're unbelievable," responded Alex, shifting his eyes and pistol toward the back door.

"You don't think this guy made it easy on purpose for us to tail him for the past couple of days?"

"Nope."

"So, you don't have a bad feeling then?" replied Kwame.

"Nope, now let's go. I'll take the left side, you take the right."

Kwame exhaled. "Fine."

Just as Alex stood up, he fell to the ground just as quickly. A quick forearm strike slammed into the left side of his neck. The impact caused a shock to the cartridge artery, jugular vein, and vagus nerve. He collapsed to the ground in an unconscious state.

The second Kwame turned to his left to check his partner and address the noise, he found himself staring down the barrel of a silenced pistol and someone inside of a well-created ghillie suit.

The camouflage clothing material known as a "ghillie suit" had been around for decades and was used by militaries all over the world. The material was typically made from net or cloth material, covered in loose strips of burlap or twine and made to look like whatever environment the user dictated. From snowcapped mountains to the Sahara Desert and every sort of foliage in between, the suit was worth its money in gold for any operator trying to hide from their enemy.

The ghillie-suited individual moved his right arm to his mouth, and held up a single finger to his lips, motioning Kwame to stay silent. Kwame did and was forced to hand over his pistol. The man in the ghillie suit then handed Kwame a black burlap sack to place over his head. Tossing zip ties to Kwame, he was made to administer them to himself.

"Turn around and walk," said the man. Kwame did as he was told. Shifting behind Kwame, the person in the suit moved his pistol from Kwame's face to the small of his back. The barrel dug into his skin underneath Kwame's thermal, causing him to wince walking into the clearing. After a very short walk, the person in the suit instructed Kwame to give a quick rap on the door. A couple of seconds went by and the door opened. The muzzle dug yet again into his back, forcing Kwame into the cabin.

"There's one more I subdued, just out beyond the clearing," said the voice behind the suit.

"Okay," said the man inside the house, yanking Kwame forward.

The door shut as the individual in the ghillie suit secretly wrapped around to the front of the cabin, concentrated hard looking around, and spotted the remaining two individuals lying prone out in the trees. He decided to wait. Should they move toward the front of the cabin, he would have a clear line of sight. As long as they made their decision before nightfall, which was just two hours away, he would be fine, but he cursed under his breath for not having his night vision goggles.

"Where the hell are Alex and Kwame?" said Nate.

"I don't know, but something isn't right," he responded.

"Fuck it then, let's breach," said Nate. Antonio nodded. Doing a quick check of their surroundings, Antonio was the first to step out into the clearing, his pistol raised just below his eye-line. Nate wasn't more than five paces behind him and was bringing his sniper rifle slowly up to his chest. They had no idea that they made perfect targets for the man in the ghillie suit.

"Damn it!" Nate shouted as three well placed paintball rounds peppered up his left arm.

Antonio heard the rounds off to his left and didn't stop to look, sprinting toward the front door of the cabin. Blind firing in the direction of the shots and picking up enough momentum, Antonio crashed through the front door and simultaneously took paintball rounds in the chest.

Slipping on the rug and falling onto his back, Antonio cried as the wind escaped his lungs. Jack Knowles set his pistol on the end table next to him, and stood up from his rocking chair.

Laughing he said, "You're an idiot." Grabbing his legs, Jack yanked Antonio out of the doorway, waving Nate to come inside.

"Index!" Jack shouted, stepping back into the house. Helping Antonio to sit up against the wall was Alex, who was still rubbing the side of his neck.

"Luckily you didn't break the door in half and just snapped the bolt," said Jack, as Max Fontaine sidestepped through the threshold into the cabin.

"I still got it," said Max.

"Screw you man, that hurt," said Alex, grabbing the ice bag sitting on the table and placing it on his neck. "And Kwame, what happened? You didn't hear him creeping up on me?"

"How could I have heard him when you didn't? He was standing right next to you," Kwame replied.

Alex shook his head. Just then Jack's phone rang. "It's Janet," he said, walking down the hallway into one of the bedrooms and shutting the door.

Janet Carrera was Chief of Clandestine Operations for the entire agency, and Jack's immediate boss. While the Bering Group and the rest of the agents were off gallivanting around the world, she was in command, running everything back home. Janet was the eyes, ears, and communications for every and all things that went "bump in the night." Anything Janet requested she received, short of a nuclear warhead. There was no mountain she couldn't climb, no obstacle she couldn't tackle, and no one who could tell her what to do. Her most prized possession, however, was the Bering Group. And to top it off, she was an attractive forty-two-year-old brunette who held multiple black belts. She was a high-octanc dynamo and none of the members wanted to mess with her. Max sat on the couch and faced the television hanging over the fireplace. Throughout his time with the agency, this training site always stuck out in his mind, drawing memories from his past.

When Ben had been kidnapped and the Bering Group had brought him back, it placed the group on the map. Max Fontaine was Jack's old partner and was asked to stop working as a rogue agent and lead the new team. Jack had long served his time at the agency, most of it while he and Max were partnered together. Together, they killed, tortured, maimed, and captured more terrorists and people of interest to the United States government than he knew what to do with. But all good times must come to an end, and when Jack reached his early fifties, blowing his knee out on a training exercise, he knew it was time trade his pistol for an instructor's ball cap.

Teaching new recruits at Camp Peary, also known as "The Farm," had become Jack's new assignment. A nine-thousand-acre US military reservation near Williamsburg, Virginia, it was a training facility run by the CIA for the sole purpose of training their clandestine officers, as well as officers of different organizations-who specialized in clandestine activities.

Max understood why, and he couldn't blame him. So Max became a full-fledged solo agent while his best friend went off and taught. It wasn't until a couple years into teaching that David Carter, the Director of the CIA, offered Jack his current role as supervisor of this new, secret group of freshly recruited operators. But when Ben was kidnapped Jack realized he needed help, and Max was called.

No one on the team besides Max had any real experience in the field, but when Ben was rescued, the Bering Group showed the agency that handling anything thrown their way would be a breeze, gaining more of David's trust and respect. There was also the fact that Jack and David had been in so long that the pair had been recruited into the Farm together. This made it easier for David to recruit Jack, and gave him a "license to work with diplomatic impunity" around the world. David built a shroud of secrecy so tightly woven around the group that the US president didn't even know about it.

Going truly anywhere on the globe, becoming anyone they needed to be, and torturing anyone they needed to, to get the information they requested, the group operated in the shadows. Jack knew the extent of what was needed to acquire information from sources around the world. He knew the public eye wouldn't approve the methods used, which is why the president didn't need to be informed. Plausible deniability.

"Well, good news, boys," said Max, standing up and beginning to take off his ghillie suit. "I don't have to wash this thing because you didn't make me work hard enough to sweat in it."

Antonio flipped him the bird. Max walked past him into the kitchen, giving him a light shove, and began opening cabinets looking for a cup. He passed Nate and Alex adjusting the front door so it would close properly, just as Courtney and Kwame entered the room. Shooting Courtney a smile and receiving one back, Max couldn't help it. He tried not to stare at her as she made her way to the couch.

It was by total coincidence the first night back in Virginia from Colombia, that Max and Courtney had met at the Irish pub up the street from Max's home in Arlington. Courtney had just broken up with her boyfriend, who happened to live in the area. She was stopping by the pub to grab a drink before her drive home, when she ran into Max. One drink quickly turned into a long night of pool, shots, and friendly laughter with the locals because Max knew everyone who worked behind the counter.

Even though Max found her attractive, and clearly she thought the same about him, he made sure he kept the conversation away from other extracurricular pleasantries as best he could. By the time they were done drinking, Courtney getting behind the wheel of her vehicle was not an option. Max closed the tab, led her back to his place to sleep in the spare bedroom, and that was that. Nothing happened. He wanted to ask her out on a date, but knew better than to mix work with pleasure. Besides, there was a redhead working behind the counter of the local coffee shop he found just as pretty, if not more so.

Just when the noise rose and fingers pointed in every direction, blaming others for their incompetence with their version of what had happened outside, the bedroom door opened. The hardwood floor squeaked underneath Jack's Converse shoes. Max went for a fist bump, but Jack responded with a concerned look.

"We have a problem that needs our immediate attention."

CHAPTER 4

"**H**is name is Khaled Ahmadi, and he is one of the heads of ISIS. He was flagged on numerous cameras in Bandaranaike International Airport in Sri Lanka Wednesday night," said Jack. Jack connected to the CIA's secure server via his work laptop and an HDMI chord. From there he connected to the television screen hanging above the fireplace. Pausing before continuing, he allowed everyone in the room to study the portrait of the individual portrayed on the screen. He waited before clicking to the next slide.

"Well, he needs to go back into the cave he crawled out of," said Max.

"I take it you two love birds have a history together?" asked Antonio, turning to face Max from across the room.

"You could say that," responded Max.

"Anyway," said Jack, clicking to the next slide, "here is the video footage of him and his accomplices walking through the airport." The screen cut to a clear video feed of a very tall individual limping with a cane and moving through the terminal. The feed went on for the next couple of minutes as different cameras throughout the airport picked up where the last ones had left off. The cameras continued following them out of the airport and into an SUV. The screen then went black, and Jack clicked back to the slide of Khaled's face, his physical attributes and statistics appearing next to the mug shot.

"I want everyone to get a good look at this man. Memorize the facial structure, the beard, the bald head, and the grey eyes. This man is a master of disguise and being able to slip in and out of places despite his six-three height. Do not underestimate him at all. Take this man seriously and treat him like the very real threat he is."

"But how did he get caught?" asked Courtney from the kitchen, where she was eating a bag of chips.

"I was just getting to that," said Jack, clicking to a second video. "You guys wouldn't know this, seeing him for the first time, but he's had lots of facial reconstructive surgery and he's been off the grid for a very long time. Before that he was responsible for orchestrating numerous terrorist attacks around the world, running drugs, sex trafficking, illegal gun smuggling, you name it."

"Believe it or not, Jack and I managed to track him down and chase him through Europe, Africa, and the Middle East. He's a pain in the ass and to top it off, he's very smart. This is a problem and now Khaled's come back to the surface for a reason and we have to find out what that is," said Max.

"Just what I was thinking," responded Jack.

"Jesus," said Kwame.

"Yep. That particular incident Max was referring to was him leading an entourage that ambushed a highly secure weapons transport, stealing a nuclear warhead."

"Wouldn't we have heard of that?" asked Kwame.

"Negative. The higher-ups knew that if the world found out a nuclear warhead was stolen there would be all-out panic on an unimaginable scale. Our only saving grace was that we found them before Khaled and his men were able expose what they did to the world.

"This was ten years ago; social media existed but was nowhere near what it is today. Long story short, after we found his hiding place, we chased him into a warehouse. A man of his caliber doesn't go down without a fight, and the warehouse just happened to house barrels and barrels of oil that were to be shipped out to countries across the world on tankers.

"Gunfire ensued and the entire warehouse went up in flames and Max and I watched him get caught underneath a beam that had landed on his leg. That, coupled with the flames engulfing the building. We stood next to him and watched him yelling in agony. We each had our weapons pointed at his head, but we decided to let him burn for the number of lives he ruined over the previous decades."

"I take it you two never saw him officially die?" asked Courtney.

"Nope," said Jack, clicking off the television screen and placing the remote on the dining room table. Jack took a seat next to Antonio, Nate, and Kwame. "We left him there. Our mistake."

"He could be anywhere," said Alex.

"The only thing we know is that he left Sri Lanka on a plane back to Syria. The information came through after the fact. He probably has personnel working in Sri Lanka who were able to buy him some time to fly in, do whatever it is he needed to do, and get out before the proper channels were notified."

"So what's our job?" asked Kwame.

"Have any of you checked your phones in the past couple of hours?" asked Jack, staring at his team, all of whom looked to him with a blank shrug as they pulled out their cell phones and powered them on. Jack's protocol was phones off during training exercises. If anyone needed to be notified Jack would be and would relay it to whomever.

A good thirty seconds passed before anyone spoke. The first was Courtney. "A drone strike from the US Border Patrol killed a former Navy SEAL and his wife. Holy shit."

"Listen to this one," said Max. "Former Navy SEAL and family ambushed on the HBRT." His eyes grew wider the further he read into the story.

"Exactly what are the chances two team members were taken out within a matter of hours? Coincidentally after Khaled Ahmadi makes his presence known?" asked Jack.

"There was also this one: two former SEALs shot dead in hotel rooms in Oahu while on vacation," said Nate.

The room fell silent and everyone continued to research the different stories. "And all of this happened today on Veterans Day," said Nate.

"Do we know for sure though that this is him? We don't want to send our resources after this guy and have it not be him," said Courtney.

"It's too coincidental," said Jack. "And as for resources, you're it. Four SEALs killed on Veterans Day? We have the green light."

Kwame crossed his arms, then looked up from his phone and back to the photo on the screen. "Won't the Special Forces take this one? I mean, it's their guys."

Jack shook his head. "Negative. This is bigger than them; they'll have to sit on the back burner on this one. We've been after this man for a long time and Janet has the guys in the command center looking into it now. When they find what we need to get started, it'll be game on for us. So for now, stand by to stand by, because when we go hot, there's no stopping."

"That's for sure," said Max. Jack walked back into the bedroom and came out seconds later with a couple of cigars and a coat on. "Any takers?"

One by one the team members refused, making every excuse until it was Max's turn. Max didn't say anything. He walked over and took a *Romeo y Julieta*. "I'll meet you outside," he told Jack. Jack nodded, zipped up the coat, and headed for the back door.

Closing the door behind him, the orange and red hue of the sun disappearing for the day lit up the sky. Jack started to walk toward the tree line and looked back at the members inside the house through the two windows. Even though the team was on the cusp of a gigantic mission ahead of them, he witnessed and heard very faintly the team cracking jokes on one another once again.

The second they left the cabin in the morning, the team would be right back to work saving the world. Tough job.

Jack had always told them or the recruits he trained briefly at the Farm one thing. Regardless of the mission you had, you had to find a way to compartmentalize your emotions and feelings and take in whatever time you had to yourself before your assignment. You never knew if you would make it back to see another day, so enjoy the ones you could.

The back door opened and Max stepped outside. The second the door closed, Max saw his breath in the air. "Shit, old man, it's freezing out here," he said, buttoning up his coat and crunching his neck down inside of it as much as he could.

"I guess I'll have to tell Courtney she'll have to look for a new man because you can't handle the cold."

Max stopped walking toward Jack and stared at him. Twisting his head and raising an eyebrow he started to speak but Jack cut him off.

"Don't even," he said. "I see you two looking at each other. You make it too obvious, Max," Jack said, waving him forward. Max laughed and hurried to catch Jack as he started to walk deeper into the woods.

They walked in silence through the trees, ducking branches and moving around boulders and large roots too stubborn to stay planted in the ground. Leaves crunched under their feet as both men slipped once or twice on flat rocks underneath the foliage.

Ten minutes later, they made it through the trees and came across a magnificent view. Golden tops of trees blanketed the landscape for miles until the horizon. It was a sight to behold. There were some green trees left, but not many. Here the sky truly looked like someone had taken a paintbrush and painted a mural of bright colors and merged them with a dark blue.

Jack unwrapped his cigar and Max followed suit. Jack took out his cigar punch and poked a hole in the opposite end of both their cigars. Placing the punch back into his coat pocket, Jack removed his torch lighter next, lit his cigar, and passed the lighter to Max. Max breathed some of the tobacco in and coughed.

"Have you never smoked a cigar before?" asked Jack, chuckling.

Clearing his throat, Max removed the cigar from his mouth. "So what do you think about this whole situation?"

Removing the cigar from his mouth, Jack said, "I think this motherfucker is going to cause some problems."

"It's not going to matter at the end of the day because when he dies, someone else is going to take his place. You and I both know this," said Max, taking another hit of the cigar. Tilting his head up and creating a small, circular motion with his mouth as if he was going to whistle, he blew a subtle smoke circle into the air. Both of them watched the circle hover above them for a couple of inches and then evaporate.

"You're correct, but he controls the norther portion of Syria. That's one of the more dangerous regions and he's been the culprit of most of the terrorist attacks across the globe in the past decade. If we chop off his head, I think it'll be a while before another one pops up in his place. You guys just need to make sure you end it for good this time," said Jack, taking a smoke   of his own cigar.

The pair chatted for another thirty minutes, standing and admiring the dark sky creeping into view and pushing the bright colors off into the distance. The air was calm but chilly. It kept putting out the cigars if the men didn't keep them continuously lit. After removing the lighter from his pocket for the fourth time, both men decided to call it quits.

Reaching down, they stubbed out the cigars on a large boulder sitting right on the edge of the cliff, and launched the small ends over the edge. "You know," said Max, "for the record, Court came onto me."

"For the record, you can do whatever you want," said Jack, turning and looking at Max. "Don't let your dick think for you; you're too smart for that," he said, patting Max on the shoulder.

"I learned everything I know from you," he responded, winking at Jack. Jack rolled his eyes and started the walk back toward the tree line. Max took one more long look at the view, barely being able to make out the color of the beautiful trees in the distance. Inhaling, he felt the cold air pierce his lungs, which sent a shiver down his spine.

"Wait up, old man!" Max said, and jogged to catch up.

CHAPTER 5

The sun set just as Khaled pulled up to the beehive-style house. His security detail helped him out of the car. Approaching the house, he instructed the detail to wait by the vehicle. He planned for this meeting to take a while. Saying a quick prayer to Allah, he knocked three times on the door. The building wasn't the biggest, but it didn't need to be.

The nation of Syria was known all around the world for harboring some of the most dangerous terrorists, people, and having some of the worst living conditions in the Middle East. Sitting below Turkey and above Iraq, the constant fighting and turmoil in the region over the course of decades plagued its people with famine, no electricity in some areas, and depleted resources throughout the war-torn country. In the middle of the desperate nation was the city of Palmyra: a small rural farming community overrun with ISIS soldiers, who included the Shura Council and the Baghdadi himself.

Khaled traveled from Ar Raqqah, not necessarily the easiest drive in the world, but at a little over three hours, it wasn't the worst either. He always packed a small side-arm and his Avtomat Kalashnikova, or AK-47; he never left home without either of them.

Built of natural local materials, the walls of the beehive structures acted as insulation against the intense temperatures of the sun. The walls were typically made of mud brick stacked in a circle, creating a three- to four-floor, high circular structure. The interior of the structures were typically very dark, most being built without any windows. However various holes were scattered throughout the outside of the cone shape to bring in some form of light. It wasn't the most luxurious of places to live, but the people in Syria weren't blessed like the rest of the world.

Resting his cane on the outside of the structure, he looked back at his security detail. Some of its members were standing outside while others sat inside the SUV. The lights were off, but the team was ready to make a quick getaway if needed. Enemies of theirs were scarce in this part of the world, but drone strikes were unpredictable. He hadn't heard of any drones in the area, but he knew the Americans were notorious for using them to spy on him or his soldiers. He didn't need to take any risks.

Sighing and looking to the horizon, he hoped this would be the last set of attacks the council would sign off on for him. He was approaching the age where it hurt just to roll out of bed, and getting older wasn't getting any easier. Having already accrued more wealth than he knew what to do with, he just wanted to be left alone. The security detail could stay, of course. There was always someone trying to kill him, retired or not. That was just the nature of the game.

The sounds of the squeaking wooden door startled him. Inhaling, then exhaling slowly, he grabbed his cane and hobbled through the threshold. The room itself was lit with an abundance of candles and a large red-and-brown prayer rug sat in the middle. Two dusty old couches that had witnessed better days sat in the back of the room. Five council members occupied the room: one on one of the couches, two on the next couch, while the other two sat in separate chairs.

Sitting alone on the couch was the Baghdadi himself, Abdullahi Mahmoud. Making his way over to the couch, the *thump thump thump* of his cane hitting the dirt was the loudest noise in the room. Everyone respected Khaled. People may disagree with some of his tactics, but everyone respected him.

Abdullahi, who was only five years older than Khaled, stood up and embraced the commander of the Ar Raqqah region. "As-Salam-u-Alaikum," said Abdullahi, stepping back, hands still on Khaled's shoulders. Standing at about the same height, the two could pass as distant cousins.

"Wa-Alaikum-Salaam," responded Khaled, nodding with a smile. Letting go of his shoulders, Abdullahi directed Khaled to sit next to him on the couch. Nodding, he braced his cane and lowered himself into the decrepit corner on the couch. Abdullahi took the opposite end.

"What do you plan to do about the last American?" asked Abdullahi, getting straight to the point.

"That's why we're here. Jack Knowles goes hand in hand with why I want your approval for the next phase of attacks I have planned."

The couch springs groaned underneath Khaled as he shifted position. The five council members, now intrigued at what was about to come, all leaned forward. Their black jalabiyas, a loose-fitting, traditional Egyptian garment worn in the region, puddled the floor beneath their feet.

"Well," said Abdullahi, with a wave of his arm, signaling for him to speak.

"I don't need to go into detail about what happened to my family," said Khaled. Everyone nodded. "Jack Knowles is the last piece to the puzzle that changed my life decades ago. My contact wasn't able to get his information, but he is the last remaining member who needs to be killed and the task is proving to be difficult.

"I'm planning to send a video message to President Harrison. I will ask that Jack be delivered to a location outside of the United States. One of my choosing. Every twelve hours an attack somewhere in the United States will happen until I get what I want. From there, I will arrange—"

"And what makes you think Harrison will go for it? He will have his military forces bomb our depots, training camps, military operation vehicles, or whatever else he deems necessary. He will not negotiate with us. We have no problems with him now and we don't want any problems. We know the infidels are monitoring us, but now they leave us alone," said Abdullahi.

"Let me ask you," said Khaled, turning to Abdullahi. "When is the last time we planned a serious attack against the United States? It has been years. The last major one was 9/11. Sure, we have had small attacks across the globe: London, Pakistan, and other various allies to the United States, but what if—"

"No." The council member sitting closest to the door on the couch interrupted him. "I already see where this is going. What makes you think their president will not retaliate with bombs? Troops? Or drone strikes! We can't afford to go to war right now."

"Let me finish," said Khaled, keeping his composure. There was a reason why he was in charge of the northern portion of ISIS's territory. He only reported to the Baghdadi himself and personally he felt he didn't need for a "council's approval" for anything. However, he knew having their approval would make Abdullahi's decision much easier for him.

"Like I said, every twelve hours an attack will happen. I have handlers in charge of cells spread across the United States," said Khaled.

"And how thinly spread are these cells?" asked the disapproving member. "How many people are each of these handlers in charge of? What cities are they all in? There are a lot of questions that need answers before we sign off on something like this."

"Calm down, brother, I assure you that you will have your answers," said Khaled, getting annoyed with the member.

If Abdullahi approved it, the council could override Abdullahi's approval and deny Khaled his request and that would be that. A checks and balances system. But again, at the end of the day,

Abdullahi's opinion was the only one that mattered to Khaled.

Staring back and forth between the Baghdadi and his council, Khaled slowed his breathing and tried to go through possible scenarios in his head, countering any negative thoughts or actions arising from anyone in the room.

"I'll give you this," said Abdullahi. "I admire your courage and constant pursuit all these years to find the murderers of your family members. I know I can speak for the council when I say it was horrible to have gone through what you did. Peace right now is what we need, but even a dog needs to be reminded who's in charge every now and then."

"How can you agree with this?" asked the council member who had spoken earlier. "We just completed resupplying all our training sites and are in the process of completing another camp. We need to reassess and plan for an attack later so we don't take casualties so swiftly and so soon."

"While I agree," responded Abdullahi, "Khaled has served Allah for decades and I do trust his judgment, that's why he's in the position he is."

The council member shook his head, leaned back, and crossed his arms in the chair.

Stroking his long grey beard, Abdullahi took a few minutes. The room was silent while he sat thinking about the proposal. After approximately five minutes he said, "Khaled, are you certain you have the handlers and cells in place?"

"I do. I just have to give the command."

"Okay, you have my approval."

"Thank you," said Khaled, sneaking a look at the argumentative council member.

"What does the council think?" asked Abdullahi.

One by one the members agreed with Abdullahi, except for the contentious member. "You will not be disappointed," said Khaled.

"We don't have to tell you what will happen to you if your attacks fail. Don't prove us wrong," said the disapproving member.

Khaled wanted to end the man's life right then and there. On the spot. He fought every urge to curse and shoot him in the small hut. "You have my word; everything will go according to Allah's will. I promise."

The ride back to Ar-Raqqah in Khaled's three-SUV convoy was silent. The desert was pitch black in every direction and the temperatures dropped rapidly in the evening this time of year. There were only two to three months left before temperatures at night dove to unbearable conditions and death from the cold would spread across the region like the bubonic plague.

Every now and then Khaled's driver would ask him a question, he would answer, and then silence ensued. The security detail would strike up a conversation with the driver, but Khaled kept to himself. Looking off into the black abyss as the small SUV bounced up and down across the dirt and sand, Khaled did his best to relax.

He had waited so many years to retaliate against the American soldiers who had taken his family members away from him. Four of them were dead and one remained alive. The more he thought about catching Jack, the more anxious he became. His heart rate steadily increased the longer he envisioned Jack's white face as Jack ran around the house with the rest of the soldiers who'd conducted the raid that night. His teeth clenched and his breathing increased.

Closing his eyes, Khaled took a few short breaths, and over the course of the next two minutes, felt his heart rate slowly return to normal. Khaled had no idea where on earth Jack was exactly, but figured he was hiding somewhere. Pressing his face against the glass in the SUV, he looked up at the stars and wondered if a satellite or drone was watching him—possibly with Jack on the other end. It didn't matter. By the time he was done executing what he had in store, Jack Knowles and countless American lives caught in the cross fire would cease to exist.

CHAPTER 6

At forty-eight, Alexis Moore still caught the attention of many younger men. Staying in shape was a must; she wasn't getting any younger. Alexis was black with caramel skin, brown eyes, and short black hair. Her business suits spared no expense curving around her athletic frame.

She rose along with the rest of the National Security Council as President Harrison entered the White House Situation Room. Waving his hand as if to shoo a fly, the council retook their seats.

President Eric Harrison had broad shoulders, a strong chin, and a smile that could light up the darkest room. Standing at six feet two inches, with dirty blond hair and a light tan, he had the physique a lot of men at his age of fifty-five would die for. However, even with lifting weights and running five times a week, the wrinkles around his face couldn't hide the amount of stress that came with his current position. Wearing a sleek, black Brooks Brothers suit with a bright blue tie, his physique mirrored that of a former Olympic level athlete.

"Okay, Alex," President Harrison said, "you called this emergency meeting so let's hear it. I have a very busy week ahead of me."

"Roger, Mr. President," she said. She sat to the left of the president around the long, stained-wood, grained table. Alexis picked up the remote and pointed to the sixty-five-inch television hanging on the wall at the other end. With one click of a button, a video of Khaled Ahmadi appeared. He was sitting poised in front of a tan background on a tattered couch. Wearing a black jalabiya, a matching kufi, and an ISIS flag hanging in the background, the image stood still.

Turning back to the president, Alexis said, "We have a new video from Khaled Ahmadi. I have files and paperwork we could go through, but to save everyone some time…" she gestured to the other individuals in the room, "…I'm going to play this video and we can go from there if that's okay with you, Mr. President?"

Nodding, Harrison flicked his hand toward the screen to play the footage. Alexis continued. "We received this video uploaded directly to our servers ten minutes ago at zero-nine-hundred hours."

Khaled sat still on the couch looking at the screen. His droopy gray eyes, wrinkled face, and extremely long gray beard added to the image of the typical terrorist that everyone in the room already envisioned in their head. Small scars stretched across his sun-beaten face. Khaled Ahmadi looked tired and worn down, yet here he was taking a breath and delivering a speech to the most powerful man in the world.

"*Sabah el Kheir*, Mr. President, we, the Islamic State of Iraq and the Levant, have a request for you. My name is Khaled Ahmadi; you undoubtedly already know who I am. Decades ago, your Special Forces came into my cousin's house and slaughtered five of my family members like dogs, tearing the house apart and huddling the rest of us into a small room while your soldiers wreaked havoc throughout. They tore shelves down and cabinets and papers were thrown everywhere. Then your soldiers left. No sorry, no good-bye, and no money left for damages. Only innocent lives lost and crying family members, like my mother, who was left to suffer the carnage left behind by your dogs without a leash.

"Now, here we are decades later and I have come up with an answer, since your nation never provided one for me. Even though you were not responsible for the raids, I'm holding you responsible and giving you one option. By the time this video is uploaded you will have heard about the four individuals who have been killed by men on my orders. However, there is one man I can't find: Jack Knowles.

"I need Jack Knowles alive and delivered to a location of my choosing outside of the United States. Not delivering isn't an option. For every twelve hours he isn't delivered, there will be an attack within your nation. If you don't think I have the resources to do so, guess again.

Naharak sa'eed."

With that, Alexis paused the video as Khaled's war-torn face sat dormant on the television. "Kill it, Alex," President Harrison said. Alexis turned off the television. She had had this position for four years going on five now and was used to the previous president taking off his glasses, rubbing his eyes, taking a second to compose himself. President Harrison was built differently.

Maybe it was the way he was raised, his political prowess, or the fact he despised terrorists, putting them on the same level of people driving the speed limit in the left lane on the freeway. She didn't know, but he was different.

"I assume he's talking about the Navy SEALs?" the president asked.

"Yes, sir, all four of them died on Veterans Day," said Alexis.

"Jesus, Alex, I know that," he retorted. "Gimme the background info on them. Tell me you have it with you."

"Yes, sir, of course. On Monday a man by the name of—" she paused. Opening her red file, she quickly rummaged through the documents before pulling out a piece of paper with a small, wallet-size photo paper-clipped to a biography about that individual's picture. Picking it up and doing a last-second check before handing it to the president, she said, "Brandon Clark. A former Navy SEAL, serving twenty-plus years on the teams, was shot multiple times on the construction ramp on the Norfolk side of the HBRT."

Taking the photo and skimming over the document, flipping it around to see if there was anything else on the back, Harrison laid it out on the table in front of him. She continued. "In addition to him, sir, there was Daniel Lazar, Clarance Smith, and Terrance Jackson also murdered within hours of Brandon's killing." She slid the photos and documents over in the same fashion as she had the previous one.

"I'm guessing this means they're linked to the drone strike?" the president asked, flipping through each document.

"We believe so, sir," Alexis said.

"Jesus," President Harrison exclaimed, lining up each document next to one another in front of him. "Have the rest of you seen these?"

Heads shook throughout the room as the president scooped up the documents into one pile and passed them to Tracy Morgan, the Secretary of State, sitting to his right. Gently taking the photos, Tracy studied each and every one before passing them to the rest of the members in the room who included Justin Weber, the Secretary of the Treasury, Ethan Cox, the Secretary of Defense, Justin Axe, the Attorney General, Jedediah Rhodes, the Secretary of Energy, Jake Bower the Department of Justice, and Hector Gutierrez, the Secretary of Homeland Security. As the photos made their way around the table the president sat back in his chair and continued.

"All four of these individuals were former SEALs?" Harrison asked one more time. It was more of a rhetorical question just to be one-hundred-percent sure.

"Correct, sir. Actually, are you familiar with Project Green-Thumb? Initiated right before the Gulf War in 1990?" Alexis asked, pulling out another document from the folder with the words *Top Secret* stamped diagonally across the entire first page of the stapled pile.

"No, but let me guess," he said, grabbing the documents. "It has to do with what Khaled was referring to?"

"Correct, sir. It has everything to do with what he was referring to," Alexis stated.

The Secretary of Defense raised his hand. "I can add some insight to that operation Mrs. Moore, if you wouldn't mind?"

"Please," Alexis said, leaning back in her chair, relieved to take a slight break. She was used to doing most of the talking ninety-nine percent of the time, so letting someone else brief the most important man in the world from time to time with important information was a godsend.

"Mr. President, Operation Green-Thumb was an off-the-books, integrated operation lead by Special Forces and involving one CIA operative and the four deceased individuals. At the time there was credible intelligence that certain high-ranking terrorists were having a sit-down. It was decided taking them out would be a huge win for us before the war even started."

"And I imagine it didn't go as planned?" President Harrison asked, folding his arms into his chest.

"Well, once the team entered the house at night, they neutralized a handful of people. I can't remember the number, but I'm sure it's in the file you just read—"

"It said five," the president said, interrupting. "Also, Khaled stated that in the video. Pay closer attention to detail, son."

"Of course, sorry, sir. Well, the SEALs neutralized five members due to orders given out by their superiors at the time, and continued to search the house for any more intel or information to use before the war kicked off. After they neutralized the targets, it took some time to relay the identification of the targets because back then there weren't video camera feeds back to this Situation Room to see in real time who was or wasn't killed. By the time word reached the team that they had hit the wrong house, about twenty minutes or so had passed. Once they heard the news, they left the scene. The team suffered zero casualties and the mission was deemed a failure.

"The intel was thought to be solid, but obviously this was not the case. However, because it was a top secret operation, only the people occupying this room at the time and a small selection of Special Forces individuals in the community had any idea it even existed. If the rest of the world knew what happened the entire Special Forces community would come under some of the worst scrutiny imaginable. All the files were taken and consolidated into that one file you have in front of you, sir, and everything else was destroyed."

"*'Everything else was destroyed.'*" The president repeated softly to himself, but his statement lingered throughout the room. "Are we one-hundred-percent sure everything else was scraped? I don't want to see this guy pull up random-ass files in the future to expose one of the world's worst cover-ups."

"There are no more files, sir. David Carter had his team at the agency search the archives in depth and trust me when I say that the only files of that mission are in your hands," Alexis stated.

"Perfect. Now, I know Khaled and ISIS have been a threat and will be a threat for the for-seeable future, but how do we take care of this? We don't need the world knowing that a team of highly skilled operators went into the wrong house, killed Muslims, and left. The world, especially the citizens of the United States, will not take lightly that a Special Forces group ran amok however many years ago, killed Muslims, and got away with it. It won't look pretty when the press, if the press, gets hold of this."

"Sir," Hector said, "we need to be prepared to act. He stated a terrorist attack every twelve hours." Hector looked at his watch, "it's ten after nine now."

"Was he talking about an attack now or twelve hours from now as the first attack?" asked Harrison. "And how bad are we talking?"

Clearing his throat, Hector said, "I don't know to be honest, sir. I think the smart move would be to act as if nine o'clock started the first set of attacks. As far as what the attacks could entail, he could be talking a mass shooting, a bombing, multiple suicidal bombers in different locations. We just don't have enough information. The only thing we do know is that there are in fact cells spread out all across the United States, and all around the world for that matter, going through their days like everything is normal. They're sleeper cells, only activating when they're woken up. There's about fifteen to twenty in any given cell. Maybe more or less."

"And not to mention, he already orchestrated a remote drone strike on a regular civilian. What happens if he controls more drones or even snipers sitting on highways?" asked Alexis.

"Do we have a location on him, or do we think we know where he is? Also, let me make this abundantly clear, we're not negotiating with anyone. Period."

The heads in the room nodded. "Who is this Jack Knowles anyway?" The president continued.

"Sir, we don't have Khaled's exact location, but it won't matter. He's high enough and old enough, where someone else would take the head of the snake if he dies," Alexis responded. "Answering your other question, Jack Knowles is a longtime operative who has done great work for the agency. He went through the Farm with David Carter back in the late eighties and is no longer active in the clandestine operations division. He works admin, vetting the new recruits coming in through the Farm, comes up with scenarios for the instructors, and oversees the program. He's not active anymore."

"He's a washed-up old man is what it sounds like," Harrison stated, frowning and stroking his imaginary beard on his clean-shaven chin. "Alexis, I want you, Ethan, and General Godwin ready to go on a conference call in my office in one hour."

The United States Special Operations Command, or USSOCOM for short, was based out of MacDill Air Force Base in Tampa, Florida. It was in charge of overseeing the special operations component commands of the military. Since it fell under DoD, the four-star general reported to Ethan Cox, who in turn would brief the president of anything of importance going on.

"Sir, the general is on emergency leave; his mother passed two days ago. I can have Vice General Allen on the line in his—"

"Did I stutter?" interrupted the president. Alexis glanced at Ethan and wondered why the president was so angry about all this new information; it wasn't like him. He was a prick, but this was unusual. Ethan took a deep breath and said, "Roger, sir, I'll get ahold of him."

Just then an attractive redhead entered the room, heading straight for the president. Leaning over, she whispered something in his ear. They chatted quietly for a couple of seconds, before he thanked her and she exited the room.

"Turn the TV on and flip to the nearest news network, now," Harrison said.

Alexis still had the remote, so she turned on the television and clicked over to CNN. A reporter was standing outside of a Barnes & Noble in the Grove shopping complex in Los Angeles. Police, firefighters, EMTs, and a host of other personnel were gathered in and around a cordoned-off, yellow tape marked with the words *Do Not Cross*. The reporter was standing approximately fifty yards away from the entrance to the building. Bodies covered with white cloths were lying on the ground, EMTs were running in and out of the building in the background, and people could be heard crying in the distance behind the reporter.

"Alexis, turn it up," said Harrison. She did as she was told.

"For those of you who are just tuning in, the scene is chaotic. I don't know how well you can see behind me, but bodies are everywhere, people are screaming still as EMS are doing the best they can to deal with the current situation. Apparently, two individuals dressed in plain clothes and a backpack, walked into this predominant bookstore behind me and started shooting. The store in question is three stories high and from what I understand, they split up.

"During the course of the firefight, there was one police officer inside who was able to kill the first terrorist, but only after he'd killed four or five people inside and outside. After that, the police officer ran out of ammunition, from what I understand, and was killed by the second terrorist who continued to shoot inside the bookstore. Around five minutes later, LAPD responded to the scene, entered the premise, and subdued the remaining terrorist. Stand by...I'm getting a live feed stating that ISIS is claiming responsibility for this attack—"

Harrison slammed his closed fist on the table. "God dammit! Turn it off, now."

Alexis turned off the television.

"Let me make myself very clear. Find this motherfucker and bring him down, and I want it done yesterday!" screamed Harrison. He stood up quickly while the rest of his cabinet stood at attention until he left the room.

CHAPTER 7

Ethan and Alexis sat on one of the handcrafted brown leather sofas, waiting eagerly for the president to enter the room. The bright yellow walls with dark trim, the old pictures of past presidents, an old grandfather clock, some random chairs along with the classic fireplace—all of it was such an old and played out decor.

If he were ever in the position to be the most powerful person in the world, the decor in this office is the first thing that would go, thought Ethan. Matter of fact, it had been swapped out three years ago from the previous president, which meant that Harrison chose this current selection. *Disgusting.*

The door behind them opened as Harrison entered the room, with the documents from the meeting in his hands. Both members rose to greet him as the secret service agent standing outside closed the door behind him. "I'll make this quick," Harrison said, sitting on the couch across from them and placing the files directly over the presidential seal on the glass coffee table. "Alexis, in the file you showed me earlier, it stated David Carter was responsible for giving the bad intel on that operation, correct?"

Looking at Ethan before answering she said, "Yes, sir, I believe he was a low-level analyst at the time."

"And now he runs the CIA. Perfect. Just perfect. So, here's what you're going to tell him to do. Quite frankly, I don't like him and never did when I took over office. He's part of the old cowboy era of shenanigans that went on for decades. Authorizing interrogations for whomever they wanted, killing whomever they wanted, overthrowing governments to meet whatever agenda they were tasked with...the olden days are done. I can't have the American people thinking I'm over here authorizing blanket killers with no repercussions. I'm not going to tolerate it and I absolutely will not allow it. No more, that shit stops now."

"Yes, sir," said Alexis.

"Now," Harrison began. "I've been hearing for a while now David still has black-sites where illegal interrogations are held, which was banned years ago, and he was the director when all the names of the assets were spilled and auctioned off to the highest bidder five years ago. How the heck is he still anywhere within a ten-block radius of any government building?"

"Sir, the names being released wasn't at all his fault," said Alexis.

"I don't care. He should have had better online security, hired better analysts to put up firewalls, dealt with better people feeding him information, et cetera. It's his fault and people just happened to look the other way? Outrageous."

Alexis was getting frustrated.

"What I want is for David to be gone and I seem to be the only one on the Hill with enough common sense to think so. But, since you speak so highly of him, I'll give him this last chance. If he fucks this up, I'll bring him in here, and fire him myself, and you along with him. Now as far as Jack is concerned, it sounds like he's done this country a great service. I looked over what I could from the files you gave me and whatever else I was able to gain access to. If Khaled wants this man so he can just kill him himself, he can't have him and I will not allow it. I want you to send him into hiding. I want him so deep below ground even Satan couldn't find him."

"Roger, sir. I'll see him in person and let him know."

"Good. Now if there's nothing else, I would like the room please. I have to speak with Ethan and the general alone."

Alexis nodded, stood, and left the room. Once the door was

shut, Harrison stood. Taking large strides to his desk to put the documents from the meeting on top of it, he said, "Is General Godwin ready to go?"

"Yes, sir, I'll pull him up on the iPad screen now," Ethan said, reaching for the device in front of him on the coffee table and clicking a few buttons conferencing the general into the conversation. Harrison walked over and sat opposite Ethan and watched as the Secretary of Defense folded the iPad stand behind the electronic device, allowing it to stand on itself. The screen beeped every so often waiting for the line to connect and when it did the president wasted no time starting the conversation.

"General Godwin, I apologize for the short notice but we have a slight problem that needs immediate attention," the president said, adjusting the iPad ever so slightly on the coffee table so both he and Ethan could have a clear line of sight to the general.

"Sir, it's fine, there's a major accident on the highway causing the hearse to be delayed for the convoy, so we're all just sitting here at the church waiting to go to the cemetery," General Godwin said. He was able to secure a small bathroom away from the rest of his family as he sat on the toilet with his phone in his hand and earbuds in.

Having more than forty years of military experience under his belt, most of it dealing with special operations, General Godwin was the sharpest tool in the president's toolbox. And although the president enjoyed having him as the commander of USSOCOM, General Godwin couldn't be clearer that he was ready to retire after the president's current term was up. He had had enough of politics and all the rigorous nonsense that came with the territory.

"Did Ethan fill you in?" the president started again.

"Yes, sir, Khaled Ahmadi and Jack Knowles."

Looking at Ethan and then back toward the general, a slight smile began to creep across Harrison's face. Evil like. "Gentleman, what I am about to tell you doesn't leave this room, is that understood?"

"Of course, sir," both men said simultaneously. Not having the slightest clue what else he possibly could be telling them.

"I'm talking to both of you when I say this and I'm only going to say this once because I know you're not going to like it. I didn't want to say anything in the Situation Room because everyone on the council doesn't need to know, but something needs to be done about Jack Knowles."

"Sir, I'm confused," said Ethan, tilting his head a bit while raising an eyebrow.

"I want you to assemble a team," said Harrison. "I don't care who you get, SEALs, Force Recon, Delta, whomever, and have them on standby to get rid of Jack. He needs to go, as of yesterday."

"Sir, you just ordered Alexis to send him into hiding and now you want us to go behind her back?" asked Ethan.

"Yes," said Harrison, his voice ice-cold.

There was a slight pause and at first neither Ethan nor General Godwin knew how to respond to such a preposterous statement. The general spoke first. "Sir, let me make sure I'm hearing you perfectly. You're asking for Ethan and I to sign off on launching an assault against an American citizen on American soil with an American Special Forces team?"

"Correct," said Harrison. "If Khaled decides to expose Project Green-Thumb to the world, the kind of exposure that would cause, the amount of pissed-off voters losing faith in their leader, cannot nor will it be tolerated. I see this as the next best thing. When I was a kid, I lived in Missouri for a brief moment of my life. During that time my parents purchased a house right across the street from an open field. This field went on for miles. Well, one day we all smelled something funny in the wall. The smell was so pungent we had to hold our noses when we walked anywhere in the house. The smell never seemed to leave us.

"So, my father called a company to come investigate the smell because it was very apparent that whatever the smell was, it was coming from the inside the walls. Sure enough, there were field mice that fucked each other, had children, and all died inside the walls. It was grotesque. We had to leave the house for a long time and stay in a hotel while they cleaned it all up. I'll never forget that. My father served in Vietnam and wanted to round up his boys and grab a couple of flamethrowers and go to work on that entire field. I don't think I've ever seen him so upset."

Ethan and General Godwin sat quietly. Not a word was said when Harrison was done telling his story. Harrison continued, "I want you two to think of David and Jack as the two original field mice that entered the house. They fucked and reproduced little agents and people for years who have the same mindset they do. We, meaning you two and myself, need to be the men in charge of the flamethrowers, except the field will be the agency. It needs to be purged of the nonsense agents running around inside. Now Alexis doesn't need to know about our little escapade. Telling her to off someone like that is like telling you to put a bullet in the head of your firstborn. I want a team to go in, take care of business, and disappear. Simple enough."

General Godwin said, "Firstborn? Why not any of your other children, sir?"

"Firstborn, General," said the president. "No one will say it, but the firstborn is always the special one. All the other kids are always accidents or parents just wanting to have another child so the first one won't be so lonely. It's the firstborn who's the important one, yet no one has the balls to admit it."

"Sir, that's out of the question. You can't send an American team after someone on American soil, that's literally against federal law. The teams you're referring to are US military and you're using them for law enforcement purposes. There's no way I'm going to sign off on letting a US Special Forces team run rampant on US soil chasing a decorated American citizen," General Godwin argued. "Sir, sorry that's a strong no."

"That's okay general, that's why I'm in this chair and you're in that one. I'm ordering you do to it. Jack is an unknown asset to the world. He's a CIA operative who has done more than enough of his time serving his country on secret yet important mission assignments. He's fifty-seven years old, he's no longer operational, and he's teaching new students how to operate, if that's truly what Alexis has him doing. He's washed-up and quite frankly the world will not miss him if they don't know he exists. When we show Khaled the dead body, Khaled is going to look like an idiot. ISIS doesn't tolerate failed plans like the one he is attempting to execute. No, all Jack will be is a star on the wall of valor."

President Harrison was referring to the infamous memorial wall in the CIA building with stars dictating fallen operatives whose stories remained classified to the public.

"Sir, this is outrageous," Ethan stated. "You can't just—"

"Do not fucking tell me what I can or can't do, Ethan! I am the goddamned president of the United States and right now I'm ordering you two idiots to order a team to hunt and kill Jack Knowles! Unless you have a better idea this is your top priority. Is that understood? Because if not I will fire you both on the spot and find someone who will fill both of your shoes, have I made myself clear?"

"Sir," said Ethan. "We get it." Ethan looked at the camera and saw General Godwin nodding, even though he knew he hated everything just as much as Ethan did. Neither one of them wanted to lose their job; they both had families to take care of. "Let me talk to a friend. He has multiple contractors he uses as security overseas who have no issues making a little extra money on the side. No need to get SF involved, especially in the states. I promise you, it won't be good publicity, especially since you're planning on running for a second term."

Harrison looked at the painting of Abraham Lincoln staring at him and said, "Go on."

"It's best if you don't know who my contact is. I'll brief them and make it look as if it was a complete accident. Just like you want," said Ethan.

"Perfect. It's settled then. And gents, again, I cannot stress enough. Not a word of this gets out to Alexis," said Harrison. Both men nodded. Ethan watched Harrison press the red button on the iPad, ending the conference. Standing up, Ethan couldn't wait to exit the room and wanted to shout, no scream. Taking a long, deep breath, he let himself out and closed the door to the Oval Office behind him, wishing there was some way President Harrison's term could end tomorrow.

CHAPTER 8

"Jack, I hope you know the severity of this situation," said David. The main portion of the seventh floor of the CIA headquarters building was reserved for the DCI, his secretary, and a handful of other staff at his beck and call. The main conference room, with its daily and weekly updates about critical intelligence around the world, was on the seventh floor. This was so the DCI didn't have to travel around the building. When Harry S. Truman signed off on creating the CIA, he wanted to make sure that whoever was in charge lifted the smallest of fingers to get things done. Only a select few were ever summoned to the seventh floor, but Jack wasn't just anybody.

David Carter was a force to be reckoned with at the agency. He had a great memory and solid head on his shoulders, which is why he was such a great selection to take charge of the CIA. He was one of the nicest people in the office, always leaving his floor to go talk with anyone on any of the floors below him who was willing to listen. He was funny, revered by his colleagues, but straightforward and to the point when he wanted something done.

David joined the agency when Jack did and was even selected into the same Farm class as Jack. The two were paired together from the start and when they were tasked with anything, they were always the first team to get the mission completed. It was quite literally a match made in heaven, which is why when David approached Jack to stand up the Bering Group over a year ago, it was an easy choice.

Being on the top had its perks, so when asking Jack to stand up the division he also asked him to hand-select his team of operators. David could have done it himself. He had a list ready to go, but trusted Jack's judgment for years and had no reason to change that up now.

Immediately Jack accepted and went to work selecting various washouts from the Farm with the intent that when their profiles were "erased" due to dropping out, anyone deciding to hack into the database for the agency wouldn't be able to find them. They were ghosts to the world. No one knew they existed. Jack also requested conducting operations from a place outside of Langley. Thus, a mansion in a high-end gated community in Gainesville, Virginia, was located, purchased, and sold to the agency, kick-starting the process of creating a full-fledged black-ops team residing in plain sight of the public.

Once the wheels were in motion, it was decided the best option was refraining from informing the president. The DNI was the only individual close enough to the president to know about the program. Alexis wanted, and knew the country needed, a program where nothing was off the table. She wanted a program involving torture, extortion, kidnapping, and killing, all to gain information from enemies or overthrow governments. Alexis didn't care what it took to keep America safe, and was willing to make the calls she knew no one else would. However, orders given were only as good as the people who followed them and in order to succeed, she needed a subordinate in her corner she knew she could trust. Janet Carrera was the perfect candidate.

At the age of forty-two she was at the top of her age bracket, competing at various

CrossFit-games with her gym during different weekends throughout the year, always pushing herself to do better. She was smart, fit, and took a while to earn Jack's respect, but once she did there was a bond between them that couldn't be broken. Pushing her glasses up on top of her head, she crossed her legs.

Her fake tan, green eyes, brunette hair wrapped in a ponytail, and toned physique caused any man to stop dead in his tracks. She was stunning with a resting bitch face, and she didn't care. She hated getting hit on, which amplified her using her RBF to her advantage, especially at the gym.

David reached into the bottom drawer of his desk and pulled out a bottle of Blanton's Bourbon with three glasses. Pouring each member a glass, starting with Janet Carrera, he plugged the bottle when he was done.

"David, you know damn well I take this threat seriously," said Jack.

"I hope so," David said, tossing a manila file onto Jack's lap.

"Jack," Janet said, leaning toward him, "Mrs. Moore, asked us to put a protective detail on you and relocate you somewhere off the grid."

"I can't say I didn't see that one coming. I'll get with the team as soon as we're done here."

"Hold on, not so fast," David said. "The president wants a small footprint around you and I agree. Alexis, Janet and I discussed in-depth what we think the most viable option for you is, and we both think just you and Max is the answer. He'll be your guardian angel. No one else."

"I like it," said Jack.

Taking a swig from his drink, David said, "We're well aware of the situation at hand and we're well aware of the circumstances. You and I have history together; you're the godfather to my children, so of course I don't want anything to happen to you. However, I want you and Max so far off the grid that even I can't track you."

"That'll be no problem at all," Jack stated.

"Good. Now, we do have a lead on where Khaled is, or at least was?" asked David.

"We do," answered Janet.

"And where is that?" Jack asked.

"Sri Lanka," Janet said. "Khaled had some constructive facial recognition and pupil removal surgery to try and fool the cameras while traveling. It seems, Jack, when you and Max took him down in the building fire all those years ago, you two made a mistake leaving him alive. I read the report; you should have just killed him and we wouldn't be in this mess."

"I don't disagree with you," Jack responded. "I think about that moment every day. He's not a small-time terrorist, but in the heat of the moment we didn't expect him to live after a steel rod shattered his leg and he laid there as the building burned around him."

"Well, in any event we're here now," said Janet. "The surgery he's had worked good enough to evade numerous questions and he was able to leave Sri Lanka. However, after he left customs, I guess something didn't sit right with the man who cleared him. He had an intuition, spider sense, or whatever you want to call it, and sent the info over to Interpol. They in turn sent it over to us and that's how we found out. Any information we find out we will relay to your team. There's not a lot of time, they've been briefed already. They know the stakes and the rules and anything goes, just get the job done. If Khaled is still as dangerous as you say he is, then we're going to have a big problem on our hands if he's not dead or at the very least captured in the near future." Everyone knew she was right.

"Alright then, we'll send everyone, and Max and I will stay stateside," said Jack.

"Roger that," said Janet.

"Perfect," Jack responded, downing the rest of his drink and setting it and the manila folder back on the desk.

David said, "You can tell them to start with finding out what you can about Matthew Siff."

"Who?" asked Jack.

"One of the world's most dangerous computer hackers, and we think he's the one responsible for the drone strike," said Janet.

"You guys wasted no time on this," said Jack.

"Hey, when a terrorist has his paws on one of my members, he's made it personal," Janet said.

"Well, I should be honored," said Jack, responding with a wink back.

"Our guys downstairs were somehow able to trace the signal of the drone to Sri Lanka. Plus that's where one of our operations chiefs claims she last saw Matthew, but only briefly. She said she tried to get a picture, but Matthew slipped away in a crowded market. He isn't stupid; he knows we're after him and will go to whatever lengths to bring him in.

"He's also been behind no less than a dozen hacks pulling personal information from thousands of military members, high-end business accounts, and fake websites to pull money from the elderly, you name it. A real scumbag. Luckily for you one of our Directorate of Operations Language Officers, Lakshani Dissanayake, who's stationed in Colombo, is already waiting for your team," Janet said.

Standing up, straightening her skirt, and pulling her glasses back down over her eyes, she said, "Good luck, Jack, and tell Max the same. I know this is going to hurt just sitting back on the sidelines, but it's part of the job and right now my main job is keeping you safe." Janet turned, nodded to David, and left the room.

David grabbed the bottle and slid it back into his drawer. "You should get going, the clock is ticking."

"When is it not?" Jack asked. Just as he finished pushing his chair in and walking toward the door, he heard David clear his throat and begin to say something else.

"By the way, the G550 is standing by on the tarmac, waiting on your team."

"They'll be there shortly," Jack said, taking a second to look at his Omega Aqua Terra world timer. Watching the seconds hand glide effortlessly in a circle around the small globe in the center was mesmerizing. He couldn't just glance at the watch to check the time. No. Every time he looked at it, it reminded him of the scene from *Raiders of the Lost Ark*, where Indiana Jones laid his eyes on the golden idol.

The price tag was close to ten thousand dollars, but it wasn't the price or the beautiful face that caught his eye every time he looked at it. The watch was the last gift he'd received from his wife before she died from cancer. It reminded him of all the time they'd spent together. Over three decades of some of the best memories of his life flashed through his memory every time he flicked his wrist to check the time.

"How long is that flight?" Jack asked.

"They'll have to make a stop in London, but that'll be it. It's a twenty-two-plus hour flight and the plane can only go twelve before it needs to refuel—"

"Fuck, so they'll lose a day before they even get started," interrupted Jack.

"Exactly, so stop chitchatting. Their asses should have been on the tarmac yesterday."

CHAPTER 9

Puerto Vallarta, Mexico

L iam Parker sat in the corner of the large lobby of the resort in Puerto Vallarta, Mexico. Reading the newest article in the *Washington Post* via his phone, he pulled his ball cap further down over his jet-black hair, which was a wig covering his dirty blond hair. His skin's complexion mirrored that of someone who, "often didn't get enough sun," causing people at first glance to think he was an outsider, or gringo. Once his fluent Spanish kicked in, trading proper English phrases for Spanish slang, the thought of an outsider was squashed by the Spanish-speaking locals. Fooling people into thinking he was someone else was part of the chessboard, and he was the king.

Looking down at the blue band and dial on his Oris Aquis GMT, the one-hour hand read 10:00 a.m. representing local time while the second hour hand read 11:00 a.m. representing Washington DC. He had been waiting patiently for the better part of an hour.

Anytime soon his target would be walking through the tall, sliding glass doors. Quick glances around the lobby from his seat revealed an abundance of vacationers entering and leaving—from young, old, families, single people, and everything in between. The lobby was massive and entertained vibrant color combinations from the furniture, front desk, and matching walls. It was a sight to see, at least for a resort, considering the area he was in.

Moving his head back down to look at his phone he scrolled his right thumb over an article about a person forgetting his password for a hard drive holding over a billion dollars in Bitcoin. *Poor son-of-a-bitch*, he thought. His mind started to wander. He thought about what he would do with that kind of money, when the sound of the motion-activated glass doors caused him to turn. And that's when Liam saw the target.

Liam's target moved through the lobby, the swaying and status of the unbuttoned shirt giving all the telltale signs of intoxication. The man kept his arm draped over a stunningly attractive Hispanic woman, and tried to guide her through the lobby and into the hallway opposite Liam. *Right on time*, he thought.

Knowing his target was his profession, and offering a quick thousand dollars to the prostitute to make his job that much easier was all part of the facade. If he had to kill her too, he didn't care. His mission was his mission and it didn't matter who got in the way at the time of execution. All that mattered was that the job got done, he wasn't seen, and people thought it was an accident. Unless of course his orders were to make it to look like murder, and this was one of those cases. Liam watched the pair walk further and further away. The click-clack of the target's shoes matching her high heels vibrated off the tan, stone tiles.

Liam read and memorized the files on the target, then burned them in his backyard before he even left his house. What would cause a man to be a part of a criminal enterprise that kidnapped and captured teenage women to sell them into sex slavery was beyond him, but this was an easy one.

He was a hired hand of a select and distinguished crew of individuals working for powerful people in Washington DC. When people needed to be bribed, beaten, extorted, or even killed, he was one of the few men to receive the call. The business was extremely dirty, but it paid well.

Liam had stumbled into it after leaving the Marines as a scout sniper after ten years. Serving his country against all enemies, foreign and domestic, was the creed. He loved what he did, but eventually the job got old. Day in day out, reconnaissance packages, protection details over important dignitaries, or taking out enemies. All overseas. When his contract was up, he he'd parted ways and moved on.

Liam wandered around for a year, surviving on his savings account, but even that was beginning to dry up. Bouncing around from job after job became the norm until one day an envelope was slid underneath his door. By the time he got to it and opened the door, there was nobody standing outside. Regardless, that's the day his life changed, and he found his current job.

Adjusting his posture, he moved his left hand around to his lower back as if to scratch it, checking to make sure his suppressed Glock 19 with the clip holster was still there. Readjusting his shirt, he moved his arm back out in front of him and stood up to stretch. His target had taken the elevator and was out of sight now. Grabbing his small bag sitting on the floor next to him, it was time.

Doing one last survey around the lobby, he was careful to avoid staring at the cameras and made his way down the same hallway as his target. He wasn't a guest at the resort, but simply explaining to the concierge when he entered the resort he was waiting for a friend to come downstairs to meet him for breakfast was a no-brainer. Nobody paid him any attention.

Passing the concierge once again, smiling and giving the proper greeting, he rounded the corner. Completing his research on the hotel itself had been easy for the most part and the majority of it had been done before he stepped foot onto the property.

Only consisting of eight floors and overlooking the beach, the resort was in a popular area of Mexico. The resort offered multiple bars and restaurants inside as well as two pools, a spa, multiple shops, and a decent gym. He didn't really need to know all of that to complete his tasking, but at the end of the day he knew better than anyone that every small detail mattered. Once he entered the lobby, it was a different ball game. Making it to the elevator and looking above the doors, he saw the digital screen stop on the eighth floor, and he smiled. Clicking the "up" arrow, the next set of doors opened and he stepped inside.

Less than a minute later, he exited the elevator on the top floor, knowing that the camera was facing not only him but the hallway leading up to the door. No worries, he knew they wouldn't have facial recognition down this far south past the border. Too expensive.

Blocking the thought of possible capture from his mind he took a deep breath and began to focus on the task at hand. The resort was designed as an outdoor hotel. Therefore, all the corridors leading to the guest rooms were outside and every floor had a view overlooking the ocean as the breeze entered the walkway to one's room. Approaching his target's room at the end, he knocked softly on the door and waited.

The door opened; it was the woman from earlier. She was still in her colorful skintight dress that stopped a couple of inches past her voluptuous waist.

"Who is it?" asked a voice from the other end of the room.

"Just the cleaning ladies, *mi amor*," came the hooker's response. Liam handed her a wad of cash for seducing the man waiting at the far end of the room. Liam stepped in as she closed the door. Careful not to make any extra noise, he let her walk past him into the lavish room. It had an ocean view, extremely large balcony, two couches, a gigantic television hanging on the wall, and a plethora of other amenities, reminding its residents of exactly the paradise they'd paid for.

The woman, Gabriela, looked at Liam and nodded while he made his way to the coffee table. "Hurry up!" spat the man who was tied on the bed, spread-eagle and blindfolded. "I have a meeting I have to get to and I don't have all day."

"*Si, mi amor, un momento,*" she said, in her best sexy voice. Winking at Liam, who was now seated on the couch slowly pulling out the contents of his bag, he gave her a subtle kiss in response.

Meeting Gabriela the night before, he'd paid her several hundred dollars for some of the best sex ever. Once the deed was done, it was that much easier to convince her of the task that he needed her to complete. Latin women were his kryptonite, and he wanted one more hour with her before his flight out later that afternoon. He was going to move heaven and earth to make sure that it happened.

Tossing her clothes purposefully next to Liam on the floor, teasing him while giving him one last sexy smile, she removed the boxers of the plump man on the bed.

"*Si mami,*" said the man, his blood slowly rushing toward his groin.

Gabriela reached onto the nightstand and pulled a condom out of her purse, slipping it on him. "*Te gusta papi?*"

Andrei Petrov didn't really know any Spanish but he understood enough. "*Si, mami.*"

Liam turned up the television, but not loud enough to cause noise complaints. Turning his attention back to the bed, Gabriela reached over to her purse one last time and pulled out a ball gag and quickly placed it over Andrei's mouth as she began to ride him. Andrei's moaning accompanying Gabriela's seductive Spanish was all he needed.

Liam stood up, grabbed the scissors on the table, and walked over to where Andrei's head was placed at the top of the bed. Standing there admiring Gabriela's hips moving back and forth caused blood to slowly rush to his own groin and reminded him of the night before. Locking eyes with her as she talked seductively to Andrei, he couldn't do anything but envision what he was going to do to her when it was his turn to be on the receiving end of her favors.

Looking at his watch one last time, he gave it twenty more seconds before he gave her the thumbs-up and put on his gloves. She nodded, hopped off, grabbed her clothes, and immediately ran into the bathroom and shut the door. Lowering himself toward Andrei's head at the top of the bed and speaking to him loudly enough for him to hear over the television, he said, "Andrei Petrov, you attempted to blackmail Senator Graceland with photos of underage girls that you trafficked for him. I'm told the relationship between you two is now severed."

The second Liam finished his sentence, Andrei tried to scream, but the sounds were useless behind the ball and gag. That's when the real thrashing to escape from the bondage began. It was useless. Liam reached over, grabbed the end of Andrei's fully erect penis, and slowly cut through the base of it with the scissors. Blood gushed everywhere, covering the white satin sheets instantly in a dark red sheen. The thrashing that happened just seconds before was nothing compared to the thrashing that had just started.

After he was done, Liam tossed the cut-off end onto the floor and turned up the television just a bit more. Walking back over to Andrei's face, he pushed the ball gag further into his mouth.

"The screaming is useless," said Liam.

Taking one slow, final breath, he removed his pistol from his waistband. He didn't want to allow the man the pleasure of passing out from shock before Liam killed him. No, that death would be too good for a person like him, and quite frankly Liam found his crimes, including Senator Graceland's, repulsive. Unfortunately, the level of crimes people in the government were willing to commit in order to stay or go higher in office held no bounds.

Yanking Andrei's pillow from underneath his head, Liam placed it on top and placed the end of the silencer on top of the pillow, then pulled the trigger twice. Destroyed pillow and brain matter instantly covered the headboard. The thrashing stopped.

Shoving the pistol back into his back, he picked up the 9mm brass casings and placed them into his pocket. He would dispose of them later. Turning the television down, he grabbed a Kleenex wipe from his bag and quickly wiped the handle of the scissors before tossing them onto the bed. "What a horrible way to go," he mumbled to himself.

"Gabriela, *tiempo vamanos.*"

Opening the door Gabriela caught a quick glance at Liam from the hallway, but didn't dare look further into the room. She left quickly. Taking one last look at his masterpiece, Liam headed for the door but stopped just shy of the threshold when he felt a vibration in his pocket. Having two phones was another perk of the job, but he only took his burner phone when conducting an actual assignment. As much as he wanted to ignore the vibration and push forward with his day, he couldn't. It was a new text notification from Ethan Cox.

Sighing, he unlocked the screen. Clicking on the newest text, he read its contents and scrolled up to see the photo of his new target at the bottom of the screen. Staring at the picture, he stopped. Liam didn't need to go any further. He didn't need to read the bio or memorize any facial features or family members because he already knew who the target was.

Closing the application and shoving the phone back into his pocket, he pushed the thought of his next job into the bowels of his mind because in the next hour he would have round two of the best sex of his life.

CHAPTER 10

Jack didn't need to be told that time was easily not on their side. He saw the news report of the bookstore shooting, and every time he turned on the news to get a new update it seemed like the death toll was rising from the incident. He above anyone wanted to strike hard and fast, but deep down he knew tracking Khaled down wasn't going to be an easy walk in the park. The last time he and Max had chased him down, Khaled had taken them on a wild goose chase all over Europe. Although currently Jack was content with just sitting back and pulling the puppet strings on the new kids he was in charge of, he did miss the Wild Wild West times of running around and practically getting away with murder. Not that they didn't do that now, but it was just easier back then.

The second Jack left David's office, he dialed Courtney. The rest of the team had already assembled at their mansion in Gainesville, also dubbed "the office" by the team. It was the closest thing to a safe house they had. Deep down he had been wanting to give each of the team members their shot at leading everyone on a mission at some point, and now the chance had landed in his lap. He knew beyond a shadow of a doubt that Max could lead a team into hell and back. However, he wanted everyone else in the Bering Group to learn how to operate with each other without a seasoned operator leading the way. Antonio was a solid addition to the team, but he had done his time killing more than enough sicarios south of the border. Courtney was next on the chopping block and for whatever mission came up after this one, he would choose someone else to lead that one.

Walking to the parking garage, Jack made his way past the typical blacked-out Chevy Tahoes and Suburbans, and found his yellow Corvette C8. Laughing to himself at the fact that Max thought he could beat him in his Porsche Cayman GTS, he opened the door and slid into the cockpit. Moving his hands around the leather steering wheel, seats, and state-of-the-art dashboard, he nodded. *This is what retirement is supposed to feel like*, he said to himself.

Pressing the start button to the bottom right of the steering wheel, the muscle car roared to life. Backing out of the space, using the backup camera displayed in the rear-view mirror, he pressed the small *D* button on his right, shifting the car into drive, and made his way out of the parking garage, down the ramp, and out of the base. Once on the main highway, he scrolled through the large touchscreen display and found Max's phone number. Pressing the number displayed, he listened as the ringtone echoed throughout the Harmon Kardon speakers in the vehicle.

"You ready, Max?" asked Jack, speeding toward his house.

"Yeah, what's the plan?"

"Meet me at my house, we'll talk in person."

"Perfect."

Thirty minutes later Max pulled into Jack's driveway, parked, and grabbed his bag out of the back seat of his 1997 Toyota Tacoma. Adjusting the bag over his right shoulder, he walked toward the front door. Jack opened it the same time Max was about to knock.

"Jesus, miss me much?" he said.

"Relax hot shot, I saw you pull up on the doorbell camera," said Jack, stepping aside so his friend could enter. Stepping inside and seeing the foyer brought back old memories for Max.

"Ah, the good ole' days," he said. Max walked into the study and paused, seeing a picture sitting on Jack's desk. Picking it up he read the words that had been scribbled on the bottom of the frame with a silver sharpie. *Congo 11.*

Around forty people stood in a half circle. In the front was Jack and Max kneeling, each with a shemagh scarf. The shemagh was a head cloth designed for desert environments to protect the wearer from sand and heat and it was covering their faces. While kneeling, both Jack and Max were holding a large Democratic Republic of the Congo flag, stretching it out to its full potential. Behind them were some paramilitary soldiers, and to the side of them were the women, men, and children who lived in the shack homes on the grass and dirt field behind them. Max smiled and set the frame back down.

"That was a crazy-ass operation," said Jack. "Lots of people died on that one."

"Yeah, I know, I was there," responded Max, pointing at the photo.

"Fuck you," said Jack, flipping him the bird. "Come on, let's get loaded up." He led Max up the stairs and through the long, carpeted hallway.

His house was a decent size for just one person and Max knew Jack long enough to know he was wanting to downsize ever since his wife passed, but had just never gotten around to it. Pictures of Jack and his wife hung staggered on opposite walls. When Jack wasn't working, he and his wife had traveled everywhere. Each photo had a silver sharpie with a year scribbled on the bottom of the frame, similar to the one in the study.

Entering the master bedroom, Max followed Jack into the massive walk-in closet where a six feet tall safe awaited. Max paused and watched his friend type the code into the digital numeric display. After a couple of beeps and clanks were heard, Jack spun the three arms extending in front of the safe.

"I know who I'm going to rob first if the zombie apocalypse comes to town," said Max, staring at the assortment of weapons and ammunition scattered throughout the shelves and the door of the safe.

"Do the newer models of operators like yourself come with a mute button feature or is that sold separately?" asked Jack.

"It's sold separately, but I heard something about the older versions needing to be put down because they've ran past their shelf life," responded Max with a wink.

Shaking his head, Jack handed Max a black Glock 19 9mm with a red dot attachment, a clip attached to the slide to act as a holster, a SilencerCo silencer, and two extra magazines. Among other items he handed Max were a couple of flash-bangs, a five-inch serrated folding pocketknife, a small blowout bag with a leg attachment that clipped to the user's belt, a burner phone, and a Kriss Vector SBR with a couple of extra boxes of .45 ACP.

Jack's load-out was almost the exact same, except he sported a Smith and Wesson 9mm pistol and a custom Colt SBR. Closing the safe, Jack followed Max out of the closet.

"I'll meet you downstairs," said Jack. Max nodded, leaving his friend to gather whatever other clothes and things he thought he was going to need.

Ten minutes went by and Max heard footsteps coming down the stairs and saw Jack enter the kitchen. Holding his own backpack and duffel bag full of clothes, Jack set them on the floor next to the garage door.

"Alright old man, where are we headed?" asked Max.

"Back in time."

CHAPTER 11

1990 – Al Rigga, Kuwait

"Two minutes out," said Daniel Lazar, the SEAL team lieutenant. Grabbing the helmet that was sitting on the floor of the taxi, he put it on and adjusted it accordingly. Daniel was as country as could be, growing up in Alabama with a deep Southern accent. His short blond hair, green eyes, and square jaw sat perfectly on his football linebacker-like frame.

"Are we one-hundred-percent sure these are the guys?" asked Terrance Jackson, the petty officer second class sitting behind Daniel in the back seat. He was a tad shorter than Daniel, standing at five feet eleven. Terrance sported a crisp flat top, brown eyes, a trimmed medium- length beard, and was just as big as Daniel, if not bigger. They often competed to see who could out bench who in the gym.

"Ladies, keep it down, we're trying to read over here," said Clarence Smith through the radio attached to his kit. He was the other second class petty officer following them in the taxi right behind them. Clarence was five feet seven, had gray eyes and black hair but was not as big as the other two. He was a cardio-Nazi and ran circles around everyone else on the team when it came time for physical fitness. His motto was "weights can't outrun a heart attack." Cardio was his life and he strived to be as healthy as he could.

Sitting in the front seat and shaking his head was Brandon Clark. The petty officer first class standing at six feet even, cool, calm, and collected. Brandon wasn't the biggest nor the smallest, but he was what the team called "just physically fit." He didn't say much unless he needed to; silence was golden in his mind. Having brown eyes, a short high and tight haircut, and a clean-shaven face he was often also nicknamed the father of the group. He was the oldest and always looking out for his teammates. Sitting next to Clarence in the back seat was a young and intel-hungry Jack Knowles looking out of the window at the quiet buildings passing them by.

It was just past eleven o'clock at night. Nearing their target, Jack reached down to put on his helmet. *These boys are hilarious,* he thought. The good part was they respected him. Not being part of the team, but a CIA operative, that's all he wanted. Their respect.

"Comms check," stated Daniel, his taxi making a sharp right, turning down the last street. The team all reported in loud and clear.

"Roger, thirty seconds out," said Daniel, racking the charging handle of his black Colt M16. Attached were its Aimpoint 5000 optic and three-inch silencer. They were ready to roll.

"Have you ever done a hit like this before?" asked Clarence Smith, leaning over to Jack. Jack looked at the dilapidated residential buildings with stone walls and shattered glass sitting on top acting as makeshift barbed wire, before responding. "I don't kiss and tell."

"Roger that," said Clarence, chuckling to himself.

Brandon Clark turned around and began to speak into his own radio. "Alright gents, get ready."

"I'm always ready," said Brandon through the headset. "I had better not have to patch you up this time, Clarence."

"That was an accident and it was just training," he responded, racking his own charging handle.

"Call it what you want, I would like to save the items in my medical kit for the people who actually need it, not for paper cuts."

"Motherfucker, I've said it once and I'll say it again, tell Blake to not shoot his teammates when he's standing behind them in a hallway. Not my fault the round grazed my arm," snapped Clarence.

"Ladies, comms dammit," said Daniel over the radio. "You two are like an old married couple."

The two taxis slowed down approaching their destination, and pulled over to the curb. The entire block was black and dead silent. *This should be an easy infiltration,* thought Jack. "I'm glad I'm on this mission, y'all are a riot," said Jack, opening his door and immediately bringing his silenced rifle to eye level. He swept back and forth for rear security while the other two SEALs hurried out of the car behind him, tapping him on the shoulder to fall in line. Jack turned around, covered the rear, and fell in line next to the stone wall that surrounded the house to their right.

The mission was simple: gather whatever intelligence they could and hightail it out of the area before anyone noticed. The taxi drivers were longtime coalition fighters and had worked with the team before. So of course when Daniel recruited them for this mission to drop them off under the cover of darkness to eliminate a top-tier terrorist and hopefully gather intel, both fighters jumped at the chance. The taxis would sit a couple of blocks away, inside the parking lot of an abandoned building, and wait for their call.

As the second taxi made a left and drove off into the distance, the team stayed glued to the pavement in the shadows for a solid extra minute until they were sure nobody saw them. They weren't too worried; they had night vision, body armor, their rifles, and Colt 45s as sidearms.

Looking over the optic, Daniel finally decided it was time. Using his right hand to reach over to his radio, keeping his eyes fixated and left hand over the pistol grip of his rifle, he gave the command.

"Let's go," he said silently to the team. Silent whispers of *roger* came through his lapel microphone as he stood up, waited for the squeeze of his left triceps, and began to move.

Clarence, who moved right behind Daniel, pushed past him on his left, establishing dominance on the corner. Sweeping the entire street for tangos—or bad guys—Jack tapped him on the shoulder, calling out last man and Clarence fell back in line, but this time as the caboose. Jack was tired but the second he stepped foot out of the sedan, his nerves were on full alert. His eyes swept past every car window, crevice, and possible dark space they passed approaching their target. His greatest fear was a tango jumping out of a dark alley, and popping him in the face. Not tonight.

The team moved down two more blocks and as they neared the end of the second block, Daniel spoke: "Approaching the gate."

No moon in the sky, the night was working in their favor. So far anyway. There were noise and lights coming from the second and third stories of the building; something was wrong. "What the fuck," said Daniel mumbling under his breath, but loud enough for Clarence to hear.

"What's wrong, boss?" he said; the train began to slow.

"You don't see those lights and hear that noise?" he asked, reaching for his radio. "Jack, what the fuck? You said it was just supposed to be a couple of guys in the house, that's it. Get the fuck up here."

The team knelt, using the stone wall of the house to lean against, and two seconds later Jack was up front. Right in front of them to their right was a gigantic, closed front gate, but they would handle that hurdle next. Jack looked at Daniel, crouched next to him, and said, "What's up LT?"

"It sounds like a full-blown party is going on in there."

"I don't know what to tell you, sir; the intel has already checked out and is pretty solid." Jack wiped a bead of sweat from his brow.

"Pretty solid? Motherfucker, we don't work well with pretty solid intel. It's either solid or it isn't," Daniel spat back. He didn't like it, something was off. Jack looked the officer dead in his eye.

"Sir, the intelligence source I've been using is sound and has been used before to conduct solid operations. We're too far in the game and have this terrorist in one location to turn around now. We either breach this gate and deal with whatever or whoever is in this fucking house, or we radio the taxis, head back, and you can explain to your superiors why you decided to halt the mission at the front gate. Whatever is in there we'll deal with it, but right now you've got me and your men sitting out here in the open. Make a call." Maybe he was a little rough on the LT, but he didn't care. He wasn't a SEAL, but he had plenty of operations under his belt that could rival any of the guys next to him.

Daniel sat for a couple of seconds debating on what to do, and thought of what he *would have done* had Jack worked directly for him. "Jack, you're fucking lucky I'm not your boss, otherwise we would be putting on the gloves and going a couple of rounds back at the base for talking to me like that. My own fucking kids don't even talk to me like that."

"Well then, I guess you should consider yourself lucky then, huh?" Jack responded.

Daniel grunted, and readjusted his rifle into the pocket of his shoulder. "Just breach the damn gate for me and don't shoot us in the back."

Jack smiled, nodded, and shifted to the other side of the gate, now looking at Daniel and holding his hand slightly above the handle. Adjusting his eyes, he met Daniel's and locked in. Daniel raised his rifle from the ground, pointing at the gate with the muzzle just resting above Jack's hand. The team radioed "ready."

Daniel lifted the muzzle higher and that was the cue. Jack slowly turned the knob; it was unlocked. *That was easy,* he thought, and pushed on the gate. The gate let out a soft moan as one by one the operators made their way through the gate. Jack did one last quick look down and around the street before following the rest of the team inside. Quickly closing the gate, he increased his speed to fall in line behind Clarence.

The complex was massive: a complete stone building housing three floors, a decent size front lawn, and five to six SUVs littered the entire driveway. Lights were seen throughout every window, yet the curtains were drawn for all of them. The team snaked its way between the Land Rovers and Mercedes G wagons, stopping against the side of the house before encroaching the backyard.

Daniel, raising his right arm and circling it twice, started the train once more, continuing around to the back of the house. There were no motion detectors, dogs barking, or people smoking outside that they had to dispose of. It was perfect so far. Moving quickly and silently, Daniel stopped five yards before the back door. "Terrance, I'm in front of the power box, kill it."

Terrance moved up, letting his rifle dangle by his sling and grabbed the bolt cutters from his backpack. Crouching in front of Daniel, he felt around for the cheap lock and snapped it in half, moving his foot quickly so the lock had something soft to land on. He then kicked it aside. Opening the grey panel cover, exposing all sorts of switches, Terrance moved his right hand over the very bottom switch and held it, just barley touching. "Start the countdown, lights out in five," whispered Terrance through the headset.

Just then the screen door slid open and out stepped a tall Middle Eastern man laughing and saying something in Arabic, with a cigarette in his hand. Terrance had not even gotten to zero before the man stepped out, but that didn't matter.

As soon as the Middle Eastern man shut the screen door behind him and took two steps off the small concrete patio, Terrance crept up behind with his rifle and bashed the butt stock into the back of his skull, knocking him out instantly. Jack watched as Brandon ran up to help his teammate pull the body away from sight of the glass sliding door. While this was going on, Daniel crouched forward and slammed the switch into the off position, killing power to the entire house. The entire process took thirty seconds and soon Jack was stepping over an unconscious and hog-tied body while getting ready to move into the dark house. The screen door slid open and Jack followed the operators inside following the flash-bang tossed into the house by the first operator.

Speed, surprise, and violence of action were the three core fundamentals Jack followed when conducting a raid. While every tactical group had their fundamental codes, he found that his particular three integrated the best no matter who he deployed with.

By the time Jack entered the threshold, it was complete and utter chaos. Children and women were screaming as a result of the ultra-bright lumens from the flash and the ear splitting noise from the bang. Anyone who was lucky enough to escape the craziness, ran upstairs, or at least tried to. In a matter twenty seconds the bottom floor was secure, two members were sprawled out on the carpet in the living room getting patted down and hog-tied, and Daniel broke off to train his rifle on the stairs.

"Hurry up, guys," he said.

"Almost done," said Clarence, finishing up with the second body.

"Jack, stay down here and watch them. That's your only job right now and don't fuck it up," said Daniel.

"Roger," said Jack. There was definitely some hatred in Daniel's voice, but he decided he would let the smartass responses running amok in his head slide away for now.

Watching the four operators move upstairs with finesse made him wonder what life would be like had he tried out for some sort of Special Forces unit, but the freedom of working for the CIA had been too good to pass up.

It was only a matter of seconds before the team was out of sight and up the stairs, and then Jack heard it. Muffled shots, one after the other. Again and again and again. Something was wrong. The two prisoners lying at Jack's feet wouldn't stop wiggling back and forth, but he ignored them. "All clear," said Daniel through the headset.

"Roger, what do you want me to do with our friends down here?" asked Jack, anxious more than ever to get upstairs to see what the heck had happened.

"Nothing, sit tight. We'll come to you," responded Daniel.

"Roger," Jack said. *Christ*, he thought. *What the heck is going on?* Jack heard more yelling and screaming before a loud door slammed shut.

Jack heard footsteps coming down the stairs and saw Brandon. He said, "Jack, run outside and turn on the breakers, quick!" Jack ran outside. Once he flipped the main breaker, he reentered the house. Removing his NVGs from his face, Jack set them down on the counter.

"Jack, get up here," said Daniel.

Jack looked at Brandon, then to the detainees, before Brandon said, "I got this. Go."

Cursing under his breath, he bolted up the steps two at a time until he reached the second floor. To his right was Terrance, stepping out into the hallway and closing the door, but not before Jack caught a snapshot of the bloodied bodies inside. Slamming it shut, Terrance wagged his finger in front of Jack and pointed him in the opposite direction, toward Daniel.

Making his way down the hallway he passed a small bathroom to his right, another bedroom to his left, empty, and the last bedroom where the remaining team was waiting inside.

He walked up to Daniel who was standing inside of the room. Daniel held up his hand for Jack to stop and stepped out of the bedroom. He shut the door just a hair, leaving Clarence inside by himself. "What happened up here? I need to interrogate the individuals," said Jack.

Taking off his helmet, Daniel said, "You had your orders, we had ours."

"What the fuck is that supposed to mean? We enter the house, interrogate the terrorists, and bring them back. End of story."

"No, Jack, those were *your* orders," he said, stepping closer to Jack. "*Ours* were to enter the building, identify anybody matching the description of our terrorists and take them out, period. Now, I did my job so I need you to do yours. I have some people up here I need information from."

Jack was furious. "And where did those orders come from? They definitely weren't passed down to me."

"They weren't passed down to you for a reason. You were brought on this op for one reason and one reason alone, to interrogate who we say, and that's it. Now stop asking questions because you're wasting time. Follow me."

CHAPTER 12

Roanoke, Virginia

It was just past noon by the time Max and Jack pulled up to the faded yellow-and-blue house nestled on Woodcliff Road, about a five-minute drive from downtown Roanoke. Stepping out of the truck, Jack stretched his legs and looked at his cell phone, even though he knew there was nothing waiting for him. He would be lying if he said he didn't miss the action.

Jack never envisioned in a million years that he would have to go into hiding. He had been through a lot over the decades, but never something like this. The fact that a terrorist, one of the worlds most dangerous ones at that, wanted to kill him and he couldn't do anything about it, drove him insane. He wanted to take the fight directly to Khaled, and even though his team was attempting to do that for him, Jack not being there in person to pull the trigger wasn't the same. On the flip side, his position in the agency allowed him the freedom to do whatever he wanted. So when he was told by his boss to go hide, as much as he didn't like it, he obeyed.

Any number of locations could have been better, or just as good, but this was the spot Jack chose. No questions asked. Stuffing his phone back into his pocket, he crossed his arms and stood staring at the house as if it would talk back. Even though he'd barely spent any personal time at the house the older he'd gotten, it brought back memories of visiting it as a child.

A breeze blew by, kicking up the leaves littered in the yard and bringing with it the smell of grilled burgers and laughter off in the distance. Someone was having a party and whatever gathering they were at sounded like more fun than they were having. Jack exhaled.

"You know," said Max, grabbing his bag out of the bed of the truck, "the longer you stare at it, the longer your bags are going to sit back here."

"Do you ever shut up?"

"You should know the answer to that question already, bud," said Max, walking around the truck bed to stand next to Jack. Setting his bag down on the ground, leaning against the truck and letting out a small sigh, Max said, "So, explain to me again why *this* is the spot you chose? You couldn't have picked a cabin in the woods? Or someplace buried deep in the back country of some poor hillbilly redneck town?"

Jack ignored him. Instead, he grabbed his bags.

"Okay then," said Max.

"Alright, let me go inside and get situated so you can pull the truck into the garage. We don't need any neighbors snooping around wondering who the new people are. And trust me, we'll stand out here, it's a small town."

As the pair walked up to the front door, Max couldn't help but pay attention to the manicured yard, green grass, and two beautiful trees sitting on opposite ends of the yard whose trunks were so thick he was certain Paul Bunyan couldn't have chopped them down. The tree's arms extended over the front of the house, their naked branches whipping against the windows. Reaching the front of the porch, Max walked over and sat down in one of the rocking chairs, instantly collapsing under his weight.

Laughing, Jack said, "Looks like you need to lose some weight."

Max frowned. "Just open the door, old man."

Rubbing his side, Max scooped up his bag and followed Jack inside. Despite the outside of the house, the inside was almost brand-new. A large open floor plan with granite countertops, dark mahogany cabinetry, and wood-grained floors covered the entire ground level. Standing at the front, he could see all the way into the living room, which held a large gray sectional that looked like it had been bought just yesterday. Custom art pieces hung on the white walls, along with a bar cart in the corner next to the television in the living room.

Setting his bag down in the kitchen, Jack placed his backpack on the barstool next to the island. Slowly making his way over to the refrigerator, he opened it and seeing it completely empty, rubbed his stomach. "We need to get some food."

"And liquor," Max said, holding up a near empty bottle of vodka and swishing around the contents. "How old is this?"

"I don't know; try it and if you die then I guess it's too old."

He opened the bottle, walked over to the sink, and poured it out. "Don't worry, dad, I'll buy you another one."

Over the next thirty minutes the two continued throwing away things that were outdated. Max brought the truck into the garage and tidied upstairs, while Jack stayed downstairs, sweeping and cleaning whatever small dust bunnies and dead cockroaches he found. When they were done, they each showered, picked out some new clothes, and met in the living room.

Backing the truck out of the garage, the two drove to the grocery store, grabbed what they needed, and headed back to the house. Once the truck had been pulled into the garage and the door was shut, Jack grabbed the cast-iron skillet from the cabinet, threw it on the stove, and grabbed the steaks from the refrigerator. Max grabbed some beers and pulled up a chair on the island to watch his friend go to work seasoning their dinner. An hour went by, dinner was eaten, and the pair wandered outside. Opening fresh beers for the both of them, Max handed Jack his and sat down on one of the patio chairs.

"Explain to me again how you acquired this place?"

Clanking the bottle with Max's, Jack said, "This used to be my grandparents' house. It's been in the family for generations and we've been renovating it over the years. They bought it decades ago, but they're both long gone now."

"Damn."

"My grandparents wrote me into the will to ensure it stayed in the family after they passed away. Ever since then, my dad would occasionally take me up here, doing this and that for repairs, and he kept telling me one day this would be mine. When I got older and joined the agency the first thing they taught us as clandestine agents was that we should have a place to go in case the inevitable ever happened. I never even told my wife about this place. Only my parents knew, no one else.

"Because of the training and constant flying overseas, I gave my parents full authority to decorate it however they liked so long as it blended into the neighborhood. I didn't want them fixing up anything on the outside of the house, but the inside they could do with what they wanted. When they died I rarely came back. I would come up here once in a blue moon to make sure things were still functioning properly, but that's about it. Outside of random visits, I would rent it out. Luckily for me, I was able to make enough money and between renting it out and saving that it's been paid off for a while now."

The pair sat in silence for a good minute or two before Max said, "So, where do you think the next attack is going to take place?"

"I don't know," said Jack. "Khaled has way too many options and the problem is he truly does have people embedded so deeply in our society that it's going to be extremely hard to predict stuff like that."

"We should have just killed him when we had the chance," said Max with a loud sigh.

"You can't beat yourself up over what happened in the past.

Sure, do I wish we'd put a couple of bullets in his skull while we watched him screaming underneath that steel bar? Of course. Not a day goes by, when all this stuff is going on, that I don't think about that moment in my life. But we didn't know he would survive, man. I mean, fuck, who would have guessed that?" asked Jack, taking a sip of his beer.

"You're not wrong, I guess," said Max.

"No, I'm not. You can only adapt and overcome in life, that's it. You can't change the past, you can only change the future. Always do well to remember that."

Max took a long sip of his beer and thought about everything before he asked, "Do you have anybody around here who you can trust in case we need back up?"

Shaking his head he said, "Nope. We're on our own kid."

Somewhere over the Pacific

In the list of options for private business jets, the Gulfstream 550 was at the top of its class. Billionaires used them, and to an extent, high-level multimillionaires. The ability to customize the interior to any plethora of different options was one of the biggest reasons why it was considered in the top five privately used jets in the world. Using two high-powered Rolls-Royce BR710 C4-11 engines, there wasn't much room for growth in the speed category, adding to the fact that it had one of the longest ranges of any business class jet in the category.

The G550 could carry up to nineteen passengers and was used by multiple military agencies across the world to transport their high-ranking officials or delegates to any destination within a reasonable amount of time, all while in style. The jet had a cruising altitude of 51,000 feet and speeds almost matching Mach 1, so it was no surprise that this was one of the most coveted private jets around.

The plush white leather seats were some of the most comfortable seats Kwame had ever sat in. The luxuries he became accustomed to in the United States were the complete opposite of what he was used to growing up in Africa. After working with the Ghanaian Special Forces and being picked up by the CIA, committing fully to the Bering Group was more than he could ask for.

"Do we even know where this dude is?" asked Kwame.

"That's what the new contact is for, big dog," said Courtney, walking back from the bathroom in the back, choosing to sit directly across from Kwame.

"Hopefully we can get this dude to tell us where Khaled is; we're running out of time," said Antonio. He was sitting to the right of Kwame on the other side of the aisle, swerving his chair to face both Courtney and Kwame. "You know, I could get used to this life. The private jet, meals on board, private bathroom, and no kids yelling and screaming to worry about."

Closing the wood-grained pantry cabinet from the front of the jet behind the cockpit was Nate. Sitting down on the white leather chair in front of Antonio, he pulled the lever backward, causing him to spill all the peanuts sitting on his stomach onto the carpet. "Dammit."

"We can't take you anywhere," said Alex. He was lying down on the couch, across from Nate.

"Bro, go fuck yourself or make yourself useful and help me clean it up."

"I choose no. Is that an option?" Alex responded.

Nate ignored him and continued to pick up the spilled peanuts.

"Alright," said Courtney, pulling up the email on her encrypted laptop. "We won't have a lot of time when we land so let's get on the same page." Alex sat up and gave Courtney his undivided attention while simultaneously kicking Nate's hands with his foot.

"*Maricon*," said Nate, punching Alex's boot.

"Y'all are children, ugh. The contact's name is Lakshani Dissayanke. She's the language specialist out here in Sri Lanka and that's all she's done for the past seven years. She gathers intelligence on the terrorist cells working out of the area and operating in the golden triangle."

"What's that?" asked Kwame, crossing his arms.

"The golden triangle consists of three main countries, Thailand, Laos, and Myanmar, meeting at the Ruak and Mekong Rivers. It encompasses over nine-hundred and fifty thousand square kilometers of land overlapping all three countries. All sorts of drugs, including heroin, opium, and methamphetamine get produced in the area and is tracked by Lakshani. The drugs aren't necessarily made in Sri Lanka, but reading her reports here, she speaks the native language, Sinhala. It also says here that she's done this so long she has contacts with local criminal organizations. She's our in and anything we need, she's going to be it."

"We should be straight then," said Nate, standing up and walking toward the trash can in the back. Pressing down on the actuator with his foot, the lid opened as he dumped the peanuts in.

"I think you're cut off from eating peanuts, bro," said Alex with a smirk.

"The only thing I'm cut off from is talking to you for the rest of the trip, *asshole*," responded Nate, sitting back down and opening up his new plastic container of Cajun-style peanuts.

Courtney closed her eyes and wished she didn't have children to deploy with before continuing. "We have a fuel and rest stop in London and then we'll be in the air until morning. When we land she'll meet us at the tarmac and get us situated."

"Are you talking to her now?" asked Kwame.

"Yep. She'll have two SUVs waiting for us and she thinks she can get us intel on our target."

"Sounds good to me," said Antonio. "Do we have a lead on where the next terrorist attacks are likely to be held?"

"I have no clue," said Courtney. "Realistically they could be anywhere—grocery stores, shopping malls—you name it."

"This is going to be a nightmare," said Nate. "It's going to be damn near impossible to stop a terrorist attack every twelve hours."

The team sat in silence, thinking to themselves about all of the potential possibilities for terrorist attacks across the United States. That there weren't any leads didn't help the situation. As general knowledge, the team figured the Federal Bureau of Investigation would handle and be working around the clock to round up anyone they suspected of terrorism, but it was still like looking for a needle in a haystack.

"Our only option is to find Khaled quickly," said Courtney.

Back in Langley at the CIA headquarters, Alexis called David and asked if he could stay later so she could talk to him. He'd had already had a long day, so naturally David was upset. Unfortunately, she was his boss so anything but a legitimate excuse to say no was out of the question. Staring out of his window and watching the sun set, he heard a vibration on his desk. Walking over and picking up his phone, he read a text from Alexis saying she was on her way.

David double- then triple-checked his white Calvin Klein shirt, making sure all the buttons were done properly. Next he made sure his brown, pointed Beckett Simonon dress shoes had not one speck of dust, dirt, or smudges on them. Last but not least, walking over to his closet in the corner of his office, he pulled his grey Calvin Klein dress jacket off the hanger and threw it on. Taking a step back, closing the closet door and admiring himself in the mirror, he was content. Just then his door opened and Ashley, his assistant, peeked inside.

"Sir, the secret service is on their way up."

"Thank you, Ashley."

"Would you like me to get some coffee or anything prepared for her in the conference room?" she asked, still clinging to the door.

"Sure, just coffee will be fine," said David, smoothing out his jacket.

Closing the door behind her, she left David to his thoughts.

Walking around his office once, and then twice as a safety precaution, he made sure his personal carry weapon was locked away in the safe in the closet. He usually just kept it within reaching distance in his drawer but with the DNI coming, and secret service within thirty seconds of knocking on his door, he wanted the place to be ready. David didn't need to play twenty-one questions of *Why is there a pistol sitting out on your desk?* The secret service didn't care, to them everyone was a target. Unfortunately, this made things a little difficult when they showed up.

David liked Alexis and was elated when he'd received news of her selection for the position of DNI. Her background made her more than capable of being assigned the responsibility of briefing the president on national security matters. The biggest reason he loved working for Alexis was because she let him run the agency with autonomy. She'd told him when she took the job that as long as everything ran smoothly, she would stay off his ass and keep the president involved in other matters so he wouldn't ask too many questions about what was going on behind closed doors. She also kept the Bering Group out of reach of the president, which was another big reason why he liked her so much. At any point she could inform President Harrison the CIA had a black-ops group conducting business, however and wherever they deemed necessary. Unfortunately, the reason she was coming to his office wasn't a pleasant one.

There was a loud knock on the door.

"Come in," said David, standing behind his desk.

"Sir," said Ashley, bringing in a tray full of coffee, creamer, and sugar, accompanied by two extremely well-dressed agents.

"Good afternoon, sir," one agent said, whose high and tight haircut alone caused David to envision him on the cover of a military pamphlet. He was young and couldn't have been older than twenty-five. A silent nod is all the agent gave as the two conducted a quick sweep of the room, checking underneath chairs, behind his desk, and in the ceiling for anything questionable.

"You know, I am the director, and you guys can trust me," said David.

"I know, sir," said agent number two. "It's not our call, and personally I don't see a reason why we need to be here sweeping your office but that's what President Harrison wants."

"Jesus. I literally have a clearance for things even the president isn't cleared for," David said.

The first agent stepped up to the door and back outside as the second one followed. "Rules are rules, sir," he said.

"Yes, yes, I know," David said, sighing and stepping around his desk. Leaning on one of his chairs he watched the agent radio into his sleeve to bring Alexis up, then stepped outside, leaving the door open.

David chanced a glance at his Professional Sangin Instruments watch. With the advent of electronic watches, David knew the chances of people recognizing popular wristwatches was slim to none. He didn't have the expensive taste in watches that Jack did. Jack never lost an opportunity to flaunt his Omega World Timer around, but David's light-blue dial with the GMT functionality kept him content.

With two hands to keep track of two time zones at the same time, one of the two-hour hands read 2:58 p.m. Janet was the most punctual person he had ever met, and rightfully so, given her position.

As if on cue, Alexis entered the room, shut the door, and walked up to David, embracing him in a light hug. "Good to see you!"

"Great to see you, Alex, although I wish it was under better circumstances, really. Would you like a seat?" He gestured to one of the chairs.

"Can I sit on the couch?" she asked, referring to the modern grey sofa adjacent to his desk.

"Sit anywhere you like; you can sit on my desk for all I care. You're the boss," he said with a smile, pretending to move stuff onto the floor. She laughed.

"Coffee?" he asked.

"Sure, thank you."

"How do you take it?"

"Black. Now stop trying to flatter me, let's talk shop. I don't have all day," she said, watching David pour the black liquid into the cup. Handing it to Alexis, David walked back to his desk.

"Okay, so what's the scoop?" asked David.

"Nothing has changed since our discussion. How's our situation?"

"That's been taken care of already," David said.

"That's why I'm here. You need to make sure he doesn't go off on his own crusade trying to capture this guy himself. I know Jack and for something like this he's going to get tired of sitting around and not doing anything."

David raised his arm. "I assure you, we talked and he's not going anywhere. He's content with sitting tight until this thing blows over."

"Good," she said. "And how's the rest of your group doing with the flight to Sri Lanka?"

"It'll take them a while to get there, but they'll hit the ground running. No worries on their end. I would be more concerned with the contact over there providing the right information."

Nodding and shifting in her seat, Alexis said, "You know, when you pitched the idea to me about the Bering Group I had my doubts. Part of the reason why Americans are safe at night is because of our operators, but honestly your team paves the way for the future. We can't keep relying on solo operators—who go out and are spread far and wide across the globe—to keep us safe anymore. I mean, we *can*, and you know as well as I do that we always will, but this new group is a great trial run for future possibilities. The Colombia mission was a success even though it came at a cost, but what's the saying? "Such is life".

On the last mission, one operator had been killed due to the lack of responsibility of another team member. David appreciated the fact that Max took care of the issue downrange and Jack accepted the resignation letter of the team member. However, losing a member due to complacency from another team member, was something neither Max nor Jack tolerated. It was a select group of individuals Jack wanted on the team and they couldn't afford any fuckups.

"What exactly did you tell the president after all of that transpired? I would imagine killing the top cartel drug lord in the world doesn't just breeze past his desk."

"No," she said. "It didn't. He had a couple of questions, one of which included being very blunt and asking if we, the CIA, were involved. We can all hate him, but he's not stupid. He knows our agency has sent people behind enemy lines and overthrown governments and set countries ablaze in the past. He just doesn't want to be tied to it, or at least if it goes down during his presidency, he doesn't want to know it happened."

"Plausible deniability," said Jack.

"Correct. So I just said we weren't involved and at the end of the day was able to point the finger to the Colombian Special Forces. Plus it helped that their own news outlet spun the story that their Special Forces disabled his entire operation," she said.

"Well, technically they're not lying."

"No, but they had the help of a more powerful nation to their north," she said.

"True. This is all true, until the next hotshot decides to take Alejandro Alvarez's place and we're back to square one," said David, walking over to his window. The view of the tall trees swaying in the wind, and leaves blowing away from their branches, caused David to shiver. It was that time of the year. Cold, miserable, and not getting any warmer.

Turning back around he said, "So, what else?"

"Well, Khaled's video said for every twelve hours Jack isn't delivered to him, he's going to set off a terrorist cell."

"A bit of a conundrum we're in, seeing as we don't know where Khaled is or have the slightest clue where the next attacks will be," said David.

"That's correct, but the FBI is working hard and have already made countless arrests."

"They can't hold them for longer than forty-eight hours unless they have a clear charge. If media gets wind of this it won't look good. All it takes are civilians comparing the rounding up of people by the FBI to remind them of what happened during World War II."

Alexis shifted positions on the couch. "David, this isn't the Gestapo. The people they're rounding up aren't innocent. Every single one of them has done something wrong—enough to warrant their being added to a watch list, period. It's because of extenuating circumstances that we even have to bring them in and start questioning them. Harrison doesn't negotiate with terrorists and he made that abundantly clear two years ago with the American reporters kidnapped and subsequently killed by ISIS in Afghanistan. Harrison wants to avoid that again, so if Jack is out of the picture and in hiding, he can spin the story however he likes. He can tell Khaled he has no idea where Jack is, and when Khaled doesn't deliver Jack to his council of elders, it means Khaled has failed. Khaled doesn't want to fail because that's time, money, resources, and energy spent and wasted for one man's conquest for revenge. That'll be his head on a silver platter."

David was silent.

"I can also tell you the other agencies are working around the clock to implement damage-control procedures. In an hour or so, FPCON levels are going to be raised."

"This has the potential to be very bad," said David, who had wandered over to his chair. Looking at his watch he said, "It's going to be a few more hours before the team arrives in Sri Lanka, but until then you guys over on Capitol Hill do realize that in two more hours it'll be nine o'clock?"

"Of course, that's why the Bering Group needs to land in Sri Lanka and find out where in the world Khaled is. Otherwise, the things lurking in the depths of our nightmares will come true."

"I'm afraid they already have," said David.

CHAPTER 14

The ambulance, no klaxon blaring, just red and blue flashing lights, made a left off S. Caldwell Street and onto West Third Street. Just ten seconds later, the ambulance made a sharp right into the driveway sloping down in front of the entrance to the Hyatt Place Hotel. Bypassing the line of expensive Mercedes and BMWs parked in line, the ambulance driver pulled up and parked directly in front of the valet.

Throwing the vehicle in park, the driver and passengers dressed as EMTs in a short sleeve black shirt and black slacks, opened their doors and stepped outside. The passenger in the rear of the vehicle opened the back doors and handed each of them a small blue duffel bag with the white star of life symbol, signifying emergency medical services, embroidered on the sides of each bag. Once the dark-haired, dark-skinned individual stepped outside of the back, he nodded at the other two people and shut the doors.

The driver, upon seeing the young valet, unzipped his bag and reached into it but stopped when he saw that the valet appeared to be of Muslim descent. Pulling his empty hand back out of the duffel bag, the driver watched as the valet just stared, blank and confused, not knowing that the color of his skin had just saved his life.

Entering the small lobby, three older Caucasian couples dressed in tuxedos and elegant dresses stared at the three men approaching them. Whispering to one another, the couples watched as one of the EMTs reached into his already unzipped bag and pulled out a suppressed Glock 19. The couples had no time to react.

The gunman unleashed a series of shots, ripping apart the chest cavities of each of the couples. Small, silenced 9-millimeter rounds tore through hearts, lungs, ribs, and bone and in a matter of seconds.

The gunman turned to look at the valet podium to see if he was still standing there. It was deserted.

The two remaining gunmen just stood silently and watched the remnants of carnage and devastation. No expression on their faces and no remorse. Just a job to do following the will of Allah and orders from Khaled Ahmadi.

Walking up to the elevator, the gunman with the pistol used his gun to press the "up" arrow. Five seconds later, a subtle ding echoed throughout the lobby as the elevator doors opened, exposing a Caucasian mother and her two children. Seeing the blood on the floor and the dead bodies, the mother instantly grabbed her two children and hugged them close as the gunman raised the pistol again, pointing it at the mother's head.

"Aasim!" said Aabid standing behind him. Aasim's index finger moved from alongside the frame of the pistol to the trigger. Taking a giant step forward, Aabid placed his free arm on top of Aasim's and gently nudged his arm toward the floor.

"There will be more than enough bloodshed tonight," said Aabid in Arabic.

"Fine," responded Aasim. All three men stepped into the elevator and let the doors close behind them. Aasim pressed the top button with the rooftop bar label next to it. As the elevator rose, Aasim walked closer and hovered over the cowering mother who was kneeling down and clutching her children. Aasim was the youngest of the three gunmen, only twenty-three. Aabid was thirty-five and Naeem was thirty-three.

Aasim ejected the semi-empty magazine and replaced it with a full one. Aabid and Naeem placed their duffel bags on the ground and each grabbed their respective short-barreled rifles. Holding their Sig MCX Rattlers, Aabid and Naeem loaded their thirty-round magazines full of 5.56 into the magazine well and stuffed their pockets with two extra magazines apiece. Aasim leaned against the back of the elevator, continuing to stare at the crying mother while tapping his pistol against his thigh. He was anxious.

Five seconds later the elevator slowed and finally stopped. Another subtle ding was heard and the doors opened, exposing a lavish and highly decorated indoor-outdoor bar. Signs that read Thank You for Donating! were displayed all over the place along with colorful balloons that filled the ceilings of the indoor portion of the large bar. The three terrorists stepped out of the elevator, Aasim in tow, still holding his duffel bag, while the other two bags now lay empty on the elevator floor. Aasim reached over and pressed the "down" arrow and said in English, "Consider yourselves lucky tonight." He watched as the doors closed, and he turned to face the bar.

There were approximately fifty or so people dressed similarly to the couples left in the lobby downstairs. They were all chatting and laughing so much with their backs toward the elevator, that no one noticed the unwelcome terrorists entering the room until the first shots rang out.

Screams, pushing, shoving, and everything in between occurred while the terrorists took their time spraying everything in the room. Reloading and shooting some more, they kept going until there was nobody left standing.

While Naeem walked back and forth through the carnage, stopping at victims who were still alive and finishing them off, Aasim pulled out the contents of the duffel bag. Gently pulling out a suicide vest and placing it around his body, Aabid helped to adjust it. "Remember," said Aabid, pulling a small switch resembling a joystick with a wire connecting it to the vest, "press this down once the elevator opens, not before."

"Yes, yes, I know," responded Aasim.

"We can't afford any mistakes," said Aabid. "You will be welcomed with open arms in the afterlife," said Aabid, embracing Aasim.

Over the next five minutes, sirens, klaxons, and what seemed like hundreds of little black dots were surrounding the bottom of the hotel. From their height, looking over the balcony, it seemed like a million little ants all moving around.

Naeem looked at Aabid and Aasim and said, "Are you ready?"

Aasim took a deep breath and nodded his head as all three terrorists headed back to the elevator.

CHAPTER 15

Colombo, Sri Lanka

By the time the Bering Group landed, unloaded everything, and met Lakshani at her house, the sun's haze began to protrude over the early morning horizon. The team entered her community, which was a series of small houses, each with their own protective wall. A gated community in a sense. Navigating the tightly paved roads was difficult, but the Range Rovers managed.

The convoy found Lakshani's house, clicked open the large iron gate from the remote in the lead vehicle, and drove inside. Lakshani was standing outside waiting.

Her long, flowing dark hair stretched past her shoulders. She had brown eyes and full luscious lips with a stomach that appeared as if it was allergic to carbohydrates. All her physical attributes added to her tan complexion. Modeling for *Vogue* could have definitely been an option if the CIA didn't work out.

"You're lucky the windows are tinted," said Courtney to Nate and Alex while shaking her head before getting out of the vehicle.

Both vehicles were driven by embassy security, and once all the bags were taken from the vehicles, the drivers walked inside and waited in the living room.

Her house consisted of four stories. A basement, swimming pool in the center of the miniature courtyard, numerous bedrooms, and a kitchen large enough to throw a decent-size birthday party with at least thirty people. It was certainly a site to behold. Working for the embassy overseas had its perks.

Sometimes.

"Sit down," Lakshani said, gesturing to the kitchen table. "Have you heard the news?"

"What news?" asked Kwame. "My phone has been searching for cell service ever since we landed."

Lakshani walked over and turned on the small television hanging on the kitchen wall to BBC World News. It was broadcasting not only the gun attack in Charlotte, but also a follow-up explosion to emergency personnel that killed ten more people and injuring twice as many.

Antonio sighed. "Fuck, this is getting out of hand."

"It's only going to be a matter of time before Harrison mobilizes the National Guard," said Nate.

"And send them where?" asked Courtney. "At this point we don't even know what cities they're attacking; it doesn't seem like there's a rhythm to the madness."

"Well, looking at this and trying to solve it in this house isn't going to help anything, and I'm sure you're all hungry," said Lakshani, pressing mute on the remote. "I have eggs, bacon, and sausage. There's coffee in the pot and had we met under better circumstances, I would have made you a Sri Lankan feast. Unfortunately, I know we don't have the time," she said.

"Thanks, next time for sure," said Courtney. Glancing at Nate and Alex, Courtney shook her head. They had turned their attention from the television and couldn't stop staring at the stunning CIA language officer as she turned around to walk toward the coffeepot on the stove. Kicking them both under the table, Courtney broke their trance. She grabbed a napkin and pretended to wipe the corners of her mouth. Kwame and Antonio snickered.

"What's wrong with you two?" asked Nate, talking to Kwame and Antonio. "There's no telling when the next time will be that we'll see someone as beautiful as she," said Nate, just as Lakshani dropped a tray off with the coffeepot and cups.

"Did you say something?" asked Lakshani, her pearly whites contrasting beautifully with her lips.

"They're just tired and incoherent right now. Don't mind these two," Courtney said, frowning at both of them.

"Thank you, Lakshani," said Kwame. She smiled again and made her way back toward the kitchen. "That's such a beautiful name," said Kwame.

"Thank you," she said. Starting the griddle and walking over to the table, she grabbed a chair and joined the group. "Okay, so Matthew Siff, right?"

"Yeah," said Antonio. "We know you said you saw him, or thought you saw him not too long ago, right?"

Nodding, she poured herself a cup of coffee. "Yes, I definitely did. The agency's been chasing him for a long time. Not only is he a very smart hacker, he's an expert in blending in. We can never snag the son of a bitch."

"When you say 'we,' do you have a partner out here?" asked Courtney.

"A partner exactly? No. I mean, I have all the help I can ask for from the embassy, but I'm my own boss out here. I mostly do field-work, surveillance, route reports, data analysis, and work with the military who deal with terrorists trafficking anything through the golden triangle they can get their hands on. One day I was sitting outside getting lunch with a friend and I saw Matthew across the street."

"And you're sure it was him?" asked Nate.

"He's public enemy number one on my list to bring in. Trust me, it was him. Which, to me is even more crazy he would risk coming to Sri Lanka, because the Maldives has no extradition."

"But Sri Lanka does?" asked Courtney, in between sips of coffee.

"Yes," she said. Looking at the griddle, Lakshani walked over to the stove and threw the bacon and sausage on. "Look, I'm sure you guys are smart enough to figure this out, but if the Maldives has no extradition, and Sri Lanka does, then there's only one reason he would be here."

"To get some of the amazing tea this place has to offer?" asked Nate.

"Or maybe to meet someone," said Antonio, leaning back in his chair and crossing his arms.

"Correct," said Lakshani. "And you're also correct, Nate, we do have some of the best tea and spices the world has to offer. Remember, the East India Trading Company used to operate in this region many decades ago, but that's neither here nor there."

The room fell silent. All you could hear for a minute was the sizzling and popping of grease on the griddle, with the metal spatula scrapping together the meat. "And if he was willing to risk it all to come over this way, that means there had to be a big player in town."

"Khaled," said Courtney.

"Bingo," Lakshani said.

"Interesting," said Alex. "Do you happen to know where he is now?"

"I know Khaled fled; it was a quick turnaround," said Lakshani.

"We know about Khaled. I was referring to Matthew," Alex said.

"Ah, of course. Well, unfortunately I don't, but I know someone who does. Now, who's ready to eat?"

Within ten minutes the breakfast was nonexistent. Alex, Nate, and Kwame helped clean the table, while Courtney and Antonio started the conversation about what the next move was going to be.

"Alright," said Courtney, "who is this person you know?"

"Have you guys heard of the LTTE, or Liberation Tigers of Tamil Ealam?" Lakshani asked.

There was nothing but blank stares.

"I imagine you're not talking about the ones in the zoo, right?" asked Alex.

"No, not those. Back in 1985, there was a separatist group fighting for independence for Hindu Tamils in northeastern Sri Lanka. They were founded in the early 1970s and carried out a number of high-profile, terrorist-style attacks all across the region. The attacks included the assassinations of not one, but two heads of state."

"Jesus," said Antonio. "It sounds like the shit we have down in Colombia."

"Exactly. The LTTE used suicide-bombing techniques, and had an elite element in their ranks who called themselves the Black Tigers. This continued until March 2004 when negotiations tried and failed. The Sri Lankan government received help from US Special Forces and in 2009 they were defeated even though a large portion of them defected along with their leader.

"I've been stationed here for a couple of years now, and I grew up here for a little before moving to the States as a child. I remember hearing random attacks of people in their tuk-tuk's in which a random grenade would be launched in their path, killing them, but as a child I didn't know what was going on. My parents saw what was happening and wanted a better life in the United States where I could grow up without the possibility of being introduced to terrorism at such a young age. We fled, I grew up, wanted to help my people, do something and make a change, and fast-forward, here I am. The individual who I was referring to is a contact of mine who used to be one of the tigers, but is in hiding now."

"Is he close?" asked Kwame.

"Yes, he's in Colombo and controls the underbelly of petty crime and illegal activity we do have. Outside of the tigers, there isn't too much to worry about, although the bases around the island still have outposts that are manned on the beaches just in case the small remnants decide to strike."

"How in the world did he become one of your contacts?" asked Nate.

"Remember how I said I monitor all the terrorism that goes on in this part of the region, or at least try to? Well, we've known where he was for a long time now and working with the local military we've raided a couple of his opium stash houses. Because this area of the world is so big with importing and exporting drugs, guns, and whatever else, I came up with an idea."

"To use him as an informant?" asked Nate.

"Yes. The Special Forces down here managed to corner him and his men. Had I not stopped them he would have been dead."

"What about the rest of his men? Where are they?" asked Courtney.

"I was getting to that."

"Sorry."

Holding up a hand, Lakshani said, "You're fine. I struck a deal with him and told him the military didn't want him moving his weapons and illegal materials through their country, but I don't care about all that. I just wanted terrorists and names so if he could supply me with a constant flow of them, I would keep the military off his back. But the second he fails to honor his part of the agreement I wouldn't be able to stop the military and they would ransack his entire operation. All warehouses, facilities, houses, everything. They would take and or kill everything he had."

"Fuck," said Alex. "You have that kind of pull around here?"

Leaning back and spreading her arms wide as if to welcome him with a hug, she said, "We work for the same agency, except I work halfway around the world and can do what I want. The agency gives me full reign out here to do as I need, so long as I keep providing them solid intel on terrorists. A lot of things get trafficked through this region, more than just the holy trinity of drugs, weapons, and money. I'm talking slavery, sex-trafficking, and every now and then there's talk of WMDs."

"Damn, it sounds like you have things on lockdown out here."

"I do." Looking at the grandfather clock sitting behind Kwame at the opposite end, she said, "It's 7:13 now; we need to get your gear so we can be on our way. Like I said, I don't know where Matthew Siff is, but my contact definitely will. No illegal activity goes on in Sri Lanka without him knowing about it, and you guys only have seven and a half hours left before the next attack."

CHAPTER 16

Fairfax, Virginia

Liam Parker drove past his target house, parked two blocks away, and killed the lights. He took a deep breath and closed his eyes. Setting the mood was key before taking a life. He'd learned that on day one. Being calm, cool, and collected was a plus, and if he couldn't do that, he shouldn't be in the field. Period. Underneath his seat was his black fanny pack full of "candy" he called it. These were extra items he might need to take down a target.

He looked up. No moon, pitch black, perfect conditions.

Picking up his Smith & Wesson 9mm shield and threading the Omega 9k silencer to the barrel, he was ready. Not seeing anyone near him, he hopped out of his vehicle, closed the door, and headed toward the house.

Liam reached the last intersection before looking both ways and crossing the street. The target house was to his left, but the front yard and side of the house were surrounded by an immense wall of shrubbery on top of a fence. Scaling the fence up ahead of him was going to be his best bet. He crept next to another gigantic tree, crouched, and opened the front pocket of his fanny pack. A small white cloud escaped his mouth as he exhaled. He hated the cold.

In a matter of seconds, Liam scaled the fence and dropped onto the other side undetected. Crouching down and surveilling the property, satisfied there were no floodlights or roving dogs, he decided to move, pistol out in front. He spotted two windows, one downstairs, one upstairs, both blocked with curtains. No lights on, another good sign.

The lawn was just large enough to hold a decent-size pool in the back and a nice-size patio with just enough excess grass around to play fetch with a dog. He covered the distance to the back door in a matter of seconds. Twisting the doorknob, it was locked. *Of course,* he thought.

Shoving the pistol into the small of his back and removing his lock-pick set from his fanny pack, he placed the instruments into the lock. A couple seconds went by as he finagled the lock and pick until he heard a faint click. Shoving the set back into his fanny pack, he quickly grabbed the pistol.

Pushing the door open with the toe of his shoe, he entered the premises. Sweeping his eyes from right to left to check his sectors of fire, he saw nothing. Reaching behind him, Liam gently closed the door and walked forward. He didn't make a sound.

Liam reached the end of the open floor plan at the base of the stairs. He took his time going up the stairs and then swept the rest of the house. Nothing. Pulling a small transmitter device from the fanny pack, he extended the antennae and swept the room while checking the transmitter's small screen. It was an electronic tracking device able to pick up specific frequencies coming from cell phones, iPads, or almost anything else.

If he could find a burner phone or any kind of electronic device, he could attempt to hack into it and find the location of all other devices. He highly doubted someone of Jack's nature would allow someone to track him so easily, but sometimes the answers to life's problems were that simple.

A radar-like circle pulsated from the center of the screen to the outside of the screen and anything caught in the crosshairs would blip, and show in a small, filled-in circle. With the amount of money on the line, he was determined to find what he was looking for.

Setting his pistol down on the nightstand, he walked from one corner of the room to the next. Sweeping back and forth, nothing. Tossing the device on the bed, he began to ruffle through drawers, under the bedsheets, underneath the bed—anywhere he thought his target might have left clues about where he'd gone. Anything at all.

Liam's pants leg vibrated. Stopping his search and leaning on the dresser, he sighed and slid the circular button to the right.

"Yeah," he answered.

"Is that how you answer the phone when the Secretary of Defense is calling you?"

"That's how I answer the phone when I'm in the middle of doing your dirty work and you won't leave me alone. Remember who is asking whom to take care of Jack Knowles."

A short pause before, "Do you have anything?"

"Negative."

"Well, find it, the president is up my ass as well as the general's, and I told him you could deliver."

Liam shoved off the dresser and continued his search, his hands pulling out the dresser drawers and rifling through the clothes, while his shoulder and ear held the cell phone in place.

"I'll find out where they went. Jack's smart, but I've done this before. There's a reason there's only a handful of us in Washington doing all your dirty work."

"Yeah, well there's also a reason I pay you so much. Just get it done and call me when you know where he is," said the SECDEF, hanging up the phone.

"What a train wreck," said Liam, under his breath. Stepping away from the dresser he took a short breath and scanned the dark room. *If I were going into hiding, and I were a CIA asset, where would I be? Where would I go?* he thought. Scratching his head, he walked over and stepped into Jack's closet. He reached the end of the walk-in closet, shuffling through the last of the clothes on the hanger, when he saw it. A safe.

Walking up to it, testing the handle and confirming it was locked, he looked on top and noticed there were papers stacked on top of each other; he grabbed them. There was also a stack of maybe ten pieces of mail; he went through all of them. Important bank documents, titles for certain vehicles, investment portfolios and the like. As much as he wanted to deep dive into all of Jack's personal information, he didn't have the time. He placed each piece of mail back on the safe when he was done going through it, until he got to the last one: a property statement.

Pulling the contents of the envelope out and unfolding the paper, he saw it was a title to a house in Roanoke, Virginia. A piece of paper attached to the title was a death notification letter for both Martha and Robert—from a family lawyer, he presumed. Taking a second to read the letter and flip back to the original title page, he paused. He took a picture of the address on the title, placed everything back where he'd found it and left the closet. Grabbing his scanner, he put it back into his fanny pack. Then he placed his pistol in the small of his back, walked to the window, and placed a return call to the SECDEF. It rang once.

"What did you find?"

"He's staying at a house in Roanoke."

"Virginia?"

"What other Roanoke do you know?" asked Liam.

"How quickly can you get there?"

"It'll take a couple of hours by car, but you're the SECDEF. Get me a helicopter and have a rental waiting for me when I land."

"People might question that."

"You're the one who wants this guy dead."

A slight pause before, "Fine."

Liam couldn't wait for this job to be over; the cold was not his friend. The second he landed, a small Nissan Rogue with the keys on the driver's seat was waiting for him. The warm memory of sleeping in a nice bed next to the prostitute in Mexico flooded back to him. *What was her name again? It didn't matter,* he thought. It was over and it's not like they would ever have a sustainable relationship. However, he would have to give her a shout whenever he went back south.

Landing at a half past midnight, the drive from the airport to the address in the picture took just about twenty or so minutes. Using the same stealth technique as before, he drove past his target house and parked several blocks up the street. It was time to execute his orders so he could get some sleep.

CHAPTER 17

Roanoke, Virginia

Jack woke up, drenched in sweat. Sitting up and looking around in the dark, he wiped the sweat from his forehead. Bad dream.

Taking a couple of deep breaths, calming his nerves, he tossed his sheets off and stood up to use the bathroom. Opening the bathroom door and reaching for his glass of water, he realized the weight of the glass was off and he saw it was empty. He headed for the kitchen.

Stepping out onto the cold hardwood floor, barefoot, he made his way over to the refrigerator on the other side of the space. The ice cold floorboards sent shivers up his spine.

Finishing filling his glass, he walked over to the sink, moved the curtains just a smidge, and looked out the window, pausing to take a sip. That's when it happened.

His cup flew out of his right hand and into the sink in front of him just as two arms reached over his head. A wire dug into Jack's throat as the stranger's hands yanked backward and the wire pressed deeper into Jack's trachea, cutting off his oxygen supply. At the same time, he felt a knee push against his lower back.

He knew he was in a bad spot.

His lungs went into overdrive, trying to deliver oxygen to his brain, but the connection wasn't there. His arms swept in every direction trying to grasp at something, anything, but nothing was within reach except the glass in the sink. Jack stretched for the glass, but with the weight of the attacker behind him it was daunting. Still, he had to get it done. Straining his right arm as far forward as possible caused the attacker to pull the wire even harder. He felt as if his arm was going to pop out of its socket, but if he could just...

Max thought he heard something downstairs, and shot up in bed. His gut was telling him something was off. He couldn't describe the feeling, but could only relate it to the Spiderman comics when Peter Parker knew something was wrong. Lifting up the pillow next to him, grabbing his pistol, he slowly slid out of bed.

Careful not to make too much noise, he crept to his door. Pointing the gun at the doorway, he opened it and heard what sounded like muffled footsteps coming from downstairs.

Jack was beginning to black out, but his fingers had almost reached the tip of his glass. He knew the attacker couldn't swat his arm away and keep the same pressure on his windpipe. The glass was almost in his reach when he felt the attacker release the grip on the right side of Jack's throat and swat his arm away from the sink. That's when Jack struck.

With his tunnel vision slowly returning back to normal due to the quick release of oxygen into the brain, Jack tilted his body to the right, dropping his weight. Twisting himself toward his attacker, he quickly established a power base and launched his head up toward his attacker's chin, throwing the man's back onto the center island. Jack heard bone crack, and a yelp. The attacker's jaw was definitely broken. From there Jack went to work.

There were various times throughout Jack Knowles's life where the ten years of boxing instruction he'd received at a young age played a major role in his life. One was sending his stepfather to the emergency room after the jackass punched his mother, two was defending his high school girlfriend against three classmates who thought it would be funny to throw spaghetti sauce on her new white dress at lunch, and three was right now.

After Jack threw the first punch to the attacker's floating ribs, Liam tried to use his arms to protect his body, but Jack acted like he was hitting a heavy bag while training for his next fight. One punch after the other, exhaling and inhaling while landing punch after punch against his opponent's body and also trying to land one or two punches on his broken jaw. The problem was, because he was so drained from being choked, his punches didn't have the force needed to incapacitate his opponent. Truth was, Jack was tired before he even started.

Blocking Jack's next right-handed punch with his arm, Liam used his left palm to strike Jack in the chin, throwing his center of balance off and knocking him back against the sink. Following up with a right cross to the chin, Liam reached across his body with his right arm and delivered a powerful elbow blow to the side of Jack's exposed neck. Jack fell in an instant, hitting the floor on hands and knees.

Liam kicked Jack's lower ribs and heard a crack and a yelp as Jack clutched his side. "The great Jack Knowles," Liam managed to mumble through his broken jaw. Liam reached behind him, pulling out his pistol.

Just then Jack heard two faint sounds and watched as they ripped through Liam's back. He began to gasp for air that never came. Liam collapsed on top of Jack, dead. Jack managed to shimmy away from the deceased body and look toward the stairwell.

"Jesus, Jack, had I known you needed to be placed in a retirement home with 'round the clock' security, I would have suggested it to Janet," said Max, walking toward his friend.

"Go fuck yourself," was all his lungs let him say. It hurt too much for anything else.

Colombo, Sri Lanka

Pulling up to the massive warehouse, Lakshani said, "Leave the guns in the car, they'll frisk us before we get to talk to him. I've spent several years building a rapport with the man, and I don't need it ruined now." The group was split up between the two SUV's. Courtney, Lakshani, and Kwame were in the first, while Antonio, Nate, and Alex rode in the second.

The warehouse reminded Courtney of the hangar they used at the executive airport to store their G550. The sliding warehouse doors were wide open as men stood in lines behind the three big empty truck beds loading crates into them. Everything from weapons and ammunition crates to expensive vehicles, to even liquor and cartons of cigarettes sat inside. Clearly, there was nothing this man wasn't involved in. The location wasn't necessarily the nicest part of the city, but it wasn't the worst part either.

"This guy isn't worried about anybody seeing this?" asked Courtney.

"I told you, as long as he keeps feeding me information, I'm keeping the law enforcement off his back. Have everyone else sit outside, he's a credible source, but he's still a criminal," Lakshani told Courtney.

Before she had a chance to respond, Kwame said, "I'll take care of it." He hopped out of the car and walked to the other SUV. After a quick chat, Kwame flashed a thumbs-up. Both females stood next to the security guards armed in military-style fatigues with AK-style rifles.

"Shall we?" asked Lakshani, gesturing toward the guards standing at the entrance. Courtney nodded.

"Arms up," said one of the guards in broken English. Courtney and Lakshani assumed the all-to-familiar TSA search position as the guards brushed their hands up and down their bodies searching for any sign of a weapon. Satisfied, the guards stepped back and one of the guards motioned for them to follow. Courtney looked back at her guys who were watching like hawks.

The pair followed the guard into the warehouse and to the right, past all of the men counting ammunition and weapons on long tables to their left. Many more guards were inside the actual warehouse that couldn't be seen from the road. "Hired help to count all of whatever he's moving," whispered Lakshani.

"Is it always the much merchandise, weapons, and ammo?"

"No, I've seen money, drugs, you name it laid out across those tables. Like I said, we have a mutual understanding."

Satisfied with the answer, she nodded and took it all in.

The guard reached the stairs in the back of the warehouse, stopped, and gestured to the ladies to walk upstairs without him. The ladies nodded as he watched them reach the top and head back to his post. From this height, Courtney was truly amazed at the size of the operation; it seemed like there were enough crates to finance a small civil war.

Immediately entering the office, cigar smoke stung Lakshani's nostrils. There wasn't much inside the office but a giant oak desk facing a round table with six chairs deeper inside the room. A television hung on the wall and a small sofa sat in the corner of the office. A small refrigerator sat behind the desk, which Courtney guessed was probably full of beer—not water—and sitting on top of the refrigerator was an AKS-74U. This was a smaller version of the weapon the guards downstairs were carrying.

Their contact stood a couple of inches taller than both of them, his gray hairs poking underneath his perfectly seated red beret. His demeanor was serious and he greeted them with a giant smile, showcasing his many gold teeth, a result of the poor dental care in the country. With a wide outstretched arm, he embraced Lakshani with a hug and smile, then stepped back.

"Courtney, let me introduce you to Asiri Perera. The man with the eyes and ears of everything coming and going in this country."

"Nice to meet you," Courtney said, stretching out her hand.

"You are very beautiful," said Asiri, bending over and kissing her hand. "Wow, I must be in great presence to be blessed by two women such as yourselves." His English was impeccable.

"If you don't mind me asking, how is your English so good?" asked Courtney as Asiri gestured for them to take a seat on the couch. Walking over to the refrigerator, he opened the door and said, "My father served as an officer in the Sri Lankan Navy, and when you're an officer, it's mandatory that you learn to speak English. That same requirement isn't made of the enlisted and they have to learn on their own if they wish. Drink?"

Courtney nodded in approval and followed Lakshani's lead. She was in unfamiliar territory, and she knew better than to go to a foreign country and turn down anything her host offered. One of the first things Jack taught the team was etiquette in foreign countries. It could mean the difference between a friendly conversation and a gunfight, often in the blink of an eye.

Asiri pulled out three Lion beers, opened them all, and brought them over to the women. Clinking glasses and taking a sip, he sat down across from them on one of the chairs next to his table and asked Courtney, "Have you ever been to Sri Lanka before?"

"No, but I've always wanted to visit," she lied.

She had never wanted to come to this country. As a matter of fact, a trip there wasn't even remotely on her radar, but it did look quite beautiful. She had told herself if she did travel this far to the other side of the world it would be to go to the Maldives for diving. That was a true passion of hers, and unfortunately she hadn't been able to dive in a long time.

"Ahh, well this is a great country. You'll have to get Lakshani to take you on one of the safaris while you're here. *If* you have time, of course."

Laughing, Lakshani took a long swig from her bottle. "Yeah, this isn't that kind of visit," she said.

"Oh, I know, I was just trying to make small talk. I know the only reasons you come here. It's always to get some kind of information; never to just come and chat," said Asiri, crossing his left leg over his right.

"You're in bed with the CIA, Asiri; we're not in the business of just chatting."

"Yes, yes, well get on with it," he said.

Courtney could see his body language and facial expressions beginning to change. He started wriggling his left foot, which was sitting on top of his right leg, and he began tapping his left finger against the bottle. She wasn't the best at spotting micro expressions, but anyone could tell this man was getting anxious.

Setting her beer down on the floor, Lakshani asked, "What do you know about Matthew Siff and Khaled Ahmadi?"

Asiri's finger tapping and foot wiggling stopped. "I know that the next time Khaled is in my country I'll shoot him myself."

Glancing at Courtney, Lakshani narrowed her eyes and raised an eyebrow. "You have my attention."

"I know he was here not too long ago and left the next day. He met with some American, who I assume is the one you guys are looking for?"

"You don't have this American's name?" asked Courtney, sitting at the edge of the sofa now.

"No, unfortunately I don't, but I know he is still here," said Asiri, taking another swig.

"Let's backtrack before we continue. Why is it you hate Khaled?" asked Courtney.

Asiri leaned forward in his chair, clasping both hands together as his facial expression went from semi-serious to deadly. He looked at Lakshani. "Do you want to explain it or should I?"

Lakshani said, "I'll explain it to you on the ride back." Satisfied with the answer, she sat back and continued. "Khaled delivered an ultimatum to the United States. One of our agency operatives was part of an assault a decades ago, accompanied by four Navy SEALs. This was back when Khaled was in his early twenties.

"They raided the house, killed some of his family, thinking they were part of a terrorist organization, but they quickly realized they had acted on bad intel. They exited the house and that was that. This was not only in the early nineties, but it was right before the Gulf War. The way we gathered intelligence was a lot different back then."

"Yes, of course, continue," said Asiri.

"The mission was deemed a failure, and they moved on," she paused to look at her watch. "All four SEALs were killed recently."

"I heard," he said. "When one of them dies in an operation, it *might* make the news. When four retired ones die within a matter of hours across the United States, it makes headlines around the world. Harrison couldn't keep that shit quiet somehow?"

"How quiet can you keep a house getting shot up by an American military-grade drone in an American suburban neighborhood? Plus, right after they were all murdered, Khaled sent a video to the president indicating if he didn't have the CIA asset at a designated location outside of the United States, then every twelve hours he would launch some sort of terrorist attack," said Lakshani.

"We're on a tight schedule," said Courtney, cutting in.

"Hmm." His fingers went back to tapping his glass and his foot returned to wiggling. Scratching the scruff on his chin he said, "How many hours do you have left before the next attack?"

"We still have a few left before the next one," Lakshani said.

"And you think that this American you seek can give you the answer to where Khaled is?"

"We know he knows where Khaled is," Lakshani said. "Sri Lanka offers extradition, the Maldives don't."

"Then why didn't he just meet them in the Maldives instead of here? He could be caught over here," asked Courtney.

Shaking his head Asiri said, "No. Khaled is too smart and won't go to the Maldives because his tentacles are far greater here, in Sri Lanka. He has a well-established network of criminals who help him smuggle things in and out of the country and are part of his operation. He doesn't know a single soul on paradise island. You have to remember, this isn't the West. Sometimes extradition rules are followed, and sometimes they're not. It all depends on who picks you up, how much money you have to offer them, and how they're feeling at that exact moment. I've known authorities to arrest people and shoot them thirty minutes later, tossing their bodies in the ocean. The sharks do the rest."

"Goddamn," said Courtney.

"Yes, welcome to the rest of the world. Outside of your precious bubble of bureaucracy, you get a small glimpse of how the actual world functions. Now, let's see if I can get you a location on this American."

Ar Raqqah, Syria

"**A**re the explosives prepared?" asked Khaled, walking through the market while talking on his cell phone. He rarely left the protection of his small town on the outskirts of the city, but this was the exception.

His security detail drove him to the other side of the city, parked, and hopped out. Two guards stayed in front and two in the rear, all brandishing AK-47's. The buildings surrounding them were either destroyed, being rebuilt, or being used as checkpoints for ISIS rebel forces. The wars over the years had completely decimated any resemblance to a working city. People on the streets were homeless and broke, and electricity was nonexistent, as was clean running water.

Khaled didn't care about the petty problems of the people living in the city. All he cared about was law and order. Someone stole something? They lost a hand. Someone talked back to any one of his leaders? Their tongue was cut out.

Keeping the civilians in constant fear was key, at least in Khaled's eyes. He ruled with an iron fist, and to him, he was the beginning, middle, and end of anyone's future in the region. Respecting the wishes of Allah was the goal, and ensuring the rest of the region did the same was his calling.

"We're good to go," said Matthew.

"Good, walk me through the process again."

"We've gone over this—"

"I know we've gone over this," interrupted Khaled, "but I'm paying you a lot of money to make certain this goes off with no issues. The other attacks will pale in comparison to this one. I don't want to hear any problems with you telling me you can't execute! You have no idea what I have gone through, who I've had to talk to, who I've had to get approval from, and how long I have waited for this. My mother was slaughtered like a dog along with other members of my family. You Americans don't understand what it's like to have another country's military go into your homes and kill your loved ones."

The line was silent. Matthew was speechless. He let Khaled continue. "Now, tell me one more time."

Matthew Siff cleared his throat and walked Khaled through every step in the plan, every person's role in it, and everything they had planned down to the precise second.

More silence. Khaled was content. Stroking his long beard and stopping in the middle of the dusty road, he said, "Good."

"They won't know what hit them," said Matthew.

"Stand by for the text," said Khaled, and with that, he hung up the phone.

Asiri surprised Courtney with the information he was able to access. His network was indeed vast and unlike any other criminal organization she had ever seen. Asiri figured because Sri Lanka extradited people and Matthew Siff didn't have the level of connections that Khaled did to escape extradition, he wouldn't be arriving by plane. Other than hearing someone was meeting with Khaled a week ago, Asiri hadn't known too much about Matthew, until he made his calls.

After thirty or so minutes of back-and-forth from different phone conversations—which seemed like an eternity to Lakshani and Courtney—he narrowed down a location. One of the lieutenants in Asiri's organization gathered intelligence from one of his subordinates, and an American matching the description of Matthew was seen in and around the fishing port. From there, Asiri talked to his contact who ran the corrupt operation overseeing the docks.

Subsequently Asiri was able to find out that his fishing port contact received a larger sum of money from one of the captains of the fishing boat because that particular captain was being compensated handsomely for escorting an American from the Maldives to Sri Lanka, and back. That same captain left an hour ago to head back to the Maldives with the American onboard. Once Asiri relayed the information to Courtney and Lakshani sitting on his couch, it all came together.

"If they already left, you know where I'm headed, which means you know what to do," Lakshani said to Asiri. Nodding, he sat down behind the desk and picked up his phone once again to make some more calls. They all said their goodbyes and headed out of the office.

"What was that about?" asked Courtney, following Lakshani back down the stairwell.

"You're about to see the extent of our relationship," she answered, grinning from ear to ear. "You know, it all makes sense in the whole scheme of things. The Maldives are beautiful, and although it's a small island operating right next to two larger cousins, they are their own country. They each enforce their laws differently, and rightfully so. Matthew could blend in—and to anyone except the locals, he would look like any other tourist."

"What if the locals start getting suspicious?" asked Courtney.

"They won't, the people there are some of the nicest people

you will ever meet. They'll welcome anyone. Plus, they have their fair share of Westerners who live there. As long as you don't disrupt the peaceful tranquility of the island no one says shit."

"That's great, but now that I know that, we have a slight problem," said Courtney. They were now within visual distance of the vehicles. The rest of the team had gotten back inside the SUVs and had the windows rolled up. As hot as it was outside, Courtney couldn't blame them if they wanted to blast the AC.

"What's the problem?" asked Lakshani.

"He left the pier over an hour ago; how do we expect to catch him?"

"Helicopter and speedboats?" she said.

"I take it you already know a guy?"

"Yeah, I know a guy."

Once they hopped inside the SUV, Lakshani made a phone call to the embassy requesting their navy's Special Boat Squadron, which was modeled after the British Special Boat Service. Courtney decided then would be the perfect time to update Janet on the information they had acquired so far.

After both phone calls had ended, Lakshani was instructed not to worry and that they would have their approval by the time they arrived at the harbor.

The SBS was based out of Trincomalee, on the other side of the island, but a small contingent of men happened to be conducting training in Colombo. The embassy briefed their commander on using them for an actual operation; it was an easy sell.

The ride was quick and allowed the team to take the opportunity to check and triple-check their gear, weapons, and ammunition. Most everyone's weapons of choice back in the states were Glocks or Smith & Wesson. Courtney took Max's advice and after a fun day of shooting at the range with the team, changed her pistol of choice to the Springfield Hellcat RDP. The RDP stood for

Rapid Defense Package, which paired nicely with a micro-red dot sight and compensator, making for faster transitioning between targets and easier follow-on shots. It suited her nicely. But because they were traveling internationally, smuggling US weapons into a country was too much of a hassle. So Lakshani had Sri Lankan military weapons waiting for them at her house, which she had her drivers load inside SUVs before they took off for Asiri's warehouse.

Accompanying them were MP5 submachine guns. Lightweight and small, they came with a collapsible stock, which wasn't the best for concealing, but it was a step up from a pistol. It also offered a little more flexibility and comfort than every member carrying a rifle and a pistol and trying to conceal both. This was the perfect alternative.

Next came their clothing, specifically their button-up shirts. For their last operation in the Amazon, they wore plate carriers. But trekking through the Amazon was extremely hot. David was able to sign off on ordering them all several pairs of bulletproof shirts in a variety of different colors. The shirts were made of the same material that was used to protect billionaire clients. This way they could blend into whatever environment they were in more easily, even though a couple of Westerners in a foreign country stood out like a sore thumb.

The pair of SUVs pulled up to the guard shack of the harbor in Colombo. The second Lakshani showed her badge, the guard waved them through. It wasn't much, but the dilapidated pier, the front office sitting inside of a small shack, and the rusty fishing boats screamed smuggler's paradise. If this was how Matthew Siff was getting in and out of the country, it was no surprise why he wasn't flagged in any of the databases for Interpol or any local military or law enforcement. Anyone with pockets deep enough could pay their way through the pier, keeping their head down and disappearing into the country once they'd cleared the guard shack.

The pier consisted of five docks and as the SUVs drove down to the very last one. Courtney could see one Cedric-style fast boat, a boat similar to the rubber crafts she'd used in training. Both vehicles came to a stop, and the coxswain alongside the bowman walked up to greet Lakshani. Wearing more of the same type of military fatigues, the coxswain greeted the crew.

After a smile and hug Lakshani said, "Okay, folks, this is Kalana and his team and they will be escorting us to the target."

"Welcome," he said, shaking everyone's hands. "We must hurry, we don't have a lot of time." His wide smile quickly disappeared and was replaced with a more serious one.

"How many people can fit on that thing, including your crew?" asked Kwame, walking over to the Cedric-style boat.

"Well," said Kalana, now standing next to him. "This one has just one seat for the Coxswain and three gunmen. On the bow is a 23mm auto-cannon, and a PKM 7.62mm machine gun for the gunman. My men will be on this one and the other one, which is the typical rubber boat I'm sure you're used to seeing."

"There are only eight seats on the rubber boat though," said Kwame.

"Correct," said Kalana.

"Then someone needs to stay back," said Nate. "There's five of us, plus your men."

"Yes, more than just one person needs to stay back, sir. If it is possible," said Kalana.

"Do all of you really need to go?" asked Lakshani, putting her sunglasses on. "I'm already staying back. I can coordinate things better from there anyway. There's no reason for me to go on a wild goose chase. No offense, but that's what y'all get paid for."

"Fair enough," said Alex.

"I'll stay back," said Kwame. "I get seasick easily anyway."

"I'll stay back also," said Nate, resting his hand on Kwame's shoulder. "Someone has to watch over him. Lord only knows what he'll get into by himself."

"Who's going to look over you?" Kwame responded, shrugging his hand off his shoulder.

"Alright, it's settled then," said Courtney.

"What about the interrogation stuff? It's going to take too much time to snag him and bring him back to a black-site," said Alex.

"Leave that to me," answered Antonio. "All that Colombian training isn't going to go to waste, believe me. When I get through with him, he'll be singing whatever song we want."

CHAPTER 20

Five minutes later both boats were underway. The coxswains pushed out of the harbor, slow and steady until they hit the sea buoy. Once past the buoy, the coxswains accelerated, outboards screaming out of the harbor as the boat rocked and rolled under the powerful engines.

From the pier Lakshani received permission to have a Mil Mi-24 attack helicopter take off from the Air Force base, which was shared with the Bandaranaike International Airport. Staying covert at five thousand feet and when the team was ready to execute, it would drop to one thousand, maybe lower. From there it would hover over the fishing boat while giving task direction to stop.

Staring out into the ocean, Courtney's face was battered by the wind. Looking to her right, she cracked a smile at Alex and at the same time admired the emptiness of the vast ocean in front of them. She imagined that this was the closest feeling to being a dog and sticking its head out of a car window.

"Test, test," said Antonio, covering his mouth from the wind.

"Test sat," responded the group.

"When we secure the boat and find this guy, leave the rest to me," said Antonio.

After about thirty minutes to an hour at sea, what seemed like an eternity, was finally over. The helicopter spotted the vessel by the numbering over the top of the boat's pilot house. Clouds overhead were nonexistent. Some other fishing boats were in sight but not many as the team went to work. Once the call on the radio came through, the team waited until they were about a mile out. Grabbing the railing of Kalana's seat, Courtney used it as a crutch to stand and prop her body, matching the movement of the boat. "Okay, tell Lakshani to send the helo in!"

Kalana nodded, reached for his radio, and went to work on his new orders. In less than a minute the team witnessed the helicopter drop down over their target, open the gunner door, and produce a manned 240 machine gun.

"I spy with my little eye, movement on the deck," said Antonio, standing next to her with binoculars.

"Any sign of an American?" asked Alex, doing a press check of his MP5.

"Negative," responded Antonio, giving the binoculars to Courtney after a tap on his shoulder.

Minutes later Kalana watched the second Cedric boat pull up, providing ample security in addition to the helicopter. Once the coxswain from the other boat gave Kalana the all clear, he turned and said, "You guys ready to board?"

"Let's do it!" said Courtney.

Kalana drove the boat up to the port side stern of the fishing vessel and Courtney and the Bering Group jumped over the gunwale after the SBS crew members. Staying out of their way, the Bering Group secured the stern while the SBS did what they did best and secured the passengers and crew on the bow and cleared the rest of the boat. They were quick and precise. A minute and a half later another all clear came across the headsets and the Bering Group was ready to go to work.

Once the initial thrill ceased, the smell of fish guts scattered all over the place stung the nostrils. As far as weapons were concerned, Courtney was pretty positive any one of the knives scattered across the deck, which the team had to sidestep over, would give her tetanus just by looking at them.

The trio walked down the port side, MP5s dancing from the strap across their shoulders, careful not to slip on the fish guts. Once they made their way onto the bow, there he was. Handcuffed to the rail running the length of the entire vessel was Matthew Siff. He was wearing a white button-up shirt, sunglasses, black slacks, matching boots, and a deep sunburn.

"Who are you?" he asked.

All three Bering Group operators looked at their captured subject and said nothing. Courtney asked the two guards up front to head around the corner and to radio Lakshani that the interrogation was about to begin. Shuffling around Alex, they disappeared from sight.

"Watch and learn, *mijo*," said Antonio to Alex.

"*Aye, cabron*," responded Alex, placing his hands on his hip.

"You got this?" asked Courtney, turning to Antonio.

"I got this," he said, handing his MP5 to Courtney. Walking the three feet to Matthew, who still had his glasses on, Antonio knelt down and assumed a "catcher's pose."

"What is it you want? And who the heck are you guys?" asked Matthew.

Hearing a bit of sarcasm, Antonio reached over and gently pulled Matthew's sunglasses off, tossing them on the ground in front of him.

"Hey, those were Balenziagas, probably cost more than your entire salary in a year."

Antonio smiled, looked down, and stepped on them. "None of that matters anymore. We know you're behind the drone strike that killed a Navy SEAL member and are working with Khaled Ahmadi orchestrating more terrorist attacks." Antonio looked at his watch. "The next one is scheduled to go off at nine o'clock in the morning, East Coast time, right around the corner. I'm going to be very frank with you. If you give me the answers I need, this can be quick. We can leave and turn you over to these fine gentle-men who handcuffed you and be out of your hair.”

“And if I say go fuck yourself?”

Antonio’s response was methodical; it all was. He knew exactly what he was doing and exactly what the subject was doing, or try-ing to. Antonio knew Matthew was toying with him and trying to buy some time. First would come the negotiation talks, second would come the information gathering, and last would be the pro-cess for handing him over. However, time was of the essence.

“I hope you enjoy this as much as I will,” Antonio said. He slid his right hand over Matthew’s right thumb and very slowly bent it backward until he heard a pop and snap. Matthew writhed in pain, but Antonio didn’t stop. He went to work with the rest of the fingers on the same hand and by the time he was done, Matthew was in serious pain. Flailing, crying, screaming— nothing was off limits.

“What is it you want to know!”

“Where is Khaled?”

Matthew met Antonio’s eyes, then darted down. “He’ll kill me!” he said between gasps of air.

“We own you now, which means you’re already dead to him,” said Antonio. Antonio took a quick shot at Courtney, who gave him a subtle nod. He continued. “Tell us what we want to know.”

Matthew’s breaths became rapid, his skin clammy, and he began to lose a sense of awareness.

“You’re not passing out on me, bud,” said Antonio. Reaching over he grabbed a handful of Matthew’s hair and slapped him a couple times in the cheek. His eyes met Antonio’s again. “Tell us where he is and we’ll get you all the help you need.”

“Move over,” said Courtney, “he’s going into shock.” Antonio stepped back and watched Courtney pull his pants down and administer a shot of adrenaline into his outer thigh.

It was a requirement for everyone in the Bering Group to have trauma training, but Courtney was the only EMT on the team. She carried any extra trauma packs, needles, or medical gear she felt she needed for whatever operation she was tasked with. Within two minutes, life was restored, somewhat, to their subject.

She stood up, grabbed Antonio's arm, and pulled him close. "I only have one more of those with me, and I didn't plan on administering that one to a terrorist."

"Check," he said as Courtney let go of his arm and moved back to her original position, leaning on the doorframe into the cabin.

Antonio knelt back down. "Where is he? We know you met not too long ago, here in Sri Lanka."

Matthew took a couple of seconds, catching his breath before responding. "You don't get it do you? He could be anywhere by now. I don't keep tabs on him, and he doesn't keep tabs on me. We come up with a location and meet. That's it."

"You meet with one of the most wanted terrorists in the world and you expect me to believe that you have no clue where he is? Where he lives?"

Matthew looked off into the distance for a couple of seconds before responding. "I already fucking told you, I don't know!"

"To bad, I don't believe you," said Antonio. Reaching down, he produced a knife from the inside of his boot and went to town on Matthew's index finger, sawing and hacking away. He only made it halfway before Matthew spat.

"He's in Syria!"

"We figured that much smart-ass; where exactly? Give us a location," said Antonio, placing the bloody knife on top of the next finger, the sawed one until it was dangling by tendons. Alex, standing in the back the entire time, made his way over to the edge of the boat and threw up. Antonio and Courtney ignored Alex and continued to pay attention to their subject.

"How do you get in contact with him?" asked Antonio.

Matthew's blood was pouring down his hand.

"His number is saved in my burner phone," Matthew began between gasps. "Go into my backpack and pull out my notebook. There's a series of codes and phrases we use. Quick and easy, that's it. No talking, just text."

Courtney stepped inside and brought his backpack out. Slamming it down on the deck next to Antonio, she began to rummage through until she found a small black notebook. Opening it, sure enough, there was an intense series of numbers that each had a corresponding word or phrase next to it. "Got it," she said. "How do we know you're not lying?"

"I have no more cards to play, I swear. Just please help me!" screamed Matthew.

Antonio turned to Courtney. "Does it look legit?"

"Do we have a choice?" she asked. Antonio shrugged. She said, "I'll get all of this info back to Lakshani and see if it checks out. If it sounds legit we'll get started with setting this meetup."

Courtney ducked inside and walked back out with a handful of rags to stop the bleeding. "You know, you can last a long time with a finger cut off without passing out," said Antonio. "Especially since we've already shot you up with adrenaline."

Matthew's face mimicked the initial expression when he mentioned Khaled's name.

"What else do you want to know?"

"These terrorist cells, where are they, how many, and what can we do to stop them?"

"You can't, only Khaled can make that call now, and it continues until Jack Knowles is handed over."

"How many are in this cell?"

"There are anywhere from fifteen to twenty. I don't know where they are, I don't know who they are, all I know is they've been sitting in the states for a long time, waiting for a moment like this from their handlers. They've been vetted, cleared, and hold jobs in positions that you can't even imagine, giving them access to all sorts of information," said Matthew, whose eyes were starting to get glassy again.

Antonio smacked him hard across his face. "Oh, no you don't. Every terrorist as a main event, a Super Bowl if you will, to all the other attacks. What's Khaled planning?"

In between heavy breaths he said, "I don't know, I swear. All I do know is that whatever they're planning, it's big. I was just required to make sure the explosives made it to its destination and fly the drone."

"Explosives? How big? Like 9/11 big?"

"Something like that, but he didn't ever tell me. My job was to get him the names of five people, and then I get paid. But when I couldn't get him info on Jack Knowles, that's when he improvised."

"What do you mean?" asked Courtney.

Matthew spat on the ground. "I wasn't able to get Jack's personal information because it's under heavy lock and key with the agency. It was too easy to get information on the others, but not on Jack. When I told Khaled I couldn't get Jack's info, he didn't pay me the full amount he'd promised and then told me he would have a plan in mind and take care of it himself. A week or two later he said he would send me the rest of the money if I could coordinate for his men in the States to get ahold of a large amount of explosives and initiate the drone strike."

Antonio stood up and looked at Courtney. "We need to get Khaled. What do we do with him?" asked Antonio, turning to Courtney.

"I'll patch him up and we'll take him back to Lakshani and let him get processed. If Lakshani finds this info in the notebook legitimate, we'll use it to set up a meet. We're going to cut the head off this snake before he gets too hungry," she replied.

"We had better hurry, this is an anaconda we're dealing with, not a harmless garter snake," responded Antonio. Courtney walked over to the side of the boat and signaled for them to pull alongside for departure. Antonio made his way over and leaned against the railing.

"How the fuck did you know he was going to tell you that stuff?" she asked.

"When you live where I lived and did the work I did for as long as I did, you know how to break people. They all have limits. The pain, the screams, the agony from the subject—you don't feel any amount of sorrow for the bad buys. They always crack, always. Maybe the low ones on the pole don't know anything, and rightfully so, but the higher ones are getting paid like this guy. Just remember that," he said.

"Noted. Now help me clean him up before he actually passes out."

CHAPTER 21

The White House

It was four in the morning when the phone rang. Harrison was careful not to disturb his wife, who'd grown accustomed to sleeping with earplugs. He reached over with his right arm and fumbled for the phone. Resting his hand on the spine of it, he cleared his throat. "President Harrison."

"Good morning, sir, it's Alexis."

"Hang on, let me transfer you," he whispered, not wanting to wake up his wife. Creeping out of bed and swinging his legs around, he landed in the White House slippers with the presidential seal on them. Tiptoeing toward the door, he grabbed the robe resting on the hook.

"Have fun," said his wife, without missing a beat. The plugs had stopped working months ago.

"Go back to sleep, babe, this will be quick."

"Uh-huh," she said, turning over and trying to fall back asleep.

Stepping outside he nodded to the secret service agent, who returned the nod while bringing his sleeve up to his mouth.

"Eagle en route to the nest," the secret service agent said.

This better be good, Harrison thought. He needed Knowles dead, Khaled gone, and the American people to see that he didn't fuck around when it came to protecting the homeland. He needed this win before the election next year and Jack Knowles's death was his meal ticket to another four years in office.

After a quick walk through the White House, he approached the entrance to the Oval Office with another agent standing by the door, ready to open it. As soon as he was close enough, the agent opened the door and the president stepped inside. The door closed behind him and he made a beeline over to the blinking red phone sitting on his desk.

"Alexis?" asked the president.

"Yes, sir, I'm here."

"Tell me something good, please."

Clearing her throat, she said, "Sir, I just received confirmation that Matthew Siff was apprehended thirty minutes ago in Sri Lanka. Our assets are taking him in as we speak."

"What about Khaled?"

"They captured a burner phone Matthew was using to make contact with Khaled. Our techs tapped into it and pinpointed the receiving VPN to a city in Syria."

"Of course. And what are we doing about it?"

"The team that snagged the phone is already en route to Syria. However, we still have to figure out where exactly he's hiding. We have some avenues of approach and have deep assets undercover in his organization we're working with, so it won't be long."

"Good, what about the cell?"

"The FBI has made some raids in the last couple of hours and brought in a few individuals in Florida, Wyoming, and South Carolina due to chatter the NSA was monitoring. They said terrorist chatter has gone up considerably within the last twelve hours, but they can't just go and arrest every person of Middle Eastern decent or ones that have ties with questionable people in the Middle East they're monitoring. That would make headlines by morning, so they have to play this one smart."

Rubbing his eyes he asked, "How long are they going to hold them if they bring them in?"

"They can only hold them for forty-eight hours, sir."

The president looked at his wrist and found it barren. Remembering he'd left his watch on the nightstand, he looked up at the grandfather clock in the corner of the office. The golden hands read 4:15 against the white background.

"Thank you, Alex, please keep me informed on any and all information regarding what your team finds on Khaled. After the Charlotte attack last night I'll be addressing the nation this morning."

"Sir, we only have roughly five hours until the next planned attack. When are you planning on addressing the nation?"

"Eight o'clock," said Harrison.

"Sir, might I suggest after nine?"

"Why?"

"If you address the nation an hour before the next attack is supposed to happen, the people won't believe anything you say about keeping them safe. If you address the nation immediately after the next attack, *if* it happens, that gives you another twelve hours to figure it all out and stop it from happening again."

There was a pause before Harrison said, "Okay, Alex, not a bad idea. I'll take you up on that one because that actually fits better with my schedule for the day. The wife of one of the SEAL members is having a funeral this afternoon and I planned on being there. However, due to the circumstances, my security detail doesn't think it's best to be in that type of environment right now."

"What time is the funeral, sir?" asked Alexis.

"Ten o'clock this morning. Like I said, my detail wants me to stay put but I'm not scared of another terrorist. I'm not a coward, and Khaled can go fuck himself."

"So you're going to attend the funeral then?"

"No, we compromised. I'm going to go earlier and drop off some flowers and pay my respects personally to the immediate family before everyone else shows up. I'll be back in the White House by nine o'clock."

"Roger, sir. Well, thank you and I'll inform you the second the team finds something."

"Thank you," Harrison said, ending the call.

Opening the drawer in his desk, he pulled out his encrypted iPad and walked over to the two couches facing each other. Choosing the one on the left, he turned the iPad on, looked for General Godwin's number in the list of contacts, and dialed. Once he saw the dial tone on the screen, he activated the three-way call feature and dialed Ethan Cox. The general answered first, with a solid black silhouette as his background instead of his face.

"Good morning, Mr. President," he said, clearing his throat.

"Is anyone next to you?" asked Harrison.

"No, sir, once I saw it was you calling I went downstairs into my—"

"Good," said Harrison, interrupting the general. "Now as soon as Ethan can get on the line we can continue this conversation."

General Godwin despised Harrison just as much as the other people on his staff did. He was arrogant and an asshole behind closed doors. Godwin hated the way that Harrison always complained about law enforcement and the way the tactics and procedures were used on people, and yet he always wanted to make sure his secret service detail was well taken care of. The other military leaders in his cabinet were not too fond of him either.

"There you are," said Harrison once Ethan had picked up the phone. "Did your guy do as he was told?"

"Negative sir, I sent him in and—"

"You said he was good to go with this? Jack is an old man. How the hell could your asset not handle him?"

Ethan paused. "I don't know, sir, but I think Jack has some help. Probably someone he trusts whose close to him and more than likely a lot younger than he is."

"How old is Jack?"

"He's fifty-seven," said Ethan.

"Fuck," said the president. He paused for a long time. "Ethan, get Jack's address for the general so he can pass it down the chain."

"Sir, I'm a little confused on what you're asking," said Ethan.

"You don't you remember our conversation yesterday about spinning up a certain group of people? You should remember it because you were the one who said we didn't have to. You were the one who said we could keep it under wraps and take care of this with *your* asset. Guess what happened? You failed, and now I'm left to clean up the mess."

"Yes, sir, but I thought—"

"That's the problem, you don't get paid to think, you get paid to do. What I'm asking you to do is get a simple address over to the general so he can assemble his men to take out a target. That's it. I don't fucking care about some stupid federal law; get me a team that can take out Jack."

General Godwin chirped up. "Mr. President, I can issue these orders, but I'm not sure the guys are going to like going after someone like Jack. Especially with his background, and especially since he really hasn't done anything wrong."

"Hasn't done anything wrong? He put us in this situation from the start, general. His actions over twenty years ago are the exact reason why we're in this predicament to begin with. Quite frankly, he's lucky he's survived this long and wasn't taken out like your SEALs were. The fact he's even in the CIA and has his identity hidden from the world is the only reason he hasn't been targeted by Khaled's men to begin with. If I have to pick hundreds of millions of lives over one CIA asset's fuckup, regardless of how long ago it was, I'm picking the lives of my people I have an oath to protect. Now I don't give a flying fuck what Special Forces group you decide to use or what story you decide to come up with to get them to scratch that particular killing itch, they need to execute their orders. And I need you to do it, and I need it done yesterday.

Understood? And that goes for that address too, Ethan.

"I have approximately seventy people killed or injured from the hotel attack in Charlotte last night, and it's approaching the end of twelve hours yet again. Right now nobody has any answers as to getting this shit wrapped up. I have to address the nation and hope to God another terrorist attack doesn't happen tonight because I don't have faith that my forces can stop it. Fuck! It's too early for this."

"Yes, sir. Understood," said the general. Ethan didn't respond.

"Ethan Cox, did I make myself clear?"

"Yes, Mr. President, but what if you had another option? One that involved a full team but not a military option just yet? There's only one caveat."

President Harrison sat back in his seat. "Why would I trust you again?"

"Because you know just as well as I do that when Godwin makes that call, no matter how much he covers it up, if the press gets wind of what we're doing and who they're going after, and why, it's all over for you. You don't want to be exposed to the world for violating military protocol. If I'm being honest, I like my job and I don't want to go down as an accessory to your crime."

"Keep talking," said the president.

"We have to involve Hector for this plan to work, sir."

Over the next five minutes Ethan explained the plan in-depth to Harrison and Godwin. Harrison still wanted to use a tried-and-true SF team, but Ethan's idea would have to do for now.

"Fine. Let Hector know, but don't tell him exactly why we need to use his men. Make up some bullshit that Jack's a high-value criminal, and he's aiding terrorism for the United States. I don't need the Secretary of Homeland Security knowing about what the fuck it is we're trying to do. The more people who know about this, the more chances of the media catching wind."

"Yes, sir," said Ethan.

CHAPTER 22

Inner Harbor, Baltimore, Maryland
That same morning

The HRT was around two hundred members in total and was deployed all around the world to complete any number of high-risk operations. Some of them worked hand in hand with the Navy's infamous SEAL teams, Army's Delta Force, and any number of other Special Forces operators. They were a full-time law enforcement group able to deploy anywhere and accomplish virtually the same as the Special Forces groups in the military. People often confused them with the Police Department's Special Weapons and Tactics Team, or SWAT.

The main distinguishable attribute between HRT and SWAT was that SWAT team members trained a couple of times a month while performing their normal policing duties. Once the HRT member completed a year of training, plus other schooling, this was their life. Day in and day out, at any point in time a call could be given to parachute over a target, take down a hostage-taker deep in the mountains, deploy overseas, or integrate with an SF team to take down a high-level ISIS member, or in this case—quickly assemble to take out a hijacker stateside.

It was pitch black just below the surface of the water as Josh Quinn and his team of seven other Federal Bureau of Investigation Hostage Rescue Team members—more commonly referred to as FBI's HRT—approached their target. Recently their dives had involved warmer climates, a 3mm wet suit, an oxygen tank, and a mask but this one was a little different.

Baltimore was known for its colder climates, especially in the winter. With the water temperature close to freezing and pitch black under the surface, without the proper protective gear, the average person wasn't surviving long.

A rebreather diving apparatus absorbs carbon dioxide of a user's exhaled breath, permitting rebreathing of the substantially unused oxygen content, and unused inert content when present with each breath. The apparatus was also extremely quiet, did not emit bubbles, and because the gas the diver was using was warm, there was an added benefit of the member's internal body temperature not dropping too quickly.

Josh Quinn approached the bottom of *David II*, which was a two-hundred-and-fifty-foot yacht belonging to a billionaire who happened to be celebrating his fiftieth birthday with his closest friends and a number of attractive women. The local SWAT team was called first until they realized the best method of approach was waterside, specifically diving.

Josh approached the hull and set up his equipment. His silenced MP5 and pistol, already tucked away and secured, allowed his hands and feet to use the four, high-powered magnetic grips to climb up the side of the boat. The lever-activated system was entirely waterproof, allowing the operator to start the climb underneath the surface. The choice was perfect.

Josh and the team made their way up the stern of the vessel, pausing just below the railing. Josh quickly poked his head over the side, pistol first, and scanned for any threats. Seeing someone with a rifle, their back toward him, Josh pulled the trigger twice. Silenced rounds screaming out of the barrel hit its target square in the back. The target dropped without a sound.

The rest of the team scurried over the railing, dropping their rebreathing apparatus. They unslung their rifles and started their journey throughout the boat. They were on a time constraint and only had four minutes left before the hostage-taker told the negotiator he would execute the first one if he didn't get his money. The call reminded Josh of something out of a novel.

Three members moved toward the engine room, two toward the pilot house. The remaining group consisted of Josh and the sweep team that was securing everything else. The team's black boots scuffed up the nice hardwood floors. *Whatever*, thought Josh, *this billionaire can afford it.*

His team encountered two more tangos, or bad guys, approaching the rear entrance to the kitchen. Dropping them was a breeze and as more bodies hit the deck, his team simply stepped over them. Pushing the silver swivel door to the kitchen, Josh turned right as his team flowed to the left. The team took charge of both walkways on either side of the massive shelving system holding various pots and pans sitting in the middle of the room. The shelving system was the same length as the kitchen, so the team wasn't able to meet up until they rounded the unit, and met on the other side. The door had a circular window in the center, but nobody dared look through it just yet.

Giving the signal to pause, Josh looked at the dial on his Doxa Sub 300t Caribbean. The orange minute-hand ticked away; two minutes left. "This is baby Yoda, teams one and two give me a SITREP, over."

"For the record, I think your name is hilarious every time I hear it," said one of the team members standing behind Josh. Josh answered by raising his middle finger with his left hand, his right still holding the rifle aimed at the door. The name Baby Yoda was ironic for Josh because he resembled a brick house more than a cuddly fictional character. Josh also had tattoos covering every space on his gigantic biceps, a thick beard with various grays, and a bald head. He looked more like a Norse god.

All clears were given, every other room was captured, so Josh and his team were all that was left. "Alright, gents, we now have a minute and a half. Remember, slow is smooth and smooth is fast."

As Josh talked he never took his eyes away from the door. A simple head movement to the right or left, and not paying attention was the difference between a random tango spotting you and shooting you, or vice versa. The operator standing behind Josh reached underneath Josh's right arm, floating his hand just above the door handle. Josh paused and raised his muzzle from the door handle to just below eye level, signaling it was time.

The team quickly made entry into the massive room. There were tables and chairs strewn everywhere, bottles broken on the floor, and a person passed out behind the bar to their right. All the patrons huddled on the ground to the left, zip tied, with the three remaining terrorists standing in the center of the room. They didn't have time to react.

The team spread out, owned the real estate across the room, and released their rounds to each target simultaneously. All three tangos dropped with relative ease. The team swept the room, yelling at the hostages to stay down, overwhelming the hostages' nerves, and taking control of the situation. Relief swept over the hostages in the dining room. A full thirty seconds passed before Josh radioed to base camp.

"Base camp, this is Baby Yoda, boat secu—" Josh was interrupted by a string of gunfire from the individual they thought was dead behind the bar. Josh and his teammate's entire left side was covered in blue paint before one of the teammates engaged the last tango.

"Dammit, Drew, I thought you checked him already?" asked one of the team members across the room.

"Fuck, rookie! Go check him, now!" screamed Josh.

Running over to the role player, who was shot more than

enough times with paint to be declared dead, Drew said, "All clear, Josh, sorry I didn't see him."

"No fucking shit you didn't see him," said Josh, moving up close and into the new member's face. "Always frisk the people in the room with a gun. I don't care if they look dead with a gun or if they're a hot chick in a bikini with a gun. Fucking check everyone, is that clear?"

A simple head nod was all he received before walking away and signaling an official all clear, halting the exercise.

"Hey, Josh, you and your guys get down here, something just came up," said their boss, standing outside on the pier.

"Stay here and release everyone from the zip ties, rook," said Josh, heading out the starboard side door.

"Just be more careful next time," said Bryce Holden, the second-in-command and more relaxed senior member. Patting Drew on the shoulder, he ran to catch his longtime teammate.

"You think you were a little hard on the new guy?" asked Bryce.

"Of course I was hard on the new guy," said Josh, smiling and turning around, facing Bryce. "You remember when we got sidetracked by the smoke-show role player they hired on the first round of training ops with the teams?"

Laughing, Bryce replied, "How could I not? You were too busy staring at her boobs while her husband pulled out a pistol from underneath the counter behind you and smoked you. I was laughing so hard on the inside that my abs hurt."

"I'm happy to know that my best friend was laughing at me while I got shot in the back."

"Well, it taught you to be more careful, right? And you shouldn't have been looking anyway, you were dating Sheryl at the time," said Bryce. They reached the bottom of the pier and walked over to their equipment table where their boss was standing. Josh and Bryce began to take off their plate carriers.

"Well, a lot of good dating *her* did," said Josh, taking his helmet off and placing it on the table. "And we were *dating*. Period. It's not like we were married or anything."

"Y'all might as well have been married with the amount of time you were dating. Jesus himself was watching y'all so long he could have come down and married you two." As the rest of the team trickled down, they took off their gear.

Sophia Rodriguez, their boss, approached them. Covering her tan skin was a dark-blue business suit and over that was a large coat. Her looks couldn't stay hidden underneath the cold weather gear. She had long black hair, brown eyes, and curves that mimicked those of a Coke bottle, causing men to salivate once they laid eyes on her. She was Ecuadorian, and the second a man heard her accent, they were usually in love.

Sophia wasn't stupid, she knew she was attractive and even though she wore a fourteen-carat diamond ring on her finger, it didn't sway anyone from attempting to get in her pants. However, the guys with HRT were built differently and considered her more of a sister than a boss, always looking out for her and treating her with all the respect she deserved. Asking for a better group of operators was out of the question.

"Morning, boss," said Josh.

"Good morning, Josh," she said, catching him squinting at her face. "What's wrong?" she asked.

"I don't see your nose bleeding from the pressure change," he said, referring to her position on the totem pole of hierarchy from being on the pier as opposed to the office. The rest of the team laughed. She shot him a smug look.

"You're lucky I'm not making you run that again. You have a couple of members shot and killed. I don't think that's grounds for laughing is it?"

Nobody said a word. "Anyway, it's too cold to stay out here, so here it is. It seems like you guys have got a real mission, a high-value one straight from the top."

Josh and Bryce looked at each other before Josh said, "Where we going?"

"Roanoke," she said. "You and Bryce come with me. The rest of you misfits, get the gear ready."

CHAPTER 23

It took Max thirty minutes to search and wrap Liam's body in the big tarp Jack conveniently had in the garage. Max spared no expense in his serial killer jokes as to why anybody would have a tarp of that size just randomly laying around in the garage unless you hunted and chopped your own meat. Which he knew Jack didn't do.

The entire time, Jack was plopped up on his couch, television on, and a frozen bag of peas on his fractured ribs. Max knew Jack wanted to do everything he could to help him dispose of the body, but working through the pain with his ribs was too excruciating. Once Max was done placing the body in the bed of his truck, he walked back into the house and into Jack's bedroom to grab his pistol. Conducting a press check and ensuring there was indeed a round in the chamber, he laid it on the couch, inches from Jack's right hand. Telling him to not hesitate to give him a call, he then left the house to get rid of the evidence. Sunrise was in an hour or so, so Max knew his chances of disposing the body somewhere in town without being seen were perfect.

After about half an hour, Jack heard the garage door open and close as Max entered the house. Throwing his keys on the countertop, he grabbed himself a glass of water and headed toward the couch. The curtains remained closed and the television was on the local news for anything relating to an increase in terrorist activity. All was quiet. A hospital would be the best answer to the situation, but right now Jack could barely move and he didn't know how far Khaled's reach extended.

Before Max sat down, Jack remembered the secret stash of OxyContin in his medical kit in the bedroom. Max handed him the pills and watched him down them with a glass of water. Jack's breaths slowed. Finally he was able to relax as the pain subsided, creating a barrier between bliss and chaos. Max looked at his friend sitting on the couch. Defeated, slouched posture, and droopy eyes. He was exhausted.

Scooting to the edge of the chair, Max said, "We need to figure out who the fuck that guy was."

"I know exactly who that was," said Jack, wincing. "Liam Parker. He's an asset used by high-ranking officials in DC when they want to cover up their dirty work or get rid of people they don't want exposing their dirty laundry."

"What? I knew DC was bad, but I didn't know they had people on standby to make individuals disappear. I always thought that was a rumor."

"No, it's as real as this cracked rib. They started around the same time I was going through the Farm. I honestly don't know too much about them, but I do know they exist. They are a handful of people, hired hitmen if you will, who will do the bidding of just about anyone for the right price. I say DC because all of those political fucks use them left and right."

"Damn."

"Yeah. From my understanding, if you want something done, somebody killed, somebody bribed, these are the guys to do it. All those stories you've heard over the years, of people involving cases that could implicate people in Washington, DC, that's them. To everyone on the outside, sure the deaths will seem suspicious, of course, but they'll never get the proof because the killers are so far removed from the hellhole that is politics."

"That doesn't exactly answer how you know the guy who just tried to kill you?"

Jack moved positions a little, wincing. "He used to work for us, solid asset. Solo type, like what you did after the agency split us up."

"If he was so good why didn't I know about him?"

"How many assets do you know by name?"

Max paused. "Not that many now that I think about it."

"Exactly. We keep you guys secluded from each other for a reason. When you go solo that's it, you're on your own. You get tasked with an assignment, you do it, and that's it until you get tasked again. We can't afford all the assets knowing where and who everyone else is that works for the agency. There's too much room for error, especially getting involved with fellow female assets, you know? Just take my word for it, he was good."

"Okay, so he used to work for the agency, then what happened?"

"Honestly, I don't know. All I know is he was doing great work and the next thing I knew, he was gone. I never heard a peep from anyone about him and I didn't care to ask either. Next thing I know he's standing behind me with a wire trying to kill me."

Max sat back, taking it all in. "Well, that leads to the next question: who sent him?"

Both men sat for a minute or two before Jack said, "I don't know, but I do know we're not going to find our answer in Roanoke."

"Where do you suggest we go?"

"We have two options. Option A, we either hunker down, fortify this place for the next guy that comes, or we choose option B."

"I'm game for option B."

"Alright then, let's get to work."

Lakshani looked through the codes, talked with a few analysts she met at the pier, and found that despite some concerns about the legitimacy of the notebook, it was the best lead they had. With Matthew handcuffed, on intense painkillers, and his hand wrapped the best that Courtney could without a hospital, he led the charge with great enthusiasm in instructing Courtney exactly what to text. The last thing he wanted was to experience another round of intense interrogations on the only working hand he had.

Matthew convinced Khaled he had Jack's location, and it was too dangerous to not hand him the information in person. It was getting down to the wire. Khaled was fine meeting in person, but didn't want to leave Syria. The last thing Khaled needed was to be caught this far in the game. No, that would be his biggest disappointment to Allah.

After ten minutes of back-and-forth, the team had their answer. They were meeting inside what Lakshani called "the heart of hell": Ar Raqqah. The only caveat was that the times were going to be between 5:00 a.m. and noon the following day. One attack was still planned to happen that evening, and another one the following morning. No pressure.

Traveling straight to Syria was an easy no-no. They couldn't land anywhere in Syria with an executive airplane and not stick out like a sore thumb. Unfortunately, intense weather conditions in the region prevented a last-minute request for a high-altitude, low-opening jump, often referred to as a HALO jump, over Syrian airspace.

ISIS had soldiers scattered all over the place in Syria. The team needed to get in, get to their target, and get out undetected. They needed help. With the problem of contacting Khaled solved, it still left another: how were they going to get into Syria? Luckily for the Bering Group, Lakshani's contacts didn't just stop in Sri Lanka.

Her hand extended across the pond and into Turkey. The chief of operations in the area happened to be one of her instructors from the Farm and coincidentally, Lakshani was his favorite student.

Whether it was because of her looks or the fact that he genuinely liked her as a person she would never know, but he was always there for her with whatever she needed. She told the team to board the plane and everything would be resolved before they landed. Once again, as promised, she delivered.

Landing in the Gaziantep Airport, just beyond the border of Syria, they met their contact, Aydin Aksoy. The team went through the same process as before. Aydin brought customs to the tarmac, "cleared the plane," quickly stamped their passports, and with a smile and nod left Aydin with his new colleagues.

"It's only been a couple of hours and I've already heard so much about you guys," said Aydin, extending his hand to each one of the Bering Group operators.

"I heard you're the guy out here who can get us into places?" asked Courtney.

"Possibly. Follow me," he said. As the team walked past the plane, Aydin led them into the two, waiting, black G-wagon Mercedes. Aydin, Courtney, and Antonio climbed in the front SUV, while Alex, Nate, and Kwame chose the back SUV. The second the doors closed, the convoy was off.

"Any new news on Jack and the situation back home?" Antonio asked.

"Negative. All anyone knows is he's off the grid. Crazy what's goin' on with him, huh?"

Courtney knew Jack had Max to protect him and the two made a dynamic duo. With the right tools, both of them could take on the world, but Jack was older now and moved at half the pace he used to. All they could do was pray everything was going to be alright.

"Here, reach into the back seat, I have some gifts for you. Courtesy of the Turkish government," said Aydin. As much as the team wanted to take the weapons from Sri Lanka with them, Lakshani had to return them. They were borrowed, and she promised they'd have more waiting for them when they landed.

Antonio reached into the cargo section behind their seats and produced two long pelican cases and two backpacks, placing them on the seat next to him. Opening the case on top, he smiled and said, "Ahhh, *gracias senior.*"

Inside the backpacks was a jilbab for Courtney and throbes for everyone else. These were long, loose outer garments used to cover the entire body from head to toe, worn by the people of the region.

Courtney strained her head from the front and caught wind of the MP5s, one MKE JNG-90 Turkish sniper rifle, various .45 caliber pistols, plate carriers, and assorted "tactical goodies." "Thanks, Aydin," Courtney said.

"No problem," he said, swerving to the right and avoiding a car that happened to step on the brakes at the last minute to avoid rear-ending the car in front of it. After looking at the driver while flooring the pedal pushing the SUV through the yellow light in the intersection, he cleared his throat and continued. "Have either you or the guys in the other vehicle been to Syria before?"

"Nope," said Courtney.

A click came from the back seat. Courtney shot her head around to see Antonio pointing the gun toward the floor while conducting a weapons safety check. "What?" he said, pausing.

She turned back to the front. "Yeah, that's a hard no for the whole team. Is that going to be a problem?"

"It's not, but you're going to be immersed in an entirely new world. Syria isn't like anything you've ever seen before in your life, so I want you guys to be mentally prepared for what you're about to encounter. It's a war-torn country, and Ar Raqqah is one of ISIS's strongholds in the country. Starting in November of 2013, the people of ISIS promised to bring security and rest from violence in the region, but their promise was short-lived. Over the course of the next several years, the city was torn apart by constant shelling from US-led coalition forces, trying to take the city back.

"First, the country used to be bustling because ISIS fighters flooded the restaurants, spending their exorbitant amounts of money on goods and services from their local markets, purchasing phones, equipment, and whatever ever else they needed at the time. Then the flour mills reopened north of the city, stabilizing bread prices in the area. Following that, ISIS members replaced imams to lead prayers at local mosques around most of the city. Along with that, they issued strict decrees for individuals to abide by the Islamic law, with harsh punishment and judgment to those who disobeyed."

"That sounds just like Hitler in World War II, offering the people of Germany a better regime and promises," said Courtney.

"Exactly, and we all know how that ended," said Aydin.

"It ended the same as this is about to end," said Antonio, "with the US long arm and dick of the law coming in to fuck them from behind."

Aydin laughed.

"You have to love American politics. Always trying to stick their noses in any country they think needs some democracy. Anyway, the moral of the story is the city is in ruins now. ISIS runs certain areas of Syria more than others, but this was and still is a sacred stronghold for them. You'll still see ISIS out and about, but all of them live in places outside the city.

"Of course they do, why would they live in the poor war-torn mess that they created?" said Courtney. "Nope, they think they're better than that and want nothing to do with the shitstorm they've caused. That being said, the fact that it's run-down doesn't mean you're safe. Watch your back constantly. I've done some critical missions in the past where we had to rescue some people and we were in and out. Trust me you don't want to spend any more time in the country than you have to. There will still be marketplaces with lots of people running around, and there's always spotters watching to make sure no undercover Americans are trying to gather information."

"Well, they clearly haven't met us," said Antonio, leaning forward between both the driver and passenger seat.

"I'm not too worried about you guys, but just remember this is a place where you absolutely don't want to attract unwanted attention."

"Copy on all," said Antonio, leaning back in his seat.

"So what's the plan? Where are we headed?" asked Courtney.

"In thirty minutes or so, we're going to take the exit from the freeway and head to Samandoken Road, which will take us through the small town, and then your ride that awaits you on the Euphrates River. There's a forty-foot fishing boat my old friend owns and he has agreed to take you into Syria. The river itself runs for miles, coincidentally right on the outskirts of Ar Raqqah. I can't guarantee what time you all will arrive, but it's probably not going to be until late tonight. My friend will continue and lead the way into the city."

"How the fuck do they survive if the city is in such disarray?" asked Antonio.

"It's a literal fight for survival there now. The war was over in 2017. They have no electricity, no clean water, and bacteria and viruses run rampant throughout the entire city. It's horrific to see. To answer your question, I don't have a solid answer. Families sleep in fear now, not from ISIS per se, but because the buildings they live and sleep in might collapse on them at any moment. What you guys are about to walk into is like something out of a Stephen King novel."

"Fuck," said Antonio. That was the last word muttered for most of the remainder of the ride.

CHAPTER 24

The team reached the pier and shook hands with Aydin's friend, Abbud. Standing at five feet nine, Abbud sported a scraggly beard to his chest, a tattered white robe, sandals, and a cheerful grin.

Courtney, Kwame, Antonio, Alex, and Nate said their good-byes to Aydin, thanking him for everything. He responded by telling them not to thank him until they were successfully out of the country. As the team walked away in the direction of the boat, Aydin called Courtney back over to the SUV.

"Take this number down," he said, gesturing for her to pull out her phone. After giving her his contact number, Courtney could tell something was still lingering on his mind.

"What are you not telling me?"

"Last time we went into this hellhole we had to shoot our way out. Like I said before, you're about to enter a city and country the likes of which you'll hope to never see again. Once you step off that boat, it's another world. The number I gave you goes directly to my own special 'bat-phone' and when that rings, I pick up. I leave it fully charged and the ringer on full blast 24/7."

"Courtney, hurry up, we're burning sunlight!" shouted Nate, from the foxhole of the boat.

Placing his arm on her shoulder, he said, "Remember, you're it. There's no one coming to rescue you if you get into heat. No SEALs, no Delta, no US military forces of any kind. Our faithful leader, President Harrison, was briefed and doesn't want any kind of Black Hawk Down incident or any kind of bad press before the election next year. He's playing all overseas operations very close to his chest. You already know the implications if you get caught, so don't. That being said, call me on that number; I have a direct line with the Turkish Special Forces. Long story short, they help the Syrian National Army in occupying northern Syria, and I'm a personal friend of their current commander. Right now, you get in, kill Khaled, find out where his cells are if you can, and get out. Khaled's compound isn't too far outside the city so you should be able to make it back quickly."

Courtney took a second to process it all before saying, "No pressure, right?"

"Yeah, no pressure. Good luck, kid." And with that, Aydin climbed into the vehicle and drove off.

The trek down the Euphrates was long and slow. The river expanded at some points and contracted at others. The boat smelled of fish guts, blood, and diesel fuel, which would make for a bad combination had they been in the middle of the ocean with rocking waves. The river provided a smooth ride down until they reached their destination. Kwame, the only real member of the group who got seasick, even enjoyed the ride.

At 6:00 p.m. Courtney gathered the team together on the fantail. They were running out of time and still had several hours to go. "Don't sweat it," said Antonio. "*Inshallah.*"

"What the fuck does that mean?" asked Alex, crossing his arms and removing his sunglasses. It was getting dark.

"If Allah wills it," Antonio responded.

"I thought you were Catholic?"

"I'm just as Catholic as the next person, but if this part of the world is as true as Aydin and everyone says it is, God's already left."

Silence crept over the team at that last sentence.

"Okay," said Courtney. "Let's go over the plan."

She had everyone's undivided attention. "Abbud said we'll reach our destination around ten o'clock tonight. Now let's map this out."

Janet barged into David's office. "Really? No drones overhead?"

David was swamped with paperwork and manila folders all across his desk. "Dammit Janet, shut the fucking door."

She turned around, shut it, and walked forward standing with her arms crossed in front of him. "Why can't we use drones? You realize the safety of the United States is resting on the team over there, right?"

David sat back and rubbed his eyes. "Yes, Janet, I realize this. Harrison wants nothing to go wrong. Nothing at all, so if anyone gets wind of anyone monitoring the team and there's a massive shootout and they die—"

"Then nobody will know. They work for us—that's one of the caveats, dammit! Nobody is supposed to know anything about where we go, what we do, or who we do it for. That's why the group was specifically created, to handle missions like this."

"Janet, I'm well aware of that."

"Then we're just supposed to sit back and not lend a helping hand of support if something goes wrong?"

"That's it right there," said David, standing up and pointing at her. "You just said it, 'if something goes wrong.' Harrison's up for reelection next year and he should have the votes he needs to secure another four-year term. He's thinking worst-case scenario, if they don't get killed and get captured that'll be a shitstorm and a half. What is the United States doing running operations overseas in Syria for?"

Janet raised her arms, "What do you mean? It's to catch this bastard before he strikes. It's an easy solution to that question, and the taxpayers know we do stuff like this."

"No, no! Have you forgotten what Harrison promised, and did, at the beginning of his term three years ago?"

Janet paused for a second before everything came together. "Shit."

David nodded and gestured for her to say what was on her mind.

She walked over and sat down on his sofa. "He withdrew all our forces from the Middle East and promised the people he wouldn't be sending anyone into that region as long as he was in office. He said we have to start policing ourselves, rebuilding this nation and then, maybe, we could start redeploying our troops to areas that need our help."

"Exactly. How would that look to the people if he blatantly lied to everyone? If video surfaced from a US drone strike occurring overseas regardless of who it killed? It wasn't even a random press conference where he said it, it was his inauguration speech. Promising millions of people across the nation, their fathers, wives, sons, and daughters are going to be stateside. Here for every Christmas, Thanksgiving, birthday, or other holidays. No more wishing they would come home or praying that someone would make it another day just so they could have one more conversation with them. He did it. It's all over." David sat down.

Janet took in a deep breath, letting it out very slowly. "David, I understand all of that, but what we're doing is the best thing we have to offer right now. They're not some chewing-tobacco beard growing Special Forces pipe hitters. They're people hand-selected for one of the top-tier programs of the three-letter agencies. They were quite literally the definition of a normal person just a year and half ago."

He just shook his head, "No can do, do you want me to lose my job? You know how serious he is about all of this. You guys will have a drone, but not armed."

"What if we get the military to casually run one of their drones over the same airspace and say they're just doing routine checks for intel?"

"Nope, he wants it radio silent."

"Let me get this straight. He authorized the team to go overseas and catch Khaled by any means necessary, but when it comes to helping them in the Middle East with authorizing a drone strike if necessary, that's where he draws the line?"

"Yes. Basically all we're going to get is a live feed for him in the Situation Room from a drone circling overhead," said David.

"Unbelievable. He knows ISIS operates in that region, right? He's aware of that?" she said, with obvious sarcasm.

"Of course he is. He never had any intention of giving the team any help after they left the States. He knew eventually where the team would end up, but he doesn't care. Casualties of war Ms. Carrera. How's Jack doing?"

Pausing before speaking, she said, "I don't have any updates."

"That's good," said David, his chair squeaking as he leaned back. "Wherever he is, we can only hope they're doing alright."

"What does Alexis think about all this?" asked Janet.

"She thinks there's something going on behind the scenes, but she can't put her finger on it just yet. We'll see sooner or later I would imagine."

Janet stood up, "Hopefully sooner rather than later."

David nodded. "Just keep me updated on everything." Looking at his watch, he said, "It's almost nine o'clock. Alex said Harrison already has a press release ready to go in preparation after this next attack. I have a feeling, depending on what he says, that people are going to start taking this threat seriously."

"They should have done that already. They shouldn't leave their faith in the government to take care of them all the time because the world doesn't work that way. We can't be everywhere, so it's up to them to make sure they're okay." And with that, Janet left the room.

At eight thirty-seven in the morning, President Harrison sat inside his protective limousine in the middle of his six-car motorcade. His vehicle in particular was a 1.5 million-dollar Cadillac Escalade limousine equipped with run-flat tires, night-vision devices, smoke screens, and oil slicks. The armor on the outside walls consisted of a thickness of eight inches, the windows at five inches, and each door believed to weigh as much as those on a Boeing 757. It was as much of a tank as you could get without having treads and a turret.

The rest of the motorcade consisted of various police motor-cycles and cruisers, medical personnel, a full, special weapons and tactics unit, and other various VIPs that chose to accompany him to the give their condolences to the family.

Harrison arrived at the house, finished giving his condolences, and the motorcade was on   its way back to the White House—all within twenty minutes.

"You seem nervous," said his wife, sitting directly across from him.

Harrison ignored her, noticing the trees and colorful houses outside the window slowing down. "What's going on?" Harrison asked the driver.

"Sir, the construction sign up ahead said there was a water main pipe that burst. Water is flooding the road," said the driver. "My apologies."

"Christ, can't you plow through it?" asked Harrison, straining his neck looking through the front windshield and trying to see the chaos for himself.

"No, sir, it looks impassable. There's trucks and workers trying to fix it it looks like.

Not to worry sir, we're going to turn around, we'll have to use the alternate route—"

Just then rifle rounds ricocheted all across the front windshield of the vehicle, creating small spider-like cracks across the bulletproof glass. "Go, go, go!" screamed the agent in the passenger seat. Turning around and facing the back seat, the same agent said, "Hold on Mr. and Mrs. President, we'll get you out of here!"

Even though the limousine could withstand rocket-propelled grenades and certain types of explosives, nobody wanted to test those limitations in a real world scenario. The noise from the vehicle getting peppered by rounds was deafening. Harrison's wife reached over and death-gripped his hand, flinching every time a round hit the vehicle.

The vehicle made a quick U-turn over the grass median and onto the other side of the two-lane street. Two police cruisers had already made the U-turn, leap frogging ahead of the president's limousine to part traffic as the rest of the motorcade of VIPs followed suit. Harrison stole a glance at the scene as the motorcade pulled further away, and saw nothing but carnage behind him.

The SWAT van had stopped as the tactical operators jumped out and engaged the construction workers, disguised as terrorists, who had fired at the president's vehicle. There were three to four bodies of police officers, all from the motorcycles, not moving and bleeding out in the street. It was a war zone right in the president's backyard.

Just then, Harrison heard something loud and obnoxious in the distance. Looking through the upper left corner of the back window, he saw a small round object barreling toward them with a rooster tail of smoke. "Incoming! Behind us!" Harrison screamed. Grabbing his wife and pulling her in close, he closed his eyes. He could feel his heart racing about to explode through his chest.

The driver, had prepped and anticipated attacks like this one. Jerking the steering wheel hard to the left, the limousine responded quickly and precisely.

The passengers in the vehicle were tossed to one side as the rocket whizzed past their right side, slamming into the back of a police cruiser in front of them and sending a two-story fireball into the morning sky.

Harrison opened his eyes, looked at his terrified wife now crying in his arms, and said to the driver, "Get us the hell out of here. Now!"

CHAPTER 25

The team rested inside the mess deck, checked gear, and donned the outfits Aydin gave them as Abbud and his son worked on mooring the vessel. The boat bobbed and weaved with the faint current and when the lines were finally tied off, the boat was still. Kwame listened to the creaking of the old fishing boat, closed his eyes, and said a quick prayer, thanking God he'd made it.

"*Mira*, we're not out at sea, we were in a river," said Antonio, sitting across from Kwame, laughing to himself.

"I know, but I'm not the best swimmer and people seem to forget that the second you fall overboard into the water, humans are the lowest on the hierarchy of food. There's no telling what kind of crazy-ass creatures are lurking underneath the surface."

"You know, for as big as you are, you're a baby," said Nate, checking his weapons one last time.

"Would you like to test the waters? I can see if you'll float with all that gear on," responded Kwame.

Nate frowned.

"You two are like an old married couple," said Courtney.

"Listen, Court, if I wanted your opinion then I would ask what rhinestones are best to bedazzle my clothes with."

Pointing her submachine gun toward Alex's knee, she replied. "Or how about I shoot your kneecap? You'll never walk right again and we'll replace you with someone else."

"You know, maybe bedazzling wouldn't be such a great idea,"

said Alex, reaching for her barrel and moving it away from his knee.

Courtney smiled. "That's what I thought."

Just then Abbud entered the mess deck. "Okay, my friends, we are here. My son will stay. I stay with you and you follow me. Stay close."

Abbud's English was not the worst, but forming complete sentences was not his strong suit. His son sat on the gunnel, nodding to the team as each one crossed the bow onto the pier. The length of the pier stretched to around fifty yards with multiple boats attached to either side.

The night was silent, the boats were quietly rocking back and forth, and with no bad guy in sight, the mission was off to a solid start at least. Once the team made their way toward the end of the walkway, Abbud gathered them all in a secluded corner of the marina.

"Okay, be right back," said Abbud as the team watched him disappear around the corner.

"Saddle up, girls," said Courtney, pulling the NVGs, or night vision goggles, down and over her face. The goggles slid and locked into the attachment on the front of the helmet, while a small, counterweight pack of a couple of pounds sat on the back. Courtney reached to the top of the device, clicked a button, and instantly her field of view turned from pitch black to grey-and- white phosphorous pictures of her surroundings.

Next she ensured her plate carrier sat nice and snug against her body, checking her extra magazines and tactical grenades. Last but not least she turned on the infrared strobe light that rested on her shoulder. This would signify to the team who friendlies were in case they found themselves in a full-on gun battle. Not that she was advocating for it to happen at all.

The rest of the team followed suit and once the team was all set, they waited. Stretched out against the wall, all members had their muzzles up and pointed in various directions, waiting and watching. They were ready. Electricity was nowhere to be found; there were no streetlights, just a half moon illuminating the sky from above and no clouds.

A full minute passed before the faint rumble of a vehicle resonated through their ears. Courtney peeked around the corner and although she couldn't see the inside of the cabin, seeing the two flashing headlights meant it was time to move.

"Roger, let's roll," said Courtney.

The team slowly stood, rotated toward Courtney, and made their way around the corner. A small pathway appeared in front of them, with a torn-down fence to their left and the dilapidated marina's main office building to the right. This led them to the small parking lot where Abbud was waiting. Abbud drove a utility van, similar to what a plumber or electrician would drive when they showed up at your house, and for such a war-torn country, it was in pretty decent shape.

Kwame reached the van first, opened the sliding door and posted guard, sweeping sectors of fire off into the distance while the rest of the team entered the vehicle. Once Antonio had tapped him on the shoulder, Kwame did a final sweep. Satisfied, with no sight of threats, he turned, jumped into the vehicle, and shut the door.

The van lurched forward and with his eyes on the road, Abbud said, "The drive will take about fifteen minutes. Sit tight."

"What about a checkpoint?" Antonio asked, sitting the closest to the front of the van. If there were one or even two more people sitting in the back of the van, the group would be squished like sardines. With three on one bench and two on the other, they would make do.

"No worries. We will be fine. I have cigarettes, and cash from Aydin," responded Abbud.

"Perfect," whispered Nate, into his earpiece.

The van bobbed and weaved down the dirt path, causing discomfort in the back for the group. Kwame hit his head on the top of the van a few times, and each time he did, he was thankful for the helmets Aydin provided.

The drive was silent and uneventful. Antonio wrapped his hands around the golden cross dangling from his neck. As Abbud drove deeper into the city, the team took turns straining and seeing out of the driver's windshield. There wasn't much but torn-down buildings, a bunch of rubble that littered the streets, and a plethora of trash as far as the eye could see.

Abbud made a left turn, drove for what seemed like a hundred feet, and killed the engine. "We are here." Opening the driver's side door, he stepped out and slid open the side door. "Come with me quickly."

Exiting the van, Courtney looked around and Aydin was right. The city, if you wanted to call it that, resembled a construction site in the desert more than anything else. The concrete slabs of what used to be high-rises were mostly, if not all, broken down to half the size of what they used to be. There were huge, gapping holes in the majority of the buildings, with support beams sticking out and hovering over the dirt street. With electricity no longer a commodity in this region, it was in complete darkness. ISIS had entered and left the city in much worse shape than they'd found it. A deep hatred for them ignited a flame inside of Courtney that would only be extinguished when she captured Khaled.

Following Abbud, they jogged between two buildings sitting across the street from where they'd parked. They approached the end of the alleyway, and they waited. Abbud was point. Looking both ways, he ushered them across the street and into the destroyed, seven-story building. There was no doorway. Only a gigantic hole of a doorframe remained as the team made their way deeper into their new home. Heading down the first floor toward the end, Courtney wished she could unsee the horrific sights around her.

The building they were in had been an apartment building of some sort before the war. Each doorway they passed, some with doors still attached and some without, told a story of some sort. There was a family—probably a mother, father, and any number of children that used to occupy each residence. The dust, smell, and rubble littering the darkness of the hallway made her think about what this place used to look like in its heyday. It also made her gag, using her arm to cover her mouth in an attempt to mask the smell.

As the train stopped, Abbud stepped into the bottom of the stairway and ushered again for them to follow him. Turning the corner and beginning her ascent, she paused, stepping on an extremely faded pink, stuffed bunny.

"You alright?" asked Nate.

Looking up at the rest of the pack in front of her move up the flight of stairs, she sighed and turned to him. "We've come this far, this fucking guy better show."

CHAPTER 26

The sun's rays hadn't poked over the horizon yet, but the darkness was starting to dissipate. The team moved up to the seventh floor of the apartment building, which had a blown-out wall overlooking the city square.

The market wasn't that big, and the dirt road circled around a decimated, tall stone water fountain that had definitely seen better days. Even though the sun wasn't out, people had started to trickle into the circle to set up their tents and stands and lay whatever merchandise they had across their tables and benches.

While Courtney, Abbud, Kwame, and Nate set up shop in the main room overlooking the square, Alex and Antonio cleared the rest of the building, doubled back downstairs from the other side of the building, and did a secondary sweep back up. Abbud told them there was nothing to worry about, but they hadn't made it this far to get shot in the back while sitting in an abandoned building. Once Alex and Antonio finished, the pair made their way back and posted guard in a room down the hallway, watching the stairs.

Once 5:00 a.m. hit, Courtney turned on Matthew's burner phone. Not seeing any missed texts or phone calls, she placed it on the ground beside her and rested it against her plate carrier. It was a little chilly, but not unbearable. As soon as the orange hue crept over the horizon, she could feel the temperature start to rise.

"I'm not seeing anything," said Nate through his binoculars. His rifle sat against the wall and within an arm's reach of him. Sweeping back and forth, he took a hard five to ten seconds on each stand he saw, trying to memorize the individuals running the stand should things get hectic later. These were nice people for the most part, but anything looking out of place would be a red flag to him in a heartbeat.

The plan was simple. Once Courtney received a text via the burner phone, she, Alex, and Antonio would head downstairs and wait while Abbud went to grab the vehicle. As much as Abbud wanted the trio to just follow him into the vehicle, even in their disguises, Courtney didn't want to chance being seen any more than was necessary.

Abbud would grab the vehicle, pick them up, and make his rounds of the city for around ten minutes, making sure a tail wasn't following them. After a confirmation that the package was there, they would head back toward the city center, snatch their subject, pick up Nate and Antonio, and head north to the outskirts of the city. Questioning their subject would take time. It would be brutal. Abbud assured them there were plenty of abandoned areas just outside the city.

The team watched the market come alive over the next hour and a half. Cars of all sorts carrying more merchandise and people, individuals walking around, donkeys, sheep—you name it, it was there. Nate carefully swept over as many people as he could, taking a mental note of anyone who was sitting in a chair for longer than they should.

"Okay, I think we're live," said Courtney, donning her black jilbab.

"Did you get a response from the text?" asked Kwame, laying down next to Nate.

"Yes. He's thirty minutes out. Kwame, can you go wake Abbud up? He needs to get to the SUV."

Standing up and stretching, he walked down the hallway and into the other apartment where Alex and Antonio were walking into what resembled a kitchen. Abbud was curled up in a corner, probably where the refrigerator used to be. Nudging the sleeping man with his shoe, he slowly moved his head. "Wake up," said Kwame.

He gave a thumbs-up and Kwame walked over to Alex, standing guard while Antonio slept, repeating the process. Five minutes later everyone was back in the main apartment and Courtney began.

"Alright. Remember, keep the chatter over the radio to a minimum. This is a snatch-and-grab, and then we head north of the city in the direction of where Khaled is believed to be staying," said Courtney.

"I can get you to the area, but I don't know which building he is staying in on the compound."

"Correct, that's why we're snatching these idiots," said Courtney. "Ten, two-story buildings with a stone wall surrounding it?" asked Courtney.

"Yes," said Abbud, "Keep in mind, if you are spotted inside the compound it will get bad very quickly."

"Just another ordinary day for the Bering Group," said Nate, turning away from his scope for some eye relief.

Courtney responded to the text five minutes later, informing the person on the other end they were okay to meet. She then assembled everyone leaving with her in the hallway, and the team was on the move.

Just as planned, when they reached the bottom of the stairs, Abbud hurried across the alleyway from whence they'd come just hours before and had the SUV out in front for the waiting operators in a matter of minutes. The team piled inside, shut the door, and Abbud gently stepped on the gas, trying not to cause attention by kicking up a plume of dirt.

"Is it hard to navigate through the city now that things are different?" asked Antonio. His head hitting the ceiling as the van drove through potholes and over large rocks.

"No, I have lived here most my life. I watched some of buildings since they were built. Since I was child. I know many people here. I was lucky I met Aydin long time ago. He helped my family escape before the war started," he said.

"Where do they live?" asked Alex.

"Do you remember where my son and I picked you up?"

"Yes, of course," replied Alex.

"There is coffee shop there, you passed it on the way to the pier. We own it. Aydin went out of his way to save and help us begin better life because I helped him and his team escape when they were cornered by ISIS a very long time ago."

"That's awesome," said Courtney. "So, you just come over here every now and then and just do favors when Aydin needs them done?"

"Yes," said Abbud, his cheerful voice and tone changing a little. "The people here need help. ISIS has checkpoints sometimes on the streets. If you don't pay, they beat you and take what they wish. I've watched them take wives from husbands and take children from families of those who could not pay."

"And what happens to them?" asked Antonio.

"They are never heard from again. I think they rape and kill the women, while recruiting children to work for them. Sometimes they do the same to the little boys, and even girls too."

"Unbelievable," said Antonio.

"These fuckers need to die," said Alex. "I'm killing every one of them I see and I can't wait to meet Khaled."

"Well, as much as I would like for you to do your worst to every one of those fuckers, we don't have the time or the ammunition to clear every one of those houses. You said there's at least ten, two-story buildings in the village. Right, Abbud?" asked Courtney.

He nodded looking in the rear-view mirror.

"We each have four magazines of MP5s apiece, and three extra magazines apiece for the pistol. The only plus is that the .45 caliber rounds are interchangeable between weapons," said Courtney.

"I would imagine that's probably why he gave us these," said Antonio.

"Yeah, and the nearest backup is at least thirty minutes away by helicopter. Aydin said not to hesitate to give him a call if needed, but other than that we're on our own. If we signal him, it needs to be quick; he doesn't want a downed bird in Syria. That will cause a shit storm on Capitol Hill, and since Washington isn't lending us any support, that will be the end of Aydin's career and probably the end of the Bering Group," she said.

"No fuckups, gentlemen," she added.

They drove around for another twenty minutes and once they were confident enough that nobody was following them, they returned to the opposite end of the market. Abbud parked the vehicle about a block away from the square, but close enough to see the very tip of the structure they'd called home for the past several hours.

"Okay, *que listo cabron?*" asked Antonio, looking at Alex.

"*Si, si,*" he responded. Unlike the movies, earpieces that transmitted and received communications as stand-alone devices and worked well were far and few between in the field. Unfortunately, this was one of those instances when the communication software decided to malfunction.

For this scenario, Nate and Kwame had a birds-eye view, and would talk to them through the earpiece. Although Antonio and Alex wouldn't be able to respond, they could use hand signals as a form of transmission received.

"Bravo, team, this is Alpha, radio check," said Courtney, from the van.

"Alpha, bravo has you loud and clear. How are the earpieces?" said Kwame.

Both Alex and Antonio gave a thumbs-up, fist-bumped each other, and opened the van door. Courtney watched the pair disappear from sight, closing the door behind them.

"You seem nervous. Why don't you step outside and have a smoke?" said Courtney. "I need you relaxed."

He agreed and followed his instructions, stepping out of the vehicle. Courtney sat the radio on the bench in front of her, cranked the volume knob to the highest setting, and stood by. There was nothing she could do now but wait and listen.

"Okay, we have eyes on our boys," came the African accent through Alex and Antonio's receivers in their ears. "Let me know if you can hear me still by adjusting your gown."

The pair did as instructed. "Good," said Nate through his scope. Vehicle traffic increased, and so did foot traffic. Any notion of thinking the city was deserted had disappeared from his brain.

Nate zoomed in on the Syrian flags blowing in the wind and made the appropriate adjustments he thought were necessary for the rifle. "There's a merchant selling something a couple of stands down. Tell them to buy something and sit at the bench in front of his boutique."

"Check," said Kwame, peering around the other buildings for counter-snipers. He could never be too careful. He repeated Nate's instructions and watched his teammates do as they were told.

"Our guy will be dropped off in a silver car with a black-and-white license plate. The car will circle around until we've made contact with him," said Courtney.

"Is that all?" asked Kwame.

"Yes," she said.

"Fuck," said Nate, who was popping sunflower seeds into his mouth. "Silver car, black- and-white license plate. Luckily there aren't too many cars running around."

"I know," said Kwame.

"Tell her I'll keep tabs on the driver. You keep tabs on the subject, and when he goes to the meet spot, I'll have a plan," said Nate.

"Roger," repeated Kwame, relaying the instructions. Five minutes later, a silver car with a black-and-white front license plate, appeared on Nate's right. It was about one-hundred yards away, coming down the side street that dumped into the square. There were only four streets, each coming from a different direction and dumping off into the roundabout.

"I have eyes on the target vehicle," said Nate. Again, Kwame relayed.

"Roger," said Courtney.

Alex and Antonio, who were still sitting and enjoying whatever it was they were drinking, glanced at Nate's position and, one after the other, looked toward the street behind them.

"Okay, boys, sit tight," said Kwame.

The pair on the street went back to what they were doing. Nate moved his sights off Alex and Antonio and zoomed into the windshield. "Yep, just a driver and passenger in the front seat. Both wearing a black robe."

Kwame repeated it for the rest of the team.

"Come on, boys," whispered Nate. "Come to Daddy. Just do as you said you were going to do; let's not get weird."

As the car drove closer to the square, it slowed down. People walked in front of it, and Nate could tell by the passenger and driver slamming and waving at the individuals that they wanted nothing to do with the pedestrians. They wanted to get to their destination, make contact, and get back to whatever it is terrorists did in their off time. Once they made it into the square, Nate watched as they made a lap around the fountain and pulled off onto the same street Alex and Antonio had emerged from. He followed the driver and passenger as they both stepped out of the car and slowly made their way back toward the marketplace.

"Status update," said Courtney. "I wish we were parked the other way but we're not facing the market."

"They just parked, and now they're walking toward the marketplace intersection. It looks like from the intersection, to where our boys are sitting, is roughly fifty yards," said Kwame.

"Tell Alex and Antonio that the pair are wearing black robes. Should be easy to spot; most of the people don't have a black robe on," said Nate, referring to the black-clad ISIS members as seen on television networks across the globe. "Okay, Courtney, it's time to move. They're about to pass our boys in two minutes," said Nate.

"Roger, everyone get ready."

Antonio grabbed his drink, looked at Alex, and nodded in the direction of the two individuals headed toward them. Alex didn't have to turn around to get the hint. They were here.

"They're looking for a white American male, which neither of you are. So let them get comfortable as they look around," said Courtney.

Alex stretched his hands as both ISIS members passed him on his right. A little boy and his mother were caught walking too slowly in front of them. One of the members grabbed the little boy, shoving him to the ground, while the other member grabbed the mother, pulled her close and yelled at her in Arabic.

"These people are disgusting," said Alex under his breath.

The pair sat silently, both downing the rest of their drinks and moving their dominant hands to underneath their garments. The

ISIS members finished yelling at the mother and continued to walk further past them into the market but stayed close to the street.

Just then Alex saw the familiar white utility van make the left toward them. The pair slowly stood up, turned, and walked at a quickened pace to catch up to their targets. People were everywhere.

They casually pushed past random people in front of them—trying not to cause too much of a scene—and closed the gap in under a minute. Now around ten paces behind their victims, the terrorists stopped and moved to the left, deeper into the market, and started harassing a boutique owner. Alex was on the inside while Antonio was on the outside as they caught sight of Abbud's face. He was conducting his first pass from behind Alex and Antonio. He knew not to stop until Alex and Antonio had somehow lured both members closer to the van. People trying to intervene, not that they would, isn't what they needed in this crucial time.

"There they go with the first pass," said Antonio, watching the back of their escape vehicle make its rounds around the circle to come back to them.

"Yeah, when they come around again, we'll be ready," said Alex.

"*Cabron*, how are you going to bring them this way?"

"Easy. We just need a diversion," said Alex, never taking his eyes off the targets.

CHAPTER 27

Alex started shouting at Antonio in English, and pushed him hard in the chest. He stumbled back and looked up at him with a confused expression, but instantly got the hint. The crowd walking around them parted, and stopped whatever they were doing to watch the show. Alex, who could now see the front of the van about ten yards away from them, started waving his arms in the air. Antonio walked closer to Alex and poking him in the chest, whispered, "They're walking toward us."

Slapping Antonio's hand away, he said, "On you," while taking his turn to poke Antonio in the chest. Before either one of them knew it, the two terrorists had moved in, shoving people aside to get a closer look at the English speakers causing a commotion. They would not have it and would make them suffer for it.

"Here we go," said Antonio, shoving Alex full-bore into both terrorists, almost hard enough to knock them over. The second Alex's back hit one of the members.

Whipping around to his left, his closed right hand connected with one of the terrorist's jaws, knocking him out cold and dropping him to the dirt. The second terrorist was so shocked at what had happened that he didn't have time to react. Antonio did.

Antonio uncovered his MP5 and slammed the stock of the submachine gun into the brachial nerve on the side of the second terrorist's throat, cutting off circulation to his brain and dropping him to the dirt just like his friend.

As if on cue, the white utility van pulled up just as Courtney jumped out of the sliding door. Pushing people out of the way was strenuous for there were way too many people gathered around now. This was more excitement than they were used to. By the time she reached Alex and Antonio, they had both members in individual fireman carries over their shoulders, hustling to the van.

"We got 'em, let's go!" Shouted Antonio.

Turning around just as quickly as she left the van, Courtney stood guard, hand underneath her garment wrapped around the handle of her weapon, waiting for a random attack that never came.

"All clear, Court!" shouted Alex from inside the van.

Jumping inside, she slammed the door shut and shouted at Abbud to step on it. Kicking up dirt on his way to pick up Kwame and Nate, he did his best to maneuver around the numerous people now staring at the van that had just kidnapped two terrorists in broad daylight.

It took about five minutes for Abbud to make it out of the square and double back to grab Nate and Kwame. After the grab, and some replanning, Abbud drove to where the terrorists had parked their vehicle. Nate and Kwame got out, borrowing the keys from the knocked-out passengers, and drove their vehicle behind the van. They now had two vehicles—and two were always better than one.

"How are the new passengers?" asked Nate, kicking one of the terrorists in the thigh. He didn't move.

"They seem to be doing just fine," said Alex, who had finished searching the second individual. Satisfied with the new pistol and large knife the terrorist had been wielding, he hog-tied him, matching his partner sitting on the floor of the SUV. Facing both prisoners, lying facedown, they placed a black burlap sack over the prisoners' heads and sat in silence for the rest of the car ride.

They kept driving until they were engulfed in rolling hills with jagged-edged rocks jutting out from the sides everywhere, while the occasional sheep walked around. Abbud kept driving until the road ended right in front of a plethora of tall trees providing shade and some comfort from the sun. Another excessively tall hill stood straight up behind the trees. At least if they were going to be seen, it was going to be from the hill behind them by somebody looking down.

Abbud parked the van next to the entrance of the abandoned wooden shack. Kwame and Nate cleared the shack, and once they'd given the thumbs-up, the rest of the team undid the hog-tie, and dragged the terrorists inside.

The shack was comprised of two rooms, a table, and a few chairs sitting on top of a dirt floor with weeds and dandelions growing throughout. There were only two windows, each facing the rolling hill behind them.

"Something about this place just gives me the creeps," said Alex, placing one of the terrorists in a chair as Antonio did the same with the second one. Using some rope they'd brought from the van, he tied the first terrorist's hands and feet to the chair.

"I'm going to head outside and relay our situation to Janet," said Courtney.

Receiving head nods, she stepped outside to stand next to Abbud. Turning to the first captive, Antonio ripped off the first sack, tossing it on the floor. Right before Alex was going to start to tie up the second victim, Antonio shook his head and pointed to the other room.

Nodding, Alex grabbed captive number two and motioned for Kwame to grab the chair as

they both pulled the victim into the other room and shut the door, leaving Antonio and Nate by themselves. Antonio took off his garb and handed Nate his weapon.

Antonio moved the terrorist so his back was facing the table. Nate sat in one of the chairs behind them and prepared himself for round two of intense interrogations. Antonio leaned forward, his arms bracing the sides of the chair next to the terrorist's thighs. He was face-to-face. "Do you speak English?"

The individual looked up at him and nodded.

"Good. I know you work for Khaled Ahmadi. I'm going to ask you a series of questions. I'm going to offer you a chance to answer before I inflict pain. And by the way, Matthew Siff? Your contact? Yeah, he's happily rotting in a cell somewhere in Sri Lanka. Do you understand what I said?" asked Antonio.

The man shrugged his shoulders.

"Good enough. This will be fun." Antonio took a step back, still staring at his subject, and glanced at his watch. It read 10:46 a.m. Just seven hours ahead of East Coast time. They were cutting it close.

"First, does Khaled Ahmadi live in the village not too far from here?" asked Antonio.

"I don't know who that is," said the subject. His English was pretty good. There was obviously more than just weapons and bomb tactics taught to these people for training. Somehow the terrorists had acquired the ability to perfect their English, probably by hiring translators, making it easier to slip through airports and past security.

"Why is it these guys always want to pick the hard way?" Antonio asked Nate.

"I don't know, man. It would make things so much easier for us if they didn't," he responded.

Reaching for the five-inch, one-sided serrated Ka-Bar knife attached to his kit, Antonio yanked it out of his sheath and placed the non serrated, sharpened end on the subject's arm. Starting at his elbow, he began to dig into the forearm, not hard but just enough to break the skin, and kept it there as blood began trickling down onto the floor.

"You know, I've worked with a lot of cartels in my day. In doing so I've learned lots of different techniques and strategies to extract information from people," he said.

The terrorist looked at him and laughed. His teeth were rotted and his scraggly beard dripped with sweat. And then there was his horrendous-smelling breath. Pushing past the smell and mentally getting into the zone, Antonio moved the blade from the crux of the subject's elbow, slowly digging into his bone, tissue, and muscle until it reached his wrist bone.

Skin and muscle tissue hung over the wrist, dangling toward the ground, as the Ex-Colombian Special Forces member worked his magic. The terrorist writhed and screamed in pain. Nate pulled a rag out of his pocket shoving it into the man's mouth.

"Shut the fuckup," said Antonio, wiping the blood-soaked knife onto the subject's shirt.

"Are you ready to talk?"

The terrorist was moving around so much he would have fallen over had Nate not held the top of the chair down. Nodding excessively, he tried to say something through the rag and then began to cry. Antonio ripped the rag out of the terrorist's mouth and tossed it on the floor.

"Yes! We work for Khaled," said the terrorist, between pants of exhaustion. His forearm muscle's bled and drooped lackadaisically while exposing pure bone, reminding Nate of a scene straight out of *Nightmare on Elm Street* with Freddie Krueger.

Taking a step back and admiring his work, Nate continued. "Okay, where is the next attack?"

"I don't know! I'm just a driver. I'm not as close to him as *he* is," the subject said, nodding to the other room. Antonio looked at Alex while picking up and placing the rag back into the subject's mouth.

"You think he's telling the truth?" Antonio asked, placing the knife on the table.

"Well, either he is or isn't, but either way he's not going to last long without that bandaged up properly."

"I thought you were a pro at this?" whispered Nate.

"I am, but maybe I went a little too hard with this bastard. We usually start off with a small sliver of skin, then take our time peeling it in layers, one by one."

"Yeah, well, half his arm muscle and skin are dangling down like marionette lines," said Nate, dry heaving.

"Well, he should have thought about that before he became a terrorist."

Nate just nodded and continued to dry heave, making sure to block the terrorist's view of him. Courtney entered the room, saw the mangled arm, and walked up to the subject. Pulling her flashlight from her belt and grabbing a handful of his hair, she pulled the terrorist's face back and shined the light into his eyes.

"Fuck, Antonio, he's going to pass out," she said. "Jesus man, just a quick question, how many of these cartel members did you kill just by torturing them?"

"Why do you ask?"

"Torturing isn't supposed to go from zero to one hundred in a blink of an eye, last I checked."

"Fuck him!" He spat at the terrorist's feet. "He said he was the driver anyway, and the other guy is who we need to be talking to," he responded, picking up the knife.

Nate said, "Look man, I respect you for doing this but maybe watch some YouTube videos on torture. Specifically, torturing slowly. Or maybe watch some movies, is all."

"Fuck you," said Antonio.

Letting go of his head and stepping back, Courtney asked, "Do you believe him?"

Antonio paused. Taking a deep breath, he looked at Nate, then back at Courtney.

"Let's try the other guy," he answered.

"Okay," responded Courtney, clicking off the flashlight and holstering it. "Get going. I'm not wasting our two last adrenaline shots on these bastards, so help me out, be gentle with the next one, please."

"No promises," Antonio said.

CHAPTER 28

Josh Quinn and his team encroached the neighborhood from the woods. Their helicopter landed and dropped them off just outside the city limits where three blacked-out Chevy Suburbans waited. Notifying the local police to set up a perimeter around the neighborhood would have been an option if it weren't for the classification of the mission. Take out the target, dispose of the body, and move on. End of story.

Woods surrounded the massive neighborhood, making the encroachment that much easier. As the team crept through the woods, they did their best to avoid the random leaves and branches on the ground, acting as if they were walking through a minefield. The team was scattered in a thin line throughout the tree line, approaching the backyard of the houses.

"Stand by," said Josh though his lapel microphone. The team knelt and awaited further instruction. Bryce, standing to Josh's right, made his way over to him. Taking cover behind a thick sugar maple tree, they both flipped their NVGs up.

"What do you think? There are quite a few houses on this side of the road," said Bryce.

"Yeah, our only advantage is the fact it's early as fuck and no one should be awake right now."

"Hopefully none of these fucks decide to wake up and turn the lights on outside. I know some of these people are going to be waking up soon, walking their dogs and getting ready for work would be my guess," said Bryce, looking around at the other operators all facing different directions as they provided security.

"We'll be alright. You see this dark-blue, two-story house in front of us?"

Bryce nodded.

"You take Drew, Zac, James, and Brian down the right side. I'll take the rest down the left. I didn't see any spotlights on either side. Call it right before you get to the front yard. We'll set up and approach the target house. It should be directly across the street," Josh added.

Bryce nodded, crouched back to his position, and listened as Josh relayed the instructions to the rest of the team. There was an eight-foot wooden fence on both sides of the house but no part of the fence was blocking the woods. There were no dogs in the backyard that they could see, and no spotlights, but there was a large wooden deck with some furniture extending from the second story of the house.

Moving his team down and up the left side of the house through the small alley-like pathway separating both houses, Josh paused once they'd reached the front of the house.

"Bravo team, check in," said Josh.

"In position, standing by," said Bryce.

"Roger, move," said Josh. Both teams crept forward silently from either side of the house. Through the front lawn, the NVG- and bulletproof-vest-clad warriors crept, across the street and through the front lawn of Jack's house. Josh's team moved through to the left side, approached his fence, opened it, and crept toward the back door. Bryce and his team made their way down the right and stacked on the front door. The roads were quiet, the moon was gone, no clouds, it was pitch black.

The subtle triceps squeeze, starting from the caboose of the train, finally made its way to Bryce. Having already checked the handle he knew it was locked so he brought his left arm above his head, tapping his helmet twice.

The person in the stack, or the line of operators getting ready to make the assault, who was designated to open any kind of door—no matter what it was made of—was known as the "breacher." He usually went to a specialty school to familiarize himself with all sorts of gizmos and gadgets to get his team through any kind of door. Seeing the signal, he stepped out of the stack, moved next to Bryce, and pulled out a can of quick-acting hydrochloric acid. Shaking the can, he knelt down and sprayed the handle and locking bolt. After ten to fifteen seconds the handle and lock disintegrated completely, detaching from the door. With no bolt to hold it in place, the door casually swung out.

The breacher shoved the can in his pocket and stood next to Bryce, bringing his rifle to the low and ready. "Making entry," said Bryce.

"Roger," repeated Josh.

Placing his hand where the handle used to be, the breacher paused. Through the NVGs the breacher saw the infrared laser from Bryce's gun move from the low and ready aimed at the wall to the door at eye level. Yanking the door open, the train moved forward into the house. Moving quickly, their rifles swept different areas. In a matter of seconds Bryce said, "Bottom floor is clear."

One of the members in the stack rushed over, unlocking the back door. Josh and his team flowed in unscathed. In another thirty seconds the house was secure with no shots having been fired. NVGs came up, resting on the helmets as men stood watch in different areas of the house. Three were downstairs, standing in different sections while the rest were upstairs. Bryce and Josh walked around, very confused.

"What the fuck?" asked Bryce. "He's supposed to be here."

"Well, he's not," said Josh, leaning on one of the walls in the upstairs bedroom.

"You going to call her or should I?" asked Bryce.

"I'll do it. Then we're getting some fucking sleep."

CHAPTER 29

Antonio walked up to the terrorist and pulled up a second chair. The man's disposition was similar to that of his friend in the other room, Antonio could tell. He had the same scraggly beard reaching down to his chest, withered skin, and dark brown eyes seeming to stare into Antonio's soul.

"English?" asked Antonio.

He nodded.

"Good. Tell us what we want to know and you won't have to end up like your friend in there on life support."

He laughed. "He is a low-level soldier. His orders were to drive me and stick by my side and answer to my every beck and call. Nothing more."

Antonio crossed his arms. "So you're the boss man in charge?"

The terrorist spat in front of Antonio. "I am not the man in charge, but yes I know the man you are looking for."

"Don't do that again," Antonio responded.

The terrorist laughed. "Silly Americans. I am not stupid. *We* are not stupid. You Americans think you are so smart, coming into our lives and destroying everything while you implement your own policies in our nations. We don't want you here and we were fine without you. Go home before Allah strikes you down." He spat in front of Antonio again.

Antonio stood up and looked at Alex and Kwame. Nate was in the other room with Courtney and Abbud, helping them with the other terrorist.

Antonio pulled his arm back and slapped the terrorist across the face. The man laughed, spitting to the side instead of at Antonio's feet. This time it was blood and not just saliva.

"You're already dead. We were supposed to report back within the hour and once we don't show up, they'll know something is wrong," said the terrorist.

"Where is Khaled Ahmadi?" asked Antonio, steering the conversation back to the main topic.

"*Where is Khaled Ahmadi...*" repeated the terrorist. "I have no idea."

Antonio smacked him again. More blood trickled down the man's face from his nose. Antonio suspected he was trying to kill time. He was being vague, offering few details, speaking in sentence fragments, failing to provide specifics when a story was challenged...All were signs that the subject in question was lying. The common myth that someone looking to the left or right with their eyes when they were lying had been debunked a long time ago.

Antonio had another idea though. "Sit tight, I'll be right back," he said to Kwame and Alex, signaling them to watch the subject.

"Oh, before I forget..." he said. He reached into his pocket, pulled out his phone, and snapped a photo of the terrorist's face.

Once he'd left, Antonio shut the door. "How's he doing?"

Courtney had the terrorist laying on the floor and his arm bandaged. "He barely has a pulse. You did a number on him for sure."

"Would you say he's useless to us now?" Asked Antonio.

Courtney looked at the injured terrorist and nodded her head. "Yeah... go ahead." Her mind already matching what Antonio was thinking.

Antonio pulled out his pistol and shot the captured terrorist in the head. The room was silent for a couple of seconds as Antonio placed his pistol behind his back again.

"Good," said Nate, standing right behind Courtney and next to Abbud, both of whom were just observing it all. Courtney stood up.

"What do you need?"

"How quickly can you get your drone up and running?" asked Antonio.

"Give me two and I'll have it in the sky."

Among EMT, Courtney was also the designated drone pilot for the group. It wasn't hard; the drone was small enough to fit inside of her backpack and piloting it was a breeze. However, none of the other team members wanted to have anything to do with it. As much as she preached that you can't always win wars with guns, and sometimes you need to use other things to your advantage, they never listened. But that was their loss. There would be a time where she wouldn't be around to fly the drone and they would have to rely on whatever other techniques were available—but not this time.

"Perfect," Antonio said, then turned to Abbud. "How far did you say the village was?"

"Only about a couple more miles down the road. There's a tall stone wall surrounding the entire village. They rarely monitor the road because they know none of the people in Ar Raqqa are stupid enough to travel down it."

"That's fine. Here's what we're going to do," said Antonio.

Ten to fifteen minutes later Antonio walked back into the room, set an iPad onto the table behind the tied-up terrorist, pulled up his chair, and sat down in front of him. "Okay, last chance. Where is Khaled Ahmadi?"

"I already told you, I don't know who that is."

"Okay," said Antonio. He grabbed the iPad and turned it on.

Giving it a second or two to boot up, he clicked a couple of buttons. An image appeared on his screen. "Let's play a game." He turned the iPad around so the terrorist could see the image displayed.

It was the village compound, just five miles up the road. Just as Abbud explained, there was a stone wall surrounding the entire compound, which consisted of ten buildings all of which had seen better days, and a handful of individuals dressed similarly to the two terrorists walking around. Outside of the complex were trees planted sporadically next to different points on the wall. The terrorist's eyes widened. "What are you doing?"

"We're going to have our drone, which is being piloted from hundreds of miles away by someone back in the States, drop a missile and blow up one building. Just one. Then we're going to drive you up to the complex and drop you off tied up. I'm sure they'll be able to put two and two together that you somehow gave up information that led to the drone strike."

"That won't work."

"You're the one in charge. While I was in the other room, I took the time to do a little asking around. Your name is Ibrahim Abdallah. You're responsible for some of the atrocities in this nation, as well as bombings and terrorist attacks in other countries. You, my friend, are just as guilty as the man we're looking for, and something tells me not only do you know exactly which building our friend is in, but we can definitely use you as a bargaining tool. If we bomb even one building and show up with you to give back to them, I'm sure they will love to hear that you sold them out," finished Antonio.

"That won't work!"

"Well, then that's a risk we're willing to take. Are you truly ready to die for Allah?"

The terrorist didn't say anything.

"I didn't think so. Now," said Antonio, turning the iPad back toward him, "Alternatively, you can tell us what the fuck we need to know."

Ibrahim hesitated. Weighing his options, only one was the clear choice. Looking at Antonio, then the iPad, he said, "I tell you which one he's in, and I stay alive? No tricks?"

Shaking his head, setting the iPad on his lap, he said, "No tricks." He showed both sides of his hands as a sign of peace.

Sighing, Ibrahim said, "Let me see the iPad."

Antonio turned it around.

Using his head as if to point, he strained his neck at the screen. "He's in the top row, third building in."

Antonio rotated the screen back toward him, "Perfect."

"How do you know I'm not lying right now?" Ibrahim asked.

Antonio stood up, "I won't know until we get inside. But you're coming with us, so if you're lying, I'm going to personally put a bullet in each of your knees, let you suffer, then I'll put one in your head."

Courtney kept her drone on station as the team left the shack. Abbud drove the van a bit further up the road and pulled off to the left behind some massive boulders and trees. It was dangerous. They didn't know if there would be spotters on the road, but it was a risk they had to take. There was no better option.

The distance between the compound and their shack was too far, and they didn't have the bodies to support such a task. The van would go to the same spot, drop off Nate, Courtney, and Abbud and continue on in the terrorist's vehicle. Ibrahim would be the driver, Kwame would ride shotgun, while Alex and Antonio would lie down in the rear. They would simply drive right through the front gate. There was no other way to do an infiltration in broad daylight. They had their plan and nothing could stand in their way because if this didn't work, the entire United States would feel the wrath of Khaled Ahmadi.

CHAPTER 30

Jack shut down the ring app monitoring the inside of his house in Roanoke and turned his phone off. Rubbing his eyes, he was getting frustrated, and this job was getting more complex. The team, whoever it was entering the house, wouldn't pay any attention to the security cameras that were sitting high above the cabinets in the kitchen.

"You should probably toss that now," said Max, motioning to the burner phone.

"Get some sleep," said Jack. "We're going to need it tomorrow when we start asking questions."

Twelve hours prior...

The pair started the drive down Route 64 mid-afternoon. Taking roughly four hours to get back to Alexandria, they needed a place to crash and make sense of all this. David was the only person who would be able to provide any insight to any of what was going on and why there were hunter-killer teams chasing them all up and down Virginia. Jack didn't like it and he wanted answers.

Ignoring the fact that there were more cameras in the DC area than in most places, if not all places in the entire country, they took the risk. Checking into the Indigo Hotel in Alexandria, they dropped their bags and rested for thirty minutes. Max watched the injured Jack pop more painkillers, which seemed to be doing the trick. When it was time to leave, hats were lowered and the team walked to the car parked across the street. Max checked his watch, which read 5:00 p.m.

Closing the driver side door, Max asked, "Which way?"

"David lives over in Falls Church, and his family should be out of town," said Jack.

"You sure this is how you want to go about this?"

"I don't see any other option to figuring out why hunter-killer teams are chasing us, do you?" asked Jack, painfully turning his head toward Max.

Shaking his head in response, he turned the ignition, gently stepped on the gas, and drove out of the parking garage. In dead traffic it took almost an hour to make it to David's neighborhood, which was nothing special...cookie- cutter houses, beige-and-blue homes, half an acre or so for land, yet most of these homes sold for 1.5million on a bad day. There weren't many places to hide an old-school pickup truck in this part of town and Jack didn't want anyone to see them pull up to the house. So he instructed Max to park at the gas station not too far outside the neighborhood, and they would walk.

"I don't know if you can make the walk, Jack," said Max. "It's about a quarter of a mile away." Shoving his door open, slowly exiting the vehicle, and using his cane to brace himself, he said, "Don't underestimate my abilities."

He tried his hardest to ignore the pain, but every breath, every step, and every motion he took to move his body reminded him of the excruciating pain radiating from his side.

Max shut the door and said, "Calm down, Superman." Max ran inside and paid the cashier two hundred bucks to leave the truck alone in the back of the parking lot until he returned, ensuring nobody messed with it and promised another two. The man obliged.

It was getting dark, and the road leading into the neighborhood was a simple, two-lane highway, with woods one on side while the beginning of the houses started just beyond the gas station on the right. Making their way down the side with the trees, Max hoped Jack was right. Max's plan B consisted of waiting in the woods, capturing whomever was in Jack's house, and conducting some high-level interrogating. This was something Max hadn't done in a long time, but this way was probably smarter, but only if they didn't get caught.

David's BMW M3 pulled into his driveway around eight o' clock. The security detachment that followed, after confirming a wave from David in the garage, continued on and left the neighborhood. There was a safe house not too far away from where David lived. Unbeknownst to his suburban neighbors, David's house was contracted out by the agency for that reason. One of the stipulations in accepting the position of running one of the most, if not *the most*, informed intelligence agency in the world was that you were now under the watchful eye of a full-time security team. No matter where you went, on vacation to another continent or to your in-laws, the security detachment was always just five or ten minutes away.

Taking his shoes off in the garage, closing the door, and stepping inside, he paused. Something wasn't right. Not only was his two-year-old blue pit bull, Bruce, not greeting him by charging him at the door, but the television in the living room was on. Lisa, his wife, was a hippie and a stickler about conserving energy, despite the fact that the new televisions did little to increase their electric bill.

Setting his bags on the ground, taking his sports coat off and laying it on top of the dryer, he reached into the cabinet.

Opening an empty laundry detergent box, he pulled out a Glock 43. Conducting a press check by pulling the slide back ever so slightly to ensure a round was seated in the chamber, he released the slide and heard a very feint audible click as it found its home. Contemplating calling security, David decided against it. Whoever was in his house was clearly not worried about *him*. That was going to be their biggest mistake.

Stepping out into his dining area, sweeping the muzzle over the living room area, he paused and blinked twice. "Jack?"

"The one and only," he responded.

"Hey, David," said Max, behind him in the kitchen pouring two glasses of Booker's Bourbon. Finishing his pour, he motioned to David with the bottle. David shook his head and lowered the gun.

"Please don't drink all my Booker's. That's the last bottle. I had to pay some poor sap three hundred dollars to give me his bottle after he'd waited for two hours outside of the local ABC store," said David, setting the gun on the kitchen table. Unbuttoning his white shirt and walking over to Jack, he fell into a La-Z-Boy recliner.

"Jack, you look like shit," he said.

"Great way to start a conversation," said Jack.

David stretched and said, "I take it you two have heard about what happened to the president?"

"Of course. It was all over the radio and the news channels," said Max from the kitchen. "But I believe Jack has something more important to ask you."

"What could be more important than the president being attacked so close to the capitol?" asked David.

"Well, for starters can you explain to me why Santa's little helpers decided to show up at

my house to kill me? Last I checked, you told me to go into hiding, and next thing I know I'm fending off—"

In the kitchen,

Max cleared his throat.

"—getting my ass kicked by an old agency asset," he finished, flipping Max the middle finger.

Smiling and delivering the two glasses of bourbon, Max sat down next to Jack. "There we go," he said. "God never likes liars."

"You're such a pain in my ass," said Jack.

"Well, to be honest, you wouldn't have an ass had I not killed your attacker," Max said, shrugging.

"Who do you think is trying to kill you?" asked David.

"You remember a man named Liam Parker?"

"How could I forget? He was one of the best. If he tried to kill you, then someone of importance was trying to get rid of you because they're trying to cover something up. In DC that could mean anything from you knowing too much about who's into child pornography to knowing that we're letting ISIS build training camps."

Max scratched his beard. "Why are we letting terrorists rebuild their training camps?"

"Getting rid of the totality of ISIS isn't as easy as it sounds when you have the wrong people in office, son," said David. "For starters, there's so much bureaucracy tied into sending troops and assets to the Middle East, it'll make your head spin. Washington wants to keep this war going because it keeps congressmen and woman alike in office. They use it to bolster their campaigns as they deem fit. Maybe they want to run for the next seat in the House or Congress, and hell, who knows, maybe, eventually, even POTUS."

"Wow," Max said.

"Oh, what a tangled web we weave," said Jack, swirling his drink.

"Exactly, now back to you, old friend," said David pointing his finger at Jack. "We need to keep you hidden until all of this blows over."

"Yeah, you said that last time and fast-forward, here I am sipping your bourbon on your couch. You have to figure out who's calling the shots and make them call off the hounds, David. In case you haven't noticed, I have Max to protect me and that's it. There's also the fact that I can barely walk."

"I can't make any promises, Jack. I have a shitstorm of other crap I have to deal with right now."

Jack was getting irritated, "David, how long have I known you?"

Thinking, he answered, "A little over two and a half decades."

"Correct, and you're telling me my best friend, the one whose wedding I attended and the first person I called when my wife passed, can't hook me up and drop everything when the world is crashing down around me?"

David looked down at the ground. He had nothing to say.

"You've changed since you took this position. I love you and will always love you like a brother, but you didn't used to be like this. I remember the David who would stick his neck out for me, or anyone else, when they knew the walls were caving in," said Jack.

"Times were different back then Jack. I wasn't this high up on the totem pole."

"Don't give me that bullshit!" Jack shot back. Max sipped his drink and remained silent. It was like watching a father and son fight, only they were both old men and Max wanted no part of this ringside match.

"Jack, POTUS can have me fired in the blink of an eye and replace me, and then what? Who's going to look after your precious Bering Group? Who's going to keep you under the radar when shit goes south? Janet? She's not even in the line of succession for my position. You'll have to pretty much get a recommendation from the president to put her in my seat. Who does that leave? Alexis Moore? The goddamn director of national intelligence? Of course she'll have your back, up until she doesn't. She's a bureaucrat just like the rest of them and takes orders from the same piece of shit who's going to occupy the White House right after Harrison leaves."

Max felt the tension in the air.

"The value of a person's life is measured by the amount of people they touch in living it. You would do well to remember that." Jack turned to Max and said, "Finish your bourbon, we're leaving."

CHAPTER 31

The White House

"President Harrison," said the voice on the other line. It was Alexis Moore. "The team is about to enter the complex believed to house Khaled."

Rubbing his eyes and looking at the clock on the nightstand, he yawned. It was early, but only an hour or so before he was usually awake anyway. "Thanks Alexis."

"We're all in the Situation Room, sir."

"Okay, I'll be right down." Two minutes later, President Harrison entered the Situation Room.

Everyone rose.

"Take your seats, what do we have?" asked Harrison, shuffling his way to the seat at the head of the table. The rest of the full cabinet, including the White House photographer, sat down and studied the live black-and-white video feed from the drone circling the compound.

"Sir, at approximately 0437 our time, one of our black-ops teams is on its way to what they believed is Khaled's compound—"

"—Are we sure this is where he is? How many buildings are there? It looks like... I count ten, is that correct?" he asked, interrupting her, and squinting at the television.

"Yes, sir, there are ten buildings, however, we don't know exactly which building Khaled is in. Also, we're not sure we know the exact amount of enemies on the compound. It could be ten or forty," said Alexis.

"How do we know he's even there and hasn't left?" asked Harrison.

"We have intelligence stating he's there, sir. I trust the intel."

Nodding and staring at the screen, Harrison said, "We'll see about that."

"Let's hope these boots on the ground can do their job this time," said Harrison.

Harrison was well aware of the espionage-wet-work side of the CIA. They operated in the shadows for decades, doing even his bidding to a certain degree. All in the name of keeping the world just a little safer. However, the identities what specifically the Bering Group was and were involved in, would always be hidden behind a shroud of secrecy. The other assets had somewhat of a leash but the Bering Group had full reign.

Syria

"Don't fuck this up, Ibrahim," said Kwame, holding his pistol below the dashboard, resting it on his leg. "How are you boys doing back there?"

"We're good," said Alex, grunting after every bump in the dirt road.

"Speak for yourself," said Antonio. "This shit sucks."

"Yeah, well, we're almost there. A little less than a mile I would say," said Kwame.

Even though Courtney and Nate were back on top of the hill and constantly scanning for threats, Antonio knew they would be on their own inside the compound. God help them if they needed backup.

"Half a mile out," said Kwame. Ibrahim once again glanced down at Kwame's pistol that was pointed at him. "You don't need to worry about this little guy. You do your job and you'll be fine. Keep driving," said Kwame.

Ibrahim remained silent. The closer the off-white stone walls got, the taller the three-story buildings were. The dirt road led to an entrance that was already wide open, and the black gates were opened toward them. Trees sat growing tall and dangling over the wall into the complex. People were scattered, though they were still a little far out to tell exactly what they were doing. Kwame figured they were just walking around from one building to the next and didn't want to know, much less cared, what was in each building but would soon find out anyway. Striking quick and fast was the key.

"Courtney, can you give me a SITREP?" asked Antonio through his throat push in order to talk underneath his head garb.

"We have no movement outside. There are a handful of people walking around down there but nothing you can't already see. I have no one on any of the rooftops, nobody going crazy, it's all yours. Going radio silent. Holler if you need us and we'll do the same," she responded.

"Good copy," said Antonio.

"Stay frosty boys, we're approaching the gate," said Kwame.

"Roger," said Alex. Gripping his submachine gun tighter than before, he did his best to wipe the beads of sweat dripping from his forehead into his eyes. It was hot, they were in the back of some fucked-up car, and riding straight into the den of the most dangerous people on earth.

What could possibly go wrong?

"You ready for this?" whispered Alex, doing his best to move into a better position. His face was only a foot away from Alex's.

"I was born ready for this shit. Let's do this."

Ibrahim slowed down and passed through the entrance of the gate. Some of the men turned their heads but overall nobody paid them any attention. They were all wearing the same black clothing yet everyone seemed to be sporting some AK-variant-style rifle slung across their shoulder.

"Passing the first building," said Kwame.

"What's it look like?" asked Antonio.

"You'll see soon enough. It looks like Satan came through here and decided to post up shop. Compared to Ar Raqqah though, these buildings look like Hilton hotels," he responded.

Other than the occasional hole in the side of the building, they were all in relatively good shape: white stone and brick buildings, none taller than three stories, and five on either side of the narrow dirt path running through the middle of the complex. Each building was separated by a tight dirt alley running into the wall. The dirt path they were driving on ran smack-dab into the other side of the wall, and more vehicles parked at the end of it. Whomever had developed this place knew what they were doing if they wanted to ensure a choke point was the primary objective. There was only one way in and one way out, and with shattered glass sprinkled over the entire top of the wall. It functioned as a poor man's barbed wire security system.

They were fucked. No question about it.

Ibrahim drove the vehicle to the end of the road, completed a U-turn, and backed up their vehicle so they were facing the direction from which they'd come. "Okay, you said third one in on the top? That would be the second one down from our right-hand side based on the direction we're facing now, correct?" asked Antonio from the back.

"Yes," said Ibrahim, gripping the steering wheel tightly.

"*Calmate amigo, calmate.* Relax. Remember, I only blow your kneecaps out if you're wrong," said Antonio. "So don't be."

"We ready?" asked Alex.

"Stand by one," said Antonio. "Okay, who all knew you and the other guy were leaving to meet us?"

"Just Khaled and his team. That's it," said Ibrahim, staring forward.

"Good. But that still leaves a problem because there's two guys standing right there," Alex said, looking over at the men standing right next to the car, just talking to each other.

"I'll solve this. Nate, come in, over," said Antonio.

"Go ahead."

"Do you see these three guys to our right, standing chatting away on the side of the building? They're about ten yards from my passenger door."

"Yep, I got them both," Nate responded through his headset.

"I'll take out the one closest to me; you got the two further ones, deal?" asked Antonio.

"Yep. What's the signal?"

"Oh, I'm just going to walk up and stab him," said Antonio.

"Well, I guess that'll work," he replied.

"Watch him," said Antonio, motioning to Alex.

"Of course," said Alex. "He moves, we'll blow his kneecaps away." Smiling, Alex looked at Ibrahim, who was sweating so much it was staining his head garb. Antonio nodded and opened the car door and stepped outside. He walked up to the men. They were so deep in conversation that they didn't pay him any attention until it was too late.

Reaching underneath his garb, pulling out his knife, Antonio covered the mouth of his victim while thrusting the knife through his kidneys. At the same time a hole was drilled into the heads of the other victims who were standing approximately ten feet in front of him. At the distance Antonio was from Nate, he didn't hear any gunshot, just the crack of bullet and bone as both subjects' souls left their bodies, which dropped lifelessly to the ground.

"*Bien gracias,*" said Antonio.

"That's what I'm here for," Nate responded.

Both Alex and Kwame, jogging behind Ibrahim, ran up and got to work, pulling the bodies closer to the side of the building, hidden from plain sight.

When the team was done, Antonio turned to Ibrahim and said, "Okay, lead the way."

Ibrahim nodded and turned around, facing the dirt pathway into the complex and said, "Follow me."

The team followed him around the corner and passed in front of the first building, then the second building. They then made a right through the alleyway between the third and second building. There were two or three more terrorists chatting across the street, but they paid little attention to the individuals moving between the buildings.

The men walked down the alleyway and up to a door at the very back.

Antonio, walking right behind Ibrahim, snagged his shoulder. "You had better be right. Just remember I'm not opposed to shooting you and leaving you here."

Ibrahim turned and said, "It is, I promise. Once I open it, it leads directly to the top floor, bypassing the second floor because this is where Khaled stays. He has his bedroom, prayer room, and a third room as a guest bedroom for the other members of the council when they come. He will be inside, I promise."

"You had better fucking be right," said Antonio.

Alex and Kwame turned around and watching the alleyway.

"Court, we're about to enter the building, over," said Antonio.

"Roger, have fun."

Kwame and Alex turned around, brandished their MP5s, and stacked up behind Antonio, who shoved Ibrahim toward the door. Hesitating for a brief moment, Ibrahim twisted the knob and pushed the door open as the team moved inside right behind him.

CHAPTER 32

Folding his arms and looking at the screen in the Situation Room, President Harrison had seen enough. "Alexis, update me with everything that happens. Ethan, General Godwin, a word in my office."

Alexis watched all three members get up and leave the room. Something was going on and she couldn't put her finger on what it was, but she needed to find out. Since when did the president of the United States not care about his men raiding a compound in the Middle East, especially if they were after a known terrorist? For now she needed to watch the drone video footage displayed on the screen.

"What's the deal with HRT?" asked Harrison, pouring a cup of coffee in his office. Sitting back, he stared at both the general and Secretary of Defense as they looked at each other before speaking.

"They came up empty-handed," said Ethan.

"Of course they did," said Harrison.

Exhaling, he sat back and blew on the top of the cup; its contents were scalding.

"This needs to end today. Never in my term as president did I think I would be attacked in my own backyard. My wife is scared shitless right now. As safe and secure as this building is, she won't come out of her room. You know what I'm going to say next, Ethan."

"Sir, give HRT some time to find Jack," Ethan said.

"Ethan, look at that fucking clock on the wall behind you and tell me what it says," said Harrison.

Turning around he read it out loud, "0515, Mr. President."

"0515. We've run out of time, gentlemen." He rubbed his eyes and turned to Godwin and said, "I want no more excuses. Between the two of you, you have access to a plethora of equipment and personnel at your disposal. Use them, find Jack, and let me know when you do. We'll go from there."

Both men nodded and left the Oval Office. The second the door closed, the president pulled out his encrypted cell phone and looked at the messages. One in particular stood out. Dialing the number, he waited for the other party to pick up.

"Good morning, sir," came the response.

"I truly wish it was a good morning," Harrison said.

"You'll never guess who showed up at my house."

"Who?"

"Jack and his little sidekick, Max."

"Oh, perfect. That makes this job that much easier," said Harrison.

"I've had my security team following them ever since they left. I can text you their exact location," said David Carter.

"Do it. I'll give Ethan and Godwin a ring and let them know."

There was hesitation on David's end of the conversation, the president could tell.

"Don't worry, David, everything will go according to plan. After Jack is killed, I'll fire Alex and promote you. Then we respond to ISIS by a confirmation of Jack's dead body and we'll get your undercover agents to talk to the Shura Council to kill Khaled. When they give us an exact location, we'll send in a strike team, and once Khaled is deceased, I'll brief to the world that we have yet again successfully killed a high-ranking terrorist to the likes of Osama bin Laden. I promised the citizens I would stay out of the Middle East, but if I deliver a blow like this one I'll win the hearts and minds of the people. No casualties of war, no dead bodies, a simple black-ops mission perfectly executed and delivering the world's most deadly terrorist right before reelections. I love it!"

Feeling a bit more confident, David said, "Okay, sir. But don't forget that Jack isn't alone, he has help."

"Two people against a full HRT? Get the fuck out of here, David. They might do well against a couple of well-trained assets, but they're not Superman and Batman. They'll both be dead before nightfall."

"But what if they aren't?"

The president took a sip of his coffee before responding. "David, I'll be honest. I wasn't happy with your little team of misfits running around under my nose doing things without my supervision, but it makes sense. Plausible deniability is a thing, and when you make it to Alexis's position you can keep your little band of merry men. As of now, as far as the Bering Group is concerned, this conversation we had didn't happen and I know nothing about them. Period."

"Understood, sir."

"Good. Now, go bring me Jack's head."

Syria

"Where is Khaled?" asked Antonio. They'd raided all three rooms, coming up empty. Kwame shoved Ibrahim against a wall in the master bedroom and pointed the submachine gun at his right kneecap.

"Where *is* he?" Kwame asked.

"He must be out praying," said Ibrahim.

"Prayer? There's a prayer room right there." Nate pointed down the hall.

Shaking his head, Ibrahim took a deep breath. "No, he sometimes leaves to go to another building, to pray with the others. It's the first building when you enter the complex on the left."

"You've got to be kidding me," said Antonio who rolled his eyes and stepped out into the hallway to pass Courtney the information. Just as he was about to round up the rest of the crew to push to the other building, their earpieces sprang to life.

"Hey, guys, you have company, over," said Courtney.

Stepping into the bedroom, Antonio looked at Kwame pinning Ibrahim against the wall, and responded. "How much company?"

"They're ten minutes out and I see six to seven Jeeps and SUVs headed in your direction. You have to get out of there now."

"We haven't found Khaled yet," said Alex. Just then the sound of a door opening below them and voices entering the stairwell echoed throughout the building.

"Court, stand by, we have visitors," whispered Antonio. She went radio silent. Antonio hustled into the closet, keeping the sliding door open and hiding between the hanging clothes, while Kwame and Alex pushed Ibrahim into the bathroom, keeping the door open. All the lights were off, so at least there was an element of surprise. There were just two voices.

The bedroom door swung open and two full-grown men in black robes entered the room.

Antonio whispered, "Now." He was first, stepping out of the closet when one of the men had his back toward him, and brandished his knife up to the man's throat. Kwame dumped into the room, his pistol out and pointed at the second man's chest. The terrorists recognized what was going on and lunged onto the bed, specifically toward the pillows.

Kwame was quicker.

Dropping his pistol arm, he dove forward, grabbing the right foot of the individual and yanking him backward. He watched him fall onto the floor onto his stomach. Jumping on top of him, keeping the subject's arms out to his sides, he ripped the facial cloth from the man's head and replaced it with his muzzle. Grabbing the terrorist's dark black hair, he forced his head into a better position in order to quickly identify his face.

"Hey, guys, I think we have a match," said Kwame. "Alex, get out here and take a photo of this guy."

Alex shoved Ibrahim forward and instructed him to take a seat next to the terrorist Antonio had already flex-cuffed and begun searching at the foot of the bed. Alex snapped a quick photo of the man's face and sent the image to Courtney, who in turn relayed it to Janet.

"Great photo. I think that's him, but it's going to take a minute or two for Janet to get back to me. Now hightail it out of there; you have five minutes before they're on top of you."

"Roger that," said Antonio. "You heard her, gents, let's go!"

The operators stood their three subjects up—each operator with their own victim—and forced them into the hallway. Pausing at the stairs, Antonio asked, "Do you two speak English?"

Neither one responded, but they did give him angry looks. Antonio kicked his victim in the nuts, hard. Kwame followed suit, as both let out a loud yelp and tried to double over but neither Antonio nor Kwame would let them. "I said, do you speak English?"

After a second of panting, Antonio's subject said, "Allah will make you pay for what you are doing."

"Good, I'll be waiting for him. I've had a bone to pick with him for a long time now. We're going to walk down these stairs and we're all going to get into the car that's waiting for us. If you do anything, and I mean *anything*, to signal to anyone that you're being forced to do this, I'll shoot you where you stand. Understood?"

The subject tried to swing his head backward to smash into Antonio's, but Antonio was quicker. Moving his left hand from the subject's shoulder to the back of his head, Antonio slammed the man's face into the wall. Blood splattered everywhere and the terrorist screamed.

"Antonio, come in," said Courtney.

"Go ahead," he said, doing his best to press his voice-to-talk while keeping his muzzle pointed at the terrorist. Antonio didn't have to try hard, given that the terrorist was literally crying and no amount of machismo could prevent someone from responding to a broken nose.

"Janet confirms it. The photo is a one-hundred-percent match of Khaled Ahmadi."

"Perfect, thanks. Alright, let's go!"

Pushing Khaled down the stairs and through the door, the sun blinded them. There were no lights inside the house, just the shades pulled back from the windows upstairs allowing whatever sunlight there was to enter the rooms. Wincing, the team pushed down the alley and made a left back toward the sedan. It was right where they'd left it.

Looking around, there were more people outside, and more AK-variant rifles adorning the bodies of several men. *This is not looking good*, thought Antonio. Moving past the next building, past the last alleyway, and past the front of the last building, he breathed a slight sigh of relief. *So far so good*, he thought. Nobody paid them any attention. Granted, their weapons were hidden underneath their garb but were close enough that the terrorists could feel the silencer's digging into their backs. Then it happened.

A couple of the terrorists behind them and across the street crossed the street and headed to the alleyway where the entrance to Khaled's residence was located. "We have about thirty seconds before they realize their fearless leader and company isn't there," said Alex, the last person to reach the vehicle.

"This is going to be a tight squeeze," said Kwame, shoving his subject into the back seat, then jumping in with him. Antonio signaled for Alex to go next, and as Alex shoved his subject into the front seat, slamming the door, Antonio paused.

Guiding his prisoner to a half beaten-up Hilux pickup with an M240 attached to the bed sitting right next to them, Antonio said, "I have an idea." He looked into the driver's seat and saw keys still in the ignition. Shoving Khaled into the bed of the truck, he turned to everyone sitting in the car. "Fuck that car, everyone out, let's go!"

Twenty seconds later the two other terrorists were shoved into the bed of the truck, stomach down, while Antonio and Kwame stood in the back. Antonio manned the mounted machine gun, while Kwame knelt down, standing over the terrorists and brandishing the MP5.

Alex started her up, and they were off.

CHAPTER 33

The second Alex stepped on the gas, all hell broke loose. The terrorists who walked into Khaled's house realized that fresh blood was strewn across the wall and their fearless leader was missing. They came running outside just quickly enough to each catch a chest full of 7.62 rounds from the mounted machine gun, dropping them instantly.

They started moving toward the incoming vehicles and could see dirt kicked up behind them in the distance.

"Nate, we're going to need some cover fire leaving this place! We're headed directly toward the caravan," said Antonio.

"Already on it!" said Nate.

The road was narrow and between two massive valleys on either side. There was only one way out and it was through the caravan. It was going to get worse before it got any better.

Nate positioned his sniper rifle toward the first victim standing in the back of a Toyota Hilus. Adjusting his sights, waiting for the natural pause at the base of his breath, Nate withdrew slack from the trigger and felt the rifle recoil. A half second after he pulled the trigger, a red cloud of blood appeared where the subject's head had been. Because of the distance, the point of aim to point of impact from the sniper rifle round to the target had to be adjusted to where the subject was going to be, not where the terrorist was at the current moment. Adjusting to the terrorist behind the second manned machine gun, two vehicles behind the first, Nate followed the same procedure and achieved the exact same result. "Two down."

"Roger," said Courtney, looking at the rest of her team headed straight for the terrorist group. From their vantage point they had the clearest view of anybody on the battlefield; the gap was closing fast. "Who's driving?" asked Courtney.

"I am," said Alex, trying to keep the truck on the road while pressing his push-to-talk.

"Slow it down; give us time to help you. You're closing the gap too fast and we only have one sniper rifle."

"Check, I'll give you some more time. I'm pulling off the road," Alex said. And just like that, Courtney watched Alex peel off to the right, through the grass, heading for the bottom of the valley. Massive rocks and boulders greeted Alex and the rest of the team in the truck the closer they got to the base and if they needed to, they would have to jump out and use them for more cover. Hopefully, it wouldn't have to come down to that.

In front of them the terrorists had no clue what was going on. All they noticed was that two of their gunners were dead from sniper fire and they needed to get to the complex as fast as they could to regroup, head back out, and find who was shooting at them.

Alex pulled the truck behind a boulder and threw the shift lever into park. Jumping out, he ran to the back of the truck. Lowering the tailgate, Alex reached over and yanked Khaled out of the truck by his feet, allowing his entire body to slam on the dirt. Kwame stayed in the bed, his MP5 pointed at the other two terrorists who didn't dare do anything but sit there and remain silent. Off in the distance, a third round was heard, just as the convoy passed where Alex had turned off the road. A third body dropped out of the bed of the truck. The convoy didn't stop; they kept moving into the complex.

"How do we deactivate the terrorist cells?" asked Alex, who was standing over Khaled, both hands on his collar.

Khaled just laughed.

Punching him in the face, Alex reenergized Khaled's bloody nose and repeated the question. The terrorist yelped. "It is too late. It cannot be stopped!"

"What are you talking about? There's always a way to stop them! Make a fucking phone call!"

Alex looked up at the path to his left in the distance and saw that the convoy was gone. They didn't have that much time. He figured another five minutes before they used the remaining bodies in the compound, plus the plethora of vehicles still parked outside, and regrouped with more people.

"The only thing you can do now is wait," responded Khaled in between spits of blood. "The calls have already been made. Things have been put into motion that can't simply be undone."

"How many terrorists are in your cell?" asked Antonio from the bed of the truck.

"Twenty," said Khaled. "I don't have the resources or the man-power to keep up these games, but it wouldn't have mattered anyway. Even if Jack was delivered to me, the attacks would still be carried out. He killed my mother. My mother! But don't worry, the other attacks will pale in comparison to what I have in store for my grand finale, as you Americans call it."

Alex glanced at Kwame, looking back at him in a four-thousand-yard stare. They were too late. The next twenty seconds seemed like an eternity as all three members sat in silence. Antonio fixated his M240 on the entrance of the compound before speaking. "We need to move now, otherwise we'll be behind the convoy and our guys will be on top of that hill. It won't take long for them to start mortaring that hill Nate and Courtney are on." His monotone voice said it all.

Ripping his cloth from his face, Antonio radioed Courtney. "We're moving; we'll meet you at the bottom of the hill."

"Roger, we're on the way," she said.

Alex picked Khaled up off the ground and handed him to Kwame, who pulled him back into the truck. Jumping back into the driver's seat, Alex stomped the gas. Thirty seconds later they were on the dirt path leading to the other side of the bottleneck where both sides of the valleys met. Seeing the familiar utility van sitting off to the side of the road in the distance, Nate and his rifle sat perched on top of the hood pointing directly at them, but aiming behind them to cover their tracks. Nate picked up his rifle, opened the van door, and moved inside the vehicle. Alex pulled alongside the utility van's passenger window and stopped.

"Did Khaled say anything?" Courtney asked, riding shotgun.

"He said there's nothing he could do. The orders are already given, and all we can do is wait," responded Alex.

"Yeah, bullshit," she said.

"I agree, but what can we do," said Alex.

Shrugging his shoulders, then pointing in the direction of Ar Raqqah, he watched Abbud peel out and he followed closely behind.

"Hey y'all, we have a problem," said Kwame, pointing to the cloud of dust picking up speed behind them.

Antonio, still manning the machine gun, turned to see the cloud of dust. "Let's go! Pick up the pace, ladies!"

Courtney instructed Abbud to go faster. "How far out do they look?"

Waiting for a response, Kwame said, "I don't know, but they're closing fast."

"Roger," she said.

She looked at Nate, who sat in the back next to the terrorist who was on the verge of passing out again.

"You think it's time to call Aydin?" Nate asked.

Nodding she said, "Yeah, I think it's about that time." Reaching into the glove box and grabbing the satellite phone, she extended the antennae and powered the device on. It wasn't like the movies where they could just call anybody they wanted to from any place on earth and get excellent service, this was the real world. And in the real world, the satellite phone acquiring enough pings from satellites in space wouldn't work inside the skin of a ship, and sometimes didn't work out in the open. It was a fickle beast and you never knew what kind of a signal you were going to get.

Bouncing on along the road, they passed the cabin on the left, and could barely make out the tarnished skyline of the city in the distance. Engaging the device, the screen read: "Acquiring signal..."

"Dammit," she said.

"You know, if you stick the phone outside the vehicle you might get better reception," said Nate from the back, using one hand to brace the ceiling to keep his head from hitting it.

Courtney placed the phone in her right hand and extended it out of the vehicle. Waiting another ten seconds, she looked at the screen and still received negative results.

"Try blowing on the antennae. You know, like the old video game cartridges," said Nate.

"Try shutting the fuck up," she spat back. "Is everything a joke to you?"

"I mean, do you really want me to answer that question?"

She screamed in frustration.

"Hey, you might want to pay attention to the phone. You might miss the signal when it comes across as good to go," he said.

"The first thing I'm going to do when we stop is punch you square in the face," she said.

CHAPTER 34

Since Alexis Moore was going to be living just outside of Alexandria, she made it a point to get to know people in her community. She was married with no kids, and her husband, a marine veteran, was a private contractor, traveling the world and teaching foreign nations. His schedule allowed her to enjoy working in the White House without being harassed by him about never being at home. It was the same for him, and when he *was* home they both understood the importance of spending what little time they had together before one of them was off again for work.

All of her alone time allowed her to spend a lot of time eating out and making acquaintances. She loved every second of it. The constant workload reminded her of simpler times in the field, gathering intelligence. That time was long gone and now that she was older, the times were definitely different. Every morning on her way to work she would drive down to King Street to go to one coffee shop that she loved the most: The local coffee house.

This morning was a little different. The drone feed was down in the Situation Room and she had no comms with the Bering Group, so she decided to sneak away to her favorite coffee shop. It was still early enough in the morning and she knew she could leave the White House, make it to her coffee shop, and be back quickly enough. Besides, it wasn't like Harrison would miss her. No, a quick drive into Alexandria would relieve some of her stress, at least for a little bit.

Arriving on King Street, she parked her cardinal-red, metallic Cadillac CLS Coupe a

block away, and around the corner from the coffeehouse. Even though she was stateside, she was always careful, never parking in front of any establishment she frequented.

Spending five minutes chatting with the barista, as well as the rest of the workers behind the counter and leaving them a generous tip as always, she waved and exited the small cafe. Turning to her right and beginning the short walk back to her vehicle, she passed two individuals sitting at a small table just outside the coffee shop, and she stopped.

"Jack? Max?" she asked, flabbergasted.

"In the flesh," said Jack, removing his hat and sunglasses and graciously bowing, still sitting down. Max smiled, nodded, and motioned for her to take a seat in the empty chair.

Looking around, she took a seat. "What the heck are you two doing in the city?"

Jack shook his head, "You see this?" he said, tapping on his cane, then his ribs.

"What happened?" she asked.

"Do you remember old Liam Parker?" Jack asked.

"No," she said.

"Probably before your time. Well, he happened. Fucking kid used to work for the agency and then got recruited to do the dirty work for all of the friendly politicians you love so much over there on Capitol Hill. I haven't had any X-rays yet, you know, since apparently I'm a wanted man by somebody now, but I'm pretty sure some ribs are fractured."

"You know, two things. One, I've heard of these guys running around and doing their bidding but I personally have never heard or seen anybody actually coming across them. Two, I would have figured Max would have been able to protect you better," she said.

Sipping his coffee, he replied, "Umm, I did. I killed him and got rid of his body. He's in Roanoke if you wanna take a look."

"No, I'll pass," she said, holding her hand up.

"Do you have any idea who would want me dead?" asked Jack.

She sat for a good long minute, thinking about the answer, only coming to one conclusion. "Jack, I honestly don't know, but I will say the president has been acting very odd recently."

Jack and Max looked at each other. "How odd?" asked Max.

"He's pulled the Secretary of Defense and General Godwin into his office on more than one occasion. Our first meeting, when all of this happened, I was sitting in his Oval Office with the other two, and he kept them back after I left."

"You think that's strange?" asked Jack.

"Look at my position. Is there anything, truly, that I'm not really aware of in terms of our national security?"

Both of them had no rebuttal.

"Exactly. And he pulled them back into his office during the hit of Khaled's compound. Something is off and I don't know what it is."

Jack looked up and down the street. The only vehicle was an SUV parked two blocks up and facing them. "Is there any way you could just strike up a friendly conversation with either of them? Aren't you close with those guys?"

"Yes, I can talk to Ethan. We actually go to the same church."

"Oh, that's cute," said Jack, sipping his coffee. "Going to church with the enemy?"

Alexis frowned. "Don't forget who your boss is, Jack. I'll have you pushing paperwork until you retire."

"I don't need this job, Alex. I'll just retire. So your theory holds no weight."

"Careful. Judging by the way you look it seems like putting you in a retirement home might be all I'll have to do to finish you off."

"Not funny," said Jack.

"Okay, so let's think this through. We don't have much time left to figure all this out," said Max. "We have some sort of threat happening in an hour and a half, with no leads, and someone is actively trying to kill Jack. I'm guilty by association."

"Sounds about right," she said.

"Do you think it could be Harrison?" asked Jack.

Alex sipped her coffee. "I mean, possibly, but what would be the motive?"

"Khaled wants me handed over to him, right?"

"Yes," she said.

"Then what would he stand to gain if he had me dead?"

A car drove past and Max looked over at it. It was a vehicle with government plates. The occupants wore Army fatigues. "How's the team doing?" asked Max.

"They have Khaled in custody. Nobody has been able to get any updates, but so far, no casualties on our end, so that's good. We're just buying time now until Khaled spills the beans on the terrorist attacks."

"Sounds like we're fucked," said Jack. Seeing Max lost in translation, he asked, "You alright?"

"I think Harrison is the one who wants you dead," Max said.

"How do you figure?" asked Alexis.

"If Khaled attacks us, Harrison will have to retaliate, which goes against what he said he would do in his inauguration speech, remember? If you're dead, he can show your body to Khaled, and the terrorist will look like an idiot. We've been at a standstill with ISIS for a very long time, and his Shura Council has to sign off on any attack he wants to do. These guys are smart; there are methods to the madness. When they see that the main target—you, Jack— is already dead, they'll more than likely be incredibly frustrated with Khaled. That's time and resources lost, all for retribution.

"And with the elections coming up next year, it won't matter why we retaliated. What *will* matter is that Harrison went back on his word. He's scared because he knows his approval rating isn't that good. He knows that if he does retaliate for a terrorist attack on US soil, he'll be sending husbands, wives, brothers, and sisters back overseas to die, which isn't what he wants, but he's doing it at the risk of making us look like cowards by sending teams out to kill Jack."

"That actually makes a lot of sense," said Alexis, taking another sip of coffee. "What about David?"

Max averted his eyes and took a sip from his cup.

"Oh boy, what is it?" she asked Jack.

"He's not the same person I went to the Farm with. If I find out he's involved in this also, I'm going to wring his neck."

"Relax," said Alexis. "Let me talk to Ethan and figure out what the heck is going on. I'll see if I can dig up any more clues to all of this. I'll talk to Janet and get her up to speed. Keep your phones on. I can't lose you two, so be on standby and don't get yourself killed."

They nodded as she rose from the table and walked back up the block. The pair looked at each other and sat before Jack said, "You see that SUV that's been sitting there since we sat down?"

Max didn't have to look, "Yep. You want to go say hi?"

"Of course," said Jack.

CHAPTER 35

Jack and Max stood up and walked down the block, passing all sorts of shops and restaurants on their left, while casually keeping an eye on the SUV. It hadn't moved, but as they eyeballed it, two people stepped out and began walking fifty yards behind them on the opposite side of the street. Each of the individuals looked like a typical government agent one would find in the heart of DC. Max and Jack knew they were packing heat, probably a pistol of some sort underneath their sports coat.

Making a left on the next block where Max's truck was parked, he quickly went to work on the minivan parked directly behind his truck. With nobody around and businesses on King Street still setting up for their morning rushes, he pulled a lock picking kit from his belt, and opened the door in five seconds.

Reaching over, he opened the passenger-side door for Jack then dropped his hand down to the steering column. He pulled off the panel, finessing the wires. Ten seconds went by and the minivan came to life. Jack looked behind them, not seeing the agents yet, but he knew they wouldn't be far behind. "Step on it," Jack said.

Max quickly pulled out and took off down the street. "Where to now?" asked Max.

"Let's head back to the hotel and stand by," said Jack

Syria

"Everyone out!" shouted Courtney as Abbud pulled up to the dock where his fishing boat was located. They managed to gain some distance between the convoy and their two vehicles once they were within the city limits.

Abbud had already called his son, who was ready to cast off. Jumping out of the van, he opened the vehicle's side door and started to help the team out, but Courtney waved him off. "Go. Be with your son and get out of here. We have our own evac on the way."

"Are you sure?" he asked.

"Yes, go. This is our mission and you two don't need to be seen with us. We'll deal with them."

Knowing time wasn't on their side, he nodded, shook their hands, and told them the next time they were in town they should connect with Aydin; he would bring them fresh fish. Abbud turned around and took off toward his boat. Five minutes later, the Bering Group stood over the terrorists and watched as Abbud and his son cast their lines and float down the river.

"Where are they picking us up?" Antonio asked Courtney. Surprisingly, there was nobody else at the pier and running from thirty to forty ISIS terrorists in broad daylight wasn't how the team wanted to spend the rest of their day.

"I sent him these coordinates, but we have to find a building with a rooftop. When they land the bird, we jump in and hope we don't get shot down," said Courtney. "All for these clowns," she added, pointing to their prisoners.

"Well, there are plenty of rooftops to choose from so take your pick," said Kwame. The more stressful the situation became, the more his Ghanaian accent made an appearance.

Kwame lifted one of the terrorists. Nate did the same, and Antonio grabbed Khaled. Courtney led the pack and Alex took up the rear as they headed to one of the old buildings across the street.

The pier was the only functioning part of business on this side of town. There were no markets, no houses, and no people on bicycles this far from the city center. Just more war-torn buildings resembling pictures from the Iraqi conflict back in the early 2000s. It resembled a nightmare for anyone growing up in this life.

The team pushed the terrorists ahead and bolted to the broken building across the street, just as rounds from a machine gun turret ripped behind Alex. He had just made it through the threshold of the blown-out front entrance.

"Keep going, I'm fine!" he shouted. The team pushed on while Alex occasionally glanced backward, making sure no one was following them inside. The corridor was gigantic. There were hallways and doors leading into rooms the team was certain were used to store all sorts of sick patients and medicine.

"I think this was a hospital," said Nate. "We need to find the rooftop, otherwise we're going to get lost in this maze of corridors if we stay on this bottom floor."

Sweat was dripping from every gland of the Bering Group as they continued to run through the building. They had no idea where to go and, with nothing in English written on the walls, Courtney was trying her best to look at the signs, curving every which way.

Reaching the end of the hallway on the bottom floor, they pushed open the door and there they were, concrete stairs leading straight up.

Ascending to the top, Courtney kicking the door open. Weapons up and muzzles sweeping, the team cleared the rooftop, slammed the door shut, and spread out. The roof wasn't big but it would get the job done for a hot extract. Pulling the satellite phone out of her backpack, Courtney did her best trying to establish a signal to tell Aydin which roof they were on.

Kwame and Antonio shoved the prisoners into the corner of the roof with them. All points were covered and the second Courtney acquired a signal, she phoned Aydin. After a minute of an intense conversation, she hung the phone up and started relaying the coordinates to him via the message system in the phone. Just as she sent the last message, all hell broke loose.

A rocket-propelled grenade exploded to her right, throwing her to the floor and sending the satellite phone flying in front of her. The phone seemed to be in one piece. Lucky break.

No other buildings around them were as tall as theirs. As they watched, a fire ignited below them. The terrorists were going to either make their way toward the rooftop and enter through the doorway or collapse the building with them on it. Neither was a great option for them and they needed an extract now.

"Give me some cover fire!" shouted Nate. He quickly looked over the edge and, seeing one of the mounted machine gunners not paying attention, pointed his rifle and pulled the trigger. Nate turned the man's head into a cloud of pink-and-red dust. In the next instant Nate dove back behind the small wall separating them from falling over the edge, as AK-47 rounds ricocheted everywhere, chipping away at the cement and concrete. The three flex-cuffed terrorists were lying down, not moving. They knew the drill, and if they wanted to stand a chance at living, they didn't want to get shot.

Just then the door swung open and two terrorists emerged, their rifles sweeping, looking for fresh targets. Alex dropped both subjects in a quick double tap to each chest. All the practice at the range with Jack working on transitioning from target to target in the scorching Virginia sun   was paying off. The door started to close but stopped on their dead bodies. Alex shot over to the door. Pulling their bodies from the landing and onto the other side of the door to block it, he quickly stripped them of their guns and remaining ammunition.

Another RPG shot just over their heads and into the sky before dropping and exploding somewhere off in the distance. Rounds kept ricocheting around them, knocking more and more of their concrete wall away and exposing more of the rooftop from the ground. It was chaos. The team couldn't lean over the roof without the possibility of taking a round to the face. Nate had gotten extremely lucky. ISIS was everywhere and it was only a matter of time before they set snipers on some of the roofs around them, effectively blocking them in.

Nate quickly spotted one side of the corner of the rooftop that wasn't taking rounds and crouched over. Leaning against what was left of the crumbled wall for cover, he saw at least seven or eight people down below in all-black, running around. Bringing his rifle to bear. Taking a chance, Nate leaned over once again and pointed his weapon at one of the terrorists.

Lining up his crosshairs with the terrorist's body, he slowed his breathing and took a shot. Miss. *Fuck.* Repeating the step, he took the shot again, remembering the old phrase *Aim small, miss small,* this time hitting his target. Quickly shifting to the next target, he knocked him to the ground with ease.

"Two down!" he said, transitioning to a third target before pulling the trigger again. "Correction, three down!"

"Keep it up!" shouted Antonio. His rifle was pointed toward the door, which began to move.

"When that door opens, step back," shouted Alex, grabbing one of the grenades and holding the pin, ready to pull it. Retreating far to the right of the door, Alex waited and, on cue, it started to open but was still impeded by the bodies. Alex pulled the pin and held the grenade for three seconds before tossing it into the small opening that the new ISIS members had created.

The explosion blew the door clean off the hinges and three more dead bodies added to the pile now strewn across the roof. Blood, extremities, rebar, and shattered concrete surrounded them.

Two more terrorists emerged through the smoke of the grenade, one moving left and one right. Alex didn't have time to bring his gun up. Lunging forward and grabbing the terrorist's muzzle with his right hand and pointing it away from his body, Alex used his free left hand to punch the man in the face. But the man wasn't fazed in the slightest.

The terrorist, who was significantly taller than him, let go of his grip on the AK and socked Alex right in the face, breaking his nose and causing him to stumble backward. The pain was excruciating. He had never broken a bone in his body growing up, and even with all the adrenaline coursing through his veins, the broken nose hurt like hell.

A second later Alex heard gunshots from the other side of the roof and immediately saw brain matter explode and the terrorist's body droop to the deck.

Still fighting his terrorist, Nate had managed to separate the rifle from the terrorist and was about to go toe-to-toe in a boxing match, when he heard an all too familiar noise to his left.

In an instant, Nate watched the terrorist in front of him turn into a bloody pulp. The calvary had arrived and with it came a machine gunner that vaporized his target. Looking up, a helicopter was hovering in the distance, while another chopper conducted a quick pass.

After the gunner helicopter conducted another pass, blowing up two more vehicles below and narrowly avoiding an RPG shot, the second helicopter was radioed in to land on the roof. The fact that they'd chosen the one building with a helicopter pad attendant to a hospital was a simple stroke of luck.

Eight Turkish Special Forces members jumped out of the bird and formed a security perimeter on the roof, taking up spots and aiming at targets below. Their more powerful rifles made dust of the men in black who were running around trying to find cover. After twenty seconds, once all members of the Bering Group were safely onboard, the helicopter conducted one more pass as both gunners on either side lit up the streets below. After the lead helicopter flew ahead of them and banked hard to the left, the extraction helicopter followed suit, taking off into the distance.

CHAPTER 36

The helicopters banked and rolled and for the next hour. The Bering Group sat inside and processed everything that had occurred over the past couple of hours. The chopper's side door had been left open on purpose and a breeze blew through the cabin as the team looked at the ground below. Once they were far enough away from the city, the machine gunners relaxed but still kept one hand on the handle. You never could rest in Syria, no matter how high you were from the ground.

"It's a little past seven o'clock back home," said Antonio, adjusting his seat. "We don't have a lot of time."

"So let's make this shit count then," said Kwame. The helicopters flew into Turkey, and ten minutes after crossing the border, they landed just inside the fence of a CIA black-site. The nearest city was Gaziantep, ten miles to the west.

Aydin and the guards ushered the Bering Group into one of the buildings and moved all three prisoners into a totally separate building. After the helicopter took off, Aydin returned after five minutes of talks with the duty officer and guided the Bering Group to the building that housed the terrorists.

Kwame, Antonio, Courtney, Nate, and Alex all stood outside the building. They were without their tactical gear, having dropped it off at the armory. They formed a half circle around the entrance of the building, which housed all three individuals in separate rooms. They were the only individuals occupying the entire building.

"What kind of technique are you going to use this time?" asked

Courtney, taking a bite into the apple that she'd grabbed earlier from the galley.

"You can come watch if you want," said Antonio, placing his hands on his hips. "I have some guards bringing me my first set of tools. It should be a good one."

"I'll pass," she said, raising a hand. "Besides, I have to update the boss on what we have going on. You just get us those locations and we'll be golden," she said, turning around and walking back toward the main compound.

The black-site was a decent size and featured a handful of different buildings all designed for different purposes. The large concrete building the team was standing outside of was strictly for highly illegal interrogations. When Aydin briefed them on where they were headed, the team knew right off the bat that if American civilians knew these types of interrogations were still happening, high-ranking officials would definitely be losing their jobs.

Then there were the fences, more like cages, directly in back of the base. These were designed to house the terrorists until they were officially transported to bigger bases. There were two-story barracks for the people stationed there, which is where they slept. And then there was the main compound, which consisted of a kitchen and a lounge with computer access, and anything else that anyone staying there might need to stay sane.

The rest of the team, besides Alex, decided to leave and head to the main building for a little downtime. For all intents and purposes, they were done. Even if Khaled Ahmadi talked, there was just nothing else physically they could do. The information would get passed to Janet and the FBI and they would move heaven and earth to figure out where the individuals were and do all they could to stop them. But they had to get there first.

Two guards walked up, delivered two large jugs of water and a rag, and handed them over. Antonio took one jug and Alex the other.

"You ready?" Antonio asked.

Alex nodded.

"Alright, let's get this over with." Alex followed Antonio through the door and into the long, dark hallway. There were six rooms, three on each side of the hallway that ran the length of the one-story building. Their individual was in the very last room on the right. Each room had one-way glass in front of it, so as they walked, they took a few seconds to look at the other two prisoners who were sitting in the corners of their respective rooms. Finally, making it to Khaled's room, Antonio stopped at the one-way glass and set his jug on the floor. Alex followed suit.

"Leave that one here, we won't need it yet," said Antonio. Alex nodded and followed the newest and scariest member of the Bering Group through the door into the room. Instantly, the pair was greeted by two massive concert-style JBL speakers blaring metal and punk rock right next to the head of their terrorist who was chained to the floor in the back of the room. A small white table sat in the front of the one-way glass, with a remote on it. Antonio walked up, picked up the remote, and hit pause on the iPad that controlled the speakers.

Antonio tossed the remote back on the table as Alex leaned against the wall. Antonio sat his jug on the floor next to the table, walked over to his subject, and ripped the black burlap sack off his head. Khaled was sitting on his knees, as if in prayer, with his arms spread-eagle as if he was nailed to a cross. His wrists were in shackles, with the chains running to the metal holes in the walls. His neck was shackled as well, with the chain running behind him into the ground. The position was very uncomfortable on his knees in particular on the cold concrete. Or as Antonio looked at it, the perfect position for a terrorist.

"Khaled Ahmadi, you're a hard man to track down."

He didn't move.

"Good," said Antonio. Khaled looked rough. His dark hair was matted and drooping over his weathered face and his beard was full of blood, saliva, and whatever other particles managed to entangle themselves within his curled hair. Without question, he looked physically and mentally worn down.

"First off, how many attacks do you have left in place?"

No answer, just mumbling.

"What was that?" asked Antonio, kneeling down and getting real close to Khaled.

No answer, just more rambling, and not in English.

"Roger." Antonio stood up, walked back to the jug, and nodded at Alex. Alex walked over, placed his gloves on, and grabbed a thick wad of hair and yanked back. His head snapped back and the pressure from the shackle around the back of his neck, plus the pressure exerted from Alex, caused the man screamed.

Pacing the rag over his face, Alex knelt down behind the terrorist. Pulling tightly on the rag from both sides, Alex sat behind him as Antonio gently poured water from the jug onto Khaled's face. For the next fifteen seconds the terrorist coughed, twisted, and did everything he could to avoid the water hitting his face. The chains were unforgiving.

The technique of water boarding was simple. Among other serious injuries, it caused extreme pain and damage to the lungs and brain from oxygen deprivation. The process sometimes led to fractured or broken bones due to the subject struggling against the restraint devices. It also caused long-lasting damage psychologically, something Antonio hoped for with someone like Khaled.

Antonio set the jug down, then Alex pushed Khaled's head forward and removed the rag, tossing it on the floor. Khaled coughed, but the tightness of the chain didn't allow him to lean forward and properly drain his lungs of water. Antonio tossed Alex the key chain, and loosened the shackles, allowing him to fall forward to the ground.

After ten seconds of continuous coughing and spitting up of water, Khaled wiped his mouth and tried to catch his breath. Just as he did so, Alex and Antonio yanked the chains back to position, causing Khaled to scream, anticipating what was to come. This time they administered it for thirty seconds. When they finished, Alex repeated the process and Khaled fell forward on his arms again and coughed for longer this time.

Antonio leaned forward, "Khaled, we can do this all day. You mentioned a grand finale. Where is the attack going to take place?"

He breathed heavily. "Virginia."

"Where in Virginia? It's a big state," said Antonio. "Give me the location and we can at least talk about getting you some food. You haven't eaten since we picked you up. We gave food and water to your other buddies already," he lied.

"It's too late," said Khaled, in between breaths.

Antonio looked at Alex; their expressions didn't change. "You have to have something set up to delay the attacks or stop them. Tell us how and I'll get you some food."

"You can't," he said.

"Khaled, don't lie to me. Do you want the water again?" asked Antonio, nodding to Alex.

They repeated the process. Khaled screamed, begging them to stop. Another thirty seconds elapsed, and once again Khaled knelt over, coughing all over the ground. By now the rag was not only soaking wet, but had dirt particles from being tossed on the ground. When the water from the jug was filling Khaled's lungs, the dirt and whatever else the rag caught flowed into his mouth, adding to the pain.

After the next round of water, Khaled shouted, "Please, no more water!"

Antonio slapped him across the face, "You're not in the business of asking for anything. You tell us what we need to know and maybe, just maybe, I'll let you eat some food like your friends in the other room. Now tell me, where is the attack taking place?"

"I don't know," he said. He began to cry. "The cells have multiple locations to choose from. I tell them three locations, they pick which one they will use. That's it. I don't know where they will pick."

Antonio looked at Alex before continuing again. "Let's start with the three locations," he said, crossing his arms.

Khaled took a deep breath before he said, "Alexandria, Norfolk, and Richmond."

Antonio stood up, leaving the terrorist's chains loose with more movement, but still chained to the wall and floor, and ushered for Alex to follow him outside. Leaving the music off but the light on, they left the room and the building altogether. "What do you think?" Alex asked.

"I think I have been doing interrogations for a very long time, and I think that man is telling the truth," said Antonio.

Alex looked at his watch, "We have ten minutes before it's nine o'clock back home."

"That's not enough time," said Alex.

Antonio stepped in front of Alex and stopped him. "We have to try. Listen, we caught the bad guy, we did our job, that's it. We did it with ten minutes to spare. That's unfortunate but the tradeoff is we captured one of the most wanted terrorists in the world. Even with taking out cartel members, the one thing I learned is you can't protect every family member from the evils out there in the real world. The quicker you realize that, the easier it'll be to sleep at night, *amigo*."

Alex took it all in and nodded. "Aright then, let's go let Courtney know."

CHAPTER 37

At precisely eight o'clock in the morning on Thursday, two eighteen-wheelers, pulling a container each, began to drive through the HBRT in Virginia, from Norfolk to Hampton. Following close behind were two blacked-out Chevy Tahoes.

The morning rush to work had just ended, however, the area was known for its heavy construction. This resulted in backed-up traffic on both sides of the bridge at all times of the day, even well into the night. This alone gave the tunnel a horrific reputation for keeping the residents on either side of the bridge from crossing to the opposite side unless it was absolutely required. Nobody wanted to get stuck in a tunnel and definitely not one running under the James River.

The semi-trucks trudged along at a snail's pace. They weren't worried about time; the drivers had worked the route numerous times in the past month. It took approximately three minutes and eleven seconds for them to get from one end of the bridge to the other and it didn't matter if they were going or coming from either side. The only other factor was always traffic and this morning there was lots of it.

The trucks approached the middle of the tunnel, speeding and slowing down with the traffic. The ISIS members sitting just two deep in the cabin of each truck, rolled down the windows and nodded to one another as they started to ascend up the tunnel and into Hampton.

Malik, the driver of the truck on the left, started to sweat and said one last prayer. His passenger, Fadel, assured him that Allah would be eternally grateful. It would all be over soon and the infidels would get exactly what they deserved.

Malik reached down and grabbed his AK and wracked a round into the chamber. The passengers of each truck and SUV repeated the same process as Malik threw on body armor and made sure they had a plethora of extra magazines for their chest rigs. The Americans wouldn't forget this day.

As the exit to the tunnel got closer and the traffic sped up to forty-five miles an hour, the truck in the left lane slowed down considerably, while the one in the right lane sped up. Both drivers turned the trucks toward each other, jackknifing the semi-trucks.

The second Malik's truck stopped moving, he opened his doors and jumped out of the cabin. Malik wasn't able to take five steps before witnessing the two blacked-out Tahoes and their armed individuals jump out and start shooting at the cars behind them. It was chaos.

The HBRT had one small walkway on the left side of the tunnel running the full length. It was elevated so that whoever was using it could oversee the traffic and move through the tunnel without getting hit. Malik grabbed Fadel, jumped over the railing to get a better view of the cars further behind them, and sprayed any people they could see.

7.62 rounds flew in every direction, tearing up windows and embedding themselves in seats, engine blocks, and parts of innocent bystanders trying to hide or run. Blood spattered on clean windshields and clean interiors, and music could no longer be heard over the yelling and screaming of people running away.

As Malik moved forward through the tunnel on the walkway, he noticed an overweight Caucasian to his left. The man jumped out of his vehicle and pointed a small pistol in his direction.

Malik felt three rounds hit his plate carrier, causing him to shudder and step backward before turning and seeing Fadel rip apart the person who'd just shot. Malik didn't need to say anything; turning and nodding to Fadel was enough.

As the pair moved down the tunnel, time ticked away and already their rifles were running low on ammunition. They had practiced many times over at a local outdoor range with transitions, magazine reloads, and external movements. This was too easy.

Ten minutes later, Malik had no more targets. There were no more bodies running, no more people trying to escape vehicles, and no more screaming. They were done and out of ammunition. Malik heard the sirens long before they reached the tunnel exit, but with abandoned cars, there was no way the police cruisers were going to make it into the tunnel. The police officers would have to approach the terrorists on foot.

Fadel gave the command, and all terrorists chose a vehicle at the mouth of the tunnel, climbed to the roof, and laid down.

It was around fifteen minutes before police officers in droves gathered together and managed to make their way on foot. Once the police officers gathered enough force, approximately fifty cops surrounded the terrorists on either side of the tunnel. Nobody moved an inch.

Another five minutes went by before they eventually started walking toward the terrorists. They got close enough to climb on top of the cars to handcuff them. Then without any heads-up, a loud eruption echoed through the tunnel, a flash of light was seen, and a gigantic fireball was visible for miles around, escaping into the atmosphere.

Alexis sat inside Ethan Cox's office, in the Pentagon. His TV was on and Alexis watched the horrific scene as the HBRT went up in smoke across CNN. "Jesus," she said to herself.

The door opened and Ethan walked in, then closed it quickly behind him. "This is a pleasant surprise," he said, walking over and shaking her hand. Alexis stood, shook his hand, and sat back down on his couch after he made his way to the other side of his desk.

"That's insane," he said, looking at the TV on the wall.

"Alright, Ethan, what's going on?" asked Alexis, crossing her legs. Her eyes were daggers into his soul.

"What do you mean?" he asked, crossing his arms.

"HRT is chasing my guys, and I didn't get notified about it. I don't like that. Also, you, Godwin, and Harrison have been very close lately. A little too close for comfort if you ask me. There's something going on. I'm not stupid. I just happened to be the only person who seems to be asking questions as to why you three are constantly having private meetings, so what is it?" she asked.

Ethan was fidgeting in his chair. He was clearly nervous.

"Nothing is wrong, Alexis," he said, standing up and straightening his suit.

"Ethan, how long have you known me?"

"A long time."

"Right. And do we go to the same church or not?" she asked.

"We do."

"Yep, that's right. So do you think it would be nice of me to let your loving and caring wife know that I saw you and that young blond leaving the hotel two years ago late at night?"

Alexis actually liked Ethan. He was very nice and was one of the first people who had introduced their family to her when she took the position of DNI. How he operated at work and his personnel life were two different things. But as long as his personal life didn't interfere with his work, she didn't care.

He sighed. "Listen, you have to keep your mouth shut on this one, Alexis, okay?"

"Ethan, as long as you're not planning to off me or my people, my lips are sealed. I just want to know what the hell is going on that involves my guys, that's it. I don't give a fuck who you decide to put your dick in. Quite frankly your relationship issues are your issues."

"Well for the record, I haven't slept with anyone since that night," he said, sitting back down.

"Ethan, I swear I will send an asset to your house myself and beat it out of you."

Holding up his hand, he said, "Two days ago, when Harrison pulled all three of us into his office, after you left, he cornered Godwin and me." He looked at his desk, then at the picture of his wife and two little girls before he continued. "He told the general and me that if we didn't comply with what he was asking, he would find someone to replace us."

"If you didn't comply with what?" she said, now leaning forward in her seat.

"He wanted us to send in the SEALs to go after your boy, Jack."

"What?" she asked.

"We both told him it was illegal. If the press received wind that the SEALs were on a mission sanctioned by POTUS to hunt and kill a CIA asset on the homeland, there would be a shitstorm from everyone—"

"So you hired an off-the-books asset?"

He averted his eyes. "Yes."

Shaking her head, she said, "Of course, but he failed."

"Yes he did."

"How many of those assets do you have on standby?"

He paused before answering, "Enough."

She sighed. "So then Harrison wanted results, so he asked you to go behind Jake Bower's back because he knew the head of the Department of Justice wasn't going to sign off on sending his boys down to do the job."

"We told Jake, and he signed off on it. We just didn't tell him exactly what it was for."

"Then they showed up and found Jack's empty house in Roanoke," said Alexis.

Ethan nodded. "For what it's worth, I apologize. I didn't want to do this, neither did Godwin, but we have jobs to keep and families to feed."

"And I also have a job to do. I can't believe Harrison is even this capable of doing something like this underneath all our noses. The nerve of you both, going behind everyone's back and launching assets to kill my guys. What the fuck is wrong with you two?"

"I told you, Alex, he was going to fire us both!" Ethan shot up from his seat. She had him right where she wanted. "Alex, I'll do anything, I promise, just name it and it's done. I know I fucked up, but he had a gun to our heads."

"Bullshit, Ethan, you should have come to me on this one. For as long as I've known you and your family, I'm very disappointed in hearing this." She pointed at the television. "We have our hands full with this right now." Again she indicated the carnage on the television. "The last thing we need is some other controversy spinning up at the White House. That is something I don't intend to see. I've worked too hard in life for everything to come tumbling down during months of congressional hearings. No, I'll think of something, and when I do, I want no questions asked, not one. I want full participation of everything and any and all help I need—to get my guys out of tough situations—from your SF guys at any time, you understand?"

He nodded. "What now?"

"What now? You're going to call Godwin and tell him the same thing I just told you. Anything I need in the future, any access to anything, any help, he's going to give it. That's it. I would speak with Jake, but I'm sure he has his hands full at the moment."

CHAPTER 38

The second the secret service received word that terrorists had massacred dozens of people inside the HRBT, then detonated their suicide vests and killed first responders, President Harrison was moved to the Presidential Emergency Operations Center. It was a bunker beneath the East Wing of the White House, serving as a secure location and shelter for POTUS and others in circumstances like these.

Once the all clear was passed, which took hours, the president went back to the Oval Office and made some calls. Two of them were to General Godwin and Ethan Cox, both of whom answered the phone but made excuses as to why they couldn't meet, which left Harrison furious to no end. He chewed them both out and hung up the phone.

He wanted results. Ever since the drone had gone off-line, nobody had heard anything, or at least no one had briefed him on it. Nobody seemed to know anything more about Khaled Ahmadi or Jack Knowles either, and for some reason he couldn't get ahold of Alexis. All of these problems and it was getting late. Looking at his watch, which read 7:00 p.m., he was about to walk out and meet his wife for a late dinner when his secretary entered.

"Sir, Alexis Moore is here to see you."

"Thank fucking God," he said, throwing on his grey sports coat. "Send her in."

His secretary nodded, closed the door briefly, and then reentered it as Alexis entered.

"Good evening, Mr. President," she said, walking over and offering a handshake.

He declined and gestured to the couch, not saying a word. The door closed and he began on his tirade. "Alex, what the fuck is going on with you? Have you lost your fucking mind! I have been waiting and waiting for any type of answer from your shitty operation to catch Khaled, and it has been radio silence. I'm the goddamn president of the United States, I shouldn't have to wait on information. It needs to come to me without me having to say anything, do you understand?"

Alexis kept her composure, crossed her legs, and leaned back in her seat. "Of course, Mr. President. I understand completely," she said in a calm voice and tone. "I understand you wanted to have a Special Forces team chase down and kill a team member of mine, just so you could look good for the next election. I understand you were told explicitly that using Special Forces on home soil was strictly forbidden, and yet you wanted to do it anyway. You gave special authorization in order to use HRT to chase down one of my operators."

President Harrison was at a loss for words. In her ranting, he had balled up his fist and clenched his jaw so tightly that she thought he was going to explode. He looked like a red balloon about to burst. "Listen here, you of all people have no authority to talk to me like that. What I do behind closed doors is none of your concern. Do you understand? You're the goddamned DNI, and definitely not even close enough on the totem pole of power to even *think* of talking to me like that."

She smiled, then looked away from him. "Mr. President, let me tell you exactly what is going on right now with your country. ISIS singlehandedly killed close to two hundred people inside the HBRT today, and injured twice as many. You have an election coming up next year and have already promised the American people you won't be sending any troops back overseas, which is why you left my assets overseas on their own. Okay, I don't agree with it;

they are CIA assets invisible to the world, so I'll let it go. The main thing I'm concerned about is how you tried to sanction an off-the-books hit against my assets, HRT I might add, but none of that matters anymore."

She had him by the balls, and he knew it. "Continue," he said, under his breath.

"That, of course, would only happen if word were to leak to the press about what kind of shenanigans you were trying to pull off behind closed doors. Do we have an understanding?"

"Yes, Alex, I understand. You're going to bring up charges of malfeasance against the office of the president of the United States as you blackmail me in my own office? Do you see the irony in that?"

"Of course I do, but I know you have deeper skeletons in your closet, sir, we all do somewhere. It's DC. No matter how nice or friendly we congressmen and women are or seem to be, there's always something hiding deep in the darkest bowels of our past that seems to be fished to the surface at the most convenient of times, wouldn't you say?"

"Yes, Alex, I get it. Is there anything else?"

"You're going to leave General Godwin and Ethan Cox alone and never speak of this incident to them again. Don't bring it up and don't mention it in passing. You've done enough damage. You need to prepare a speech to address the country, and that's the only thing you should be concerning yourself with. Are we clear?"

"Yes," he said.

She stood up, nodded, and headed for the door. Reaching for the handle she paused. "I'm looking forward to your speech tonight."

He stared at her, trying to wish her into oblivion, but it didn't work. She then said, "One more thing. Stop calling me Alex. I let my friends call me that, and now that we both know where we stand, you can use my full name, which I was given at birth. Alexis." With that, she stepped outside and shut the door. Two seconds later she heard glass shatter against a wall somewhere in his office. The secret service agents standing outside gave her a wary look.

"He's going to need a moment," she said as she left to meet her husband.

CHAPTER 39

"Alright, folks," said Jack, standing in the corner of the sound-proof room, upstairs in the Bering Group's office. His ribs still hurt, but unfortunately there was nothing the doctors could do besides prescribe him some high-level painkillers, tell him to get lots of rest, and not to move too much.

Jack was cleared, as promised, by Alexis. No more foot chases. Over the next couple of days, Jack was in direct contact with Janet and, seeing as the rest of the team no longer needed to be overseas with all that was going on, they flew home. It wasn't until Sunday that enough information had been complied and Jack was able to scrounge up the tired and exhausted squad in the room for an update on current events.

"And here I was hoping Jack was mustering us all here to buy us brunch for such a great job we did overseas," said Alex, who was sitting in Jack's recliner next to Antonio in the back of the room. Everyone laughed.

"I wasn't the one in charge of this one. Court was, so take it up with her. Max and I had our own issues we had to work out," he said turning to Max who was sitting in the front row next to Courtney.

Courtney turned around and, leaning over Kwame so that she could see Alex, she said, "Go fuck yourself. You're a big boy, and we just got a nice paycheck from this one also, so I know you have money."

"*Mira*, you're so rude. I was just asking you a question," said Alex. Courtney rolled her eyes.

"Settle down, children, we have one last mission to go over," said Jack, pointing the remote in his hand at the blank screen on the projector. One click and an image of a Middle Eastern man populated the screen.

"As you know, a little less than seventy-two hours ago, there was a massive terrorist attack on the HBRT. Estimates now put the casualties, which include the dead and the injured, at almost two hundred and fifty.

"Jesus," said Nate, sitting next to Kwame.

Jack continued. "That's not including the police officers who were killed, and many more who were injured when the bomb went off, which this jackass had detonated from a distance." He pointed to the image of the young-looking man with dark hair, brown eyes, and a clean-shaven face that occupied the screen. He looked no older than twenty-four.

"So these asshats drive semis, block off the exit going into Hampton, then get out and start spraying? This guy watches the whole thing and waits until the shooting stops, the police show up, and click?" asked Max.

"That's what it looks like Janet said. Her team has been working around the clock to find this guy after the FBI figured out who it was."

"How did they find out?" asked Courtney, sipping her coffee.

"There was a traffic jam, obviously, due to the blockade with the semi-trucks. People were fleeing from inside the bridge to back out of it, and some people were just sitting there filming the whole thing on their phones instead of helping," said Jack.

"Not surprised," said Max.

"No, not at all. There was a teenager, filming, and after the explosion, he witnessed some random guy toss a cell phone over the bridge and walk away, almost directly past him."

"Makes sense. The radio signal has to be close enough to the vest and whomever detonates it is going to want to be within eyesight so they don't blow it too late or too soon," said Antonio.

Pointing to their newest member, Jack said, "Bingo."

"But how in the world did they find the phone in the James River and track it down to him? Wouldn't his fingerprints be gone?"

"Not necessarily. Fingerprints can last for up to ten days in the water, probably a little bit longer, without getting too ruined. It all depends on how quickly you can get the device out of the water. Also, fresh water versus salt water is going to play a role in the recovery of prints. The kid contacted the police because he felt something was off. The little "spider-sense" in the back of your neck I keep telling you guys about. Everyone was running around and this dude just stares at the tunnel as it explodes, throws something in the river that resembles a phone, and casually walks away? Not normal."

"Not at all, good shit," said Max.

"Kid calls cops, cops contact FBI, and within two hours after the fact, they had divers beyond divers in the river searching for that phone. They recovered it, out of sheer luck in my opinion, after thirty-six hours. The phone was brought back to a lab and underwent testing with black powder, small particle reagent and cyanoacrylate fuming. It's best on nonporous surfaces such as glass, rubber bands, woods, and of course plastic, which is what the low-grade phone was made out of."

"No shit," said Courtney. "Note to self: if I decide to kill Alex, take a boat far offshore and dump it."

"Correct," said Jack, smiling. "Anyway, HRT would have gotten the call but Janet said

Alexis personally contacted her, and told her we have control of this one."

"How upset was HRT?" asked Antonio.

"She said Alexis doesn't know for sure, but she didn't want to be the one to tell them that they were standing down. Especially since they're a unit specifically tasked with stuff like this, or at least can be. That's why she's in the position she's in and Ethan Cox is in the position he's in, but he's also not going to tell them. He's just going to pass the information to whomever runs them and they're going to do it. Sometimes it pays to be the highest on the totem pole in your organization."

"Got that right," said Kwame, adjusting in his seat.

"So we know this guy, what's his name?" asked Nate.

Reaching for a file on the desk next to him, Jack opened it and said, "Mohammed Osman."

"Okay, so Mohammed Osman attempts to blow up the bridge, makes a run for it, and here we are three days later. Do we know where this guy is?" asked Nate.

"Yep. Janet did a background check on the guy, he's just a low-level ISIS member. They have these guys scattered all through-out the United States, just random members willing to die for the cause to do this sort of stuff when needed. Sleeper agents if you will. All so the higher- ups can make, plan, and try to execute their attacks all while they sleep soundly in their beds halfway around the world," responded Jack.

"What's the famous quote?" asked Max, "Old men wage wars, young ones fight them?"

"Sounds about right," said Jack. "The second we found out who he was, HRT did make the initial hit to his residence, but of course it was empty. We tracked him via drones and found his vehicle fleeing on I-95 South in Florida just an hour or so ago. No passport was flagged, so he's probably headed to an island somewhere in the Caribbean."

"Or maybe the Keys?" asked Max.

"That too," said Jack, staring at the photo of the straight-faced killer. "So what do you guys say? You up for one last run before I give you some serious downtime?"

"Does a bear shit in the woods?" asked Alex. The team got up and exited, but not before Jack asked Max to stay behind.

Once the door was closed, Jack said, "Hey, so Alexis also told me she blackmailed the president, but she thinks it's not enough. He still might need a stern talking to in order to keep him in line."

"Before we go that high up, what about David?" asked Max, crossing his arms. "We now know he can't be trusted."

"That's done. Alexis is preparing to fire him and promote Janet next week. She said she's had it out for him for a while now, and this was the last straw."

"How in the world are we supposed to talk to him, after he knows we know it was him who sent teams after us to kill us? We're just supposed to waltz into his office and tell him not to do that again?" asked Max.

"Doctor said I have about another month or so for these ribs to heal. They're not broken, just fractured. You let me handle all those logistics. You just go deal with Mohammed, come back, and get some rest. In a month's time I'll have an answer for you."

"Fair enough," responded Max. As he turned to leave, Jack grabbed his shoulder.

"And tell the guys, if you guys capture him, you'll be turning him over to HRT."

"If?' Max asked.

Nodding, Jack responded, "Yes, if."

Taking a second to process everything, Max smiled.

"Keep me posted," said Jack as his friend walked out the door.

Mohammed Osman checked into his hotel room in Nassau, overlooking the gorgeous view of the ocean running over the pristine sand. For a low profile, this wasn't the worst thing Allah had provided for him. Khaled did say he would be taken care of for this, and taken care of he was.

He was provided a brand-new passport, new name, and one hundred thousand dollars in his bank account. By the time he had to use the passport he had a nice long and very clean beard to go along with his golden skin and warm smile. He directed his smile at any young lady caught giving him the thousand yards stare. Dressing like a tourist wasn't the hard part, staying out of sight and away from the Shura Council was. Although he knew he could get used to this life, he knew it wasn't forever, and at some point he would have to face the music and fly back to Syria and undergo rigorous training once more. Preparing for his next mission in which he wouldn't be just a foot soldier anymore, he would work his way up and possibly run his own cell. Maybe not in the near future, but an ultimate goal of his was forming in his imagination.

On his drive he listened to the radio stations all the way down to Florida, and there was no positive identification of him at all. As of right before he boarded the cruise ship, he was a ghost. This was just how he liked it and just how he wanted it to go down. The perfect plan. Khaled was right. Falling into his king-size bed, he figured if he was going to be thrown back into the ringer in a couple of weeks when he flew back overseas, he might as well take advantage of his short new vacation. Opening the double doors leading onto the balcony, he opened the blinds and let the breeze carry him to sleep.

Several hours later, Mohammed woke from his slumber, took a shower, and threw on some new clothes. If he was going to act the part, at least for a little while, he might as well dress the part and try and fuck one of these infidels. He knew he should be praying and thanking Allah for saving him and keeping the police off his back, but he was going to enjoy this. It wasn't often that the lower-tiered soldiers were given opportunities like the one he'd been given. Although it also wasn't often that he was able to work for a man as famous and as revered as Khaled Ahmadi. One day he would live up to Khaled's expectations.

Three hours later, he stumbled back upstairs to his hotel room. Reaching into his pants, he fumbled for his room key, and dropped it. *Maybe I drank too much,* he thought. Nonsense. He was just enjoying the fruits of his labor.

Leaning over, he picked the room key up and swiped it against the lock. Hearing a click, he opened the door and walked inside. Stumbling forward and taking off his shoes, he fell back into his bed, closed his eyes, and drifted off into a new world.

A couple of hours later, Mohammed awoke to something biting him. Or was it sticking him? He jerked his leg up, eyes still closed. He had to be dreaming. There it was again. Something was definitely poking him, but he couldn't see anything. Still feeling groggy, he reached over and turned on the bedroom lamp. His eyes widened as he instantly sat up against the headboard.

"Mr. Osman, how are you?" asked Max, leaning on the dresser with a Ka-bar knife in his hand. As Mohammad sat up, all he saw were different figures in the room. He had no idea who they were or why they were there, but he didn't like it.

"Who are you?" Mohammed stuttered. His head was killing him. Those damn women he had tried to impress by buying shots for them, and they didn't even follow him to his room.

"You don't get to ask the questions here, boss. Word on the street is you helped contribute to taking a massive amount of lives a couple of days ago in Virginia," said Antonio, walking over and sitting on the chair next to the bed. "Does that ring a bell, *pendejo?*"

"It wasn't my idea, I swear!" Mohammed said. He was shaking and clearly felt threatened. His eyes darted all around the room. He didn't know where to look. Granted, waking up to seven individuals staring at you in the dark would scare anyone.

Max leaned forward, yanked the sheets from off the bed and onto the floor, then went back to leaning against the dresser.

"What is it you want?" the man asked them.

"We already have all of the answers we need," said Max. "You were employed by Khaled Ahmadi, right?"

The low-ranking terrorist nodded.

"Mohammed Osman, twenty-five years old, three brothers and two sisters, mother and father are both doctors working at the prestigious New York-Presbyterian Hospital," said Courtney, clearly impressed. She was reading from his file. "Your family is from Syria, but you yourself have never lived there. You spent all your life over here in the states, being raised in New York. Your siblings seem to be doing well for themselves. Your two brothers are going to law school, your other one is in medical school, as well as both of your sisters. Jesus bro, how did you end up so fucked up?"

He didn't say anything. A million different thoughts ran through his mind. He was assured nobody would find him, and yet here he was, being asked a million questions by the same infidels he was trained to kill.

"Says here, you were going to medical school and dropped out. Why on earth did you do that?" she asked, closing the file and handing it to Antonio to look through. She pulled out her pistol and slowly threaded her silencer to the barrel.

Mohammed started to sweat. "I was walking home from college one day, and witnessed two Americans beating up a Muslim. I ran over to help, yelling and screaming at them to stop, and told them the police were on the way. They ran away. They had to be around my age, probably younger. I couldn't tell, it was very late. After talking to the man, I brought him to a nearby bar, and we sat down and had a long conversation. He told me how he hated Americans and couldn't wait to leave this country."

Max looked at other members in the room. He could see where

this was going. They all could. "So then what happened?"

"He said he was from Iran and all the American people had done over the course of time was destroy where he was from and beat on all our people. He was much older than me," said Mohammed, stuttering and wiping away tears between sentences. "Are you going to kill me? I can give you money—all the money I have in my account—and I'll catch the next flight out I promise!"

Antonio laughed, "Ahh, *mi amigo*, that's not how this works."

"Keep talking," said Kwame, leaning against the wall.

"He had my attention and gave me a website link to go to and the rest was pretty much how I ended up here."

"He gave you a website and you were hooked because naturally your parents didn't talk about the atrocities that were going on because they didn't want you to have to experience any of it. So, you went online, did your own research, and came to your own conclusions about how bad we Americans are?" said Max. "Sounds about right."

It was quiet. Max watched Mohammed's eyes dart from member to member, confused.

Alex stood up from the chair. "I'm getting bored, lets get this over with," he said. He pulled out his own pistol and began threading the barrel with his own silencer.

"You can't kill me! I didn't even threaten any of you! I know your policies, and I know you have to feel threatened before you shoot. You can't just kill me in cold blood!" he said.

"*Callate cabron*, you'll wake the neighbors. People paid lots of money to be here," said Antonio, pulling out his pistol, silencer already attached. Max did the same, except he also pulled out a second pistol from behind his back, tossing it onto the bed.

"Oh, don't worry," said Max, "we have that part covered. Now, pick up the gun."

He couldn't move. His limbs that had moved just hours prior, throwing shots into his mouth, were stuck and frozen to his sides. Courtney walked up, grabbed the pistol, and thrust it into his hands. Stepping back, she walked over to Antonio and raised her gun toward the bed.

"Pick the gun up and point it toward us," said Max. Mohammed's tears were flowing, the top of his shirt was drenched in sweat.

The team arrived stateside later that night, their Gulf Stream 550 pulling into the hangar. Tired, all the members retreated to their vehicles, anxiously waiting to get some sleep and the promised R & R time from Jack. Once the last car had pulled away, the only ones left were Max and Courtney.

"Hey, Max," Courtney said, opening the door of her brand-new Ford Bronco Wildtrak. "You want to go for a nightcap?"

Rubbing his eyes, he said, "You know, it's a little late, Court. I still have about a forty- minute drive home."

"So do I, did you forget? I live in Alexandria now," she said, standing on her running board. "Besides, the last time we drank you promised you would show me the inside of your place to give me suggestions of how people decorate over there." She rolled her eyes.

"Slick line, right?" he said with a smile.

"Clearly, because it didn't work last time," she said. "Come on, lets go, I know a bar that's open late. Maybe, if you get lucky, you can make me some of your pancakes you keep bragging about in the morning." She winked, closed the door, and started the ignition. The rumble of the exhaust echoed through the darkness.

Max closed the door to his Porsche GTS, and did the same, his aftermarket exhaust echoing over hers. Waiting for her to pull out, he followed her into the night.

EPILOGUE

When the president of the United States went for a run, he was covered from head to toe in secret service. They wore jogging gear and traveled in pairs in front of and behind him. There was even a chase car standing by along with the usual team of tactical operators standing by in their own bulletproof SUV, in addition to the car he actually rode in to the park. The vehicles would park on Seventeenth Street, let the president and his detail out, and be on standby to pick him up.

Harrison had a couple of routes mapped out to run—which was a secret service agent's nightmare—but Constitution Garden was his favorite. Random runners would occasionally run by his entourage, a couple of them would ask to join but of course, secret service always shooed them away. Every time Harrison went for a run in the park, the secret service pleaded to shut it down just while he was there, but he was a people person and he wanted some resemblance of normalcy when he left the Oval Office.

In the middle of the park there was a lake with different routes wrapping around it, with routes branching off of it. It was evening and Harrison had done this route more times than he could count over his tenure as president. Once he stepped out of the lead vehicle in the motorcade, he knelt over, untying and retying his shoes. When he was done, he looked up to see four agents, dressed in sweatpants and sweatshirts, jumping up and down, trying to stay warm. Running in the winter in Washington DC was not for the faint of heart. There weren't too many people outside at dusk, but Harrison didn't care. He loved staying fit.

"Are you ready, sir?" asked the lead agent, sporting a blue sweat suit.

"Ready as I'll ever be," said Harrison. He knew his personal protective detail like the back of his hand, although they had to switch agents constantly. Not all the agents the secret service provided were good runners and not all the agents who were good runners were even capable of keeping up with Harrison in the cold. New faces were a constant when he left the safety of the Oval Office. Especially on evenings like this.

Harrison saw the back of the lead agent, glanced at him, took one last look around, and was satisfied he was going to be the only one running through the park. He nodded to the rest of the agents. The lead agent raised his wrist, with a small mouthpiece wired through connected to a small radio on the back of his hip, up to his mouth and said, "We're moving."

"Roger," came the response.

The four-man team stepped off and made their way down the trail, running further away from the vehicles sitting on the street. There were two agents in the front and two in the rear. Each agent gave the president some space. The air was crisp and their breath showed with every exhale as they ran deeper into the park. Once they hit the lake, they made the left and kept going. Typically they would run for a solid thirty minutes. In this cold, it was half that. Harrison limited it to just a mile or two. Nothing crazy.

Harrison had his headphones on and looked at the lake to his left. Peaceful. Not one ripple in the water or a cloud in the sky. More calm and tranquility. This was truly the perfect night and the perfect end to a stressful day in the White House. Up ahead, about one hundred yards away on the right, they passed a park bench with two individuals dressed in similar warm weather gear.

"Look alive, guys, two runners ahead," said the lead agent.

"Roger," came the response from everyone. Including the

president. The two runners stood up and did various movements to stretch their legs. One was leaning over to touch their toes, while the other had a leg on the bench and stretched touching their toes. The running path was more than wide enough to accommodate a huge running group, but since there were only five total, the group swerved to the left, closer to the lake and further from the bench. The president and the two agents taking up the rear followed the two lead agents further from the bench while waving to the runners. They waved back.

Harrison turned his attention back to what was in front of him. He cranked his iPod volume up louder, listening to heavy metal, giving him more momentum and energy to continue the run. He was so into the next song that he didn't notice the two rear runners who swapped positions with the two runners on the bench. Harrison continued to smile and sing along to the song, his breath forming more small clouds in front of his mouth with every breath.

As the trail curved toward the left, and they were in the most secluded part of the park, the lead agents slowed down and stopped. Harrison, totally confused, ripped his earbuds out. "What the heck?"

"Relax, sir, this will only take a second," said a new person who Harrison didn't recognize. The president was leaning over, hands on his hips, still confused. His breath slowed down but not enough to form full sentences just yet as his heart was still beating at the running pace he'd set. On the left of the individual talking was an attractive blond, and in front were an athletically built African American and a Hispanic man.

"Who the heck are you guys? And where the fuck are my agents?" asked Harrison.

"Ask him," said the African American, pointing to the older white individual walking toward them. The president squinted and, as the figure got closer and closer, the president recognized him.

"Jack Knowles?"

Jack was now within striking distance of the president, which is exactly what he did. A clean left hook across the face caused Harrison to double over. His body, in an attempt to try to catch a breath from the cold, in addition to the punch, almost put him on the ground. Almost.

"The next time you decide to send people after me, to kill me to fit your own agenda, it'll be more than a hook to the chin."

Harrison was startled. Rising up slowly and starting to catch his breath, he turned to face Jack. "What else could you want, Jack? David was fired and I already talked to Alexis. I'm not going to put myself on the ballet for reelection. What else is it you want?"

"We want you to know you're not untouchable and if we have to do this again, it'll be more than a quick sucker punch," said Jack. "You know we exist now, but we exist to serve the citizens, doing whatever it takes. You'll grant whatever request Alexis Moore has going forward, and when it comes time to leave the Oval Office, you'll erase all knowledge you have of the Bering Group. We don't exist once you leave the White House. Understood?"

Harrison looked at the five members circling him, breathing, panting, tired, and exhausted. "Fine. Now, get me my security detail."

Jack looked in the direction the team had run, then looked at his watch. As if on cue, four agents dressed similarly to those of the Bering Group were running toward them. "Get out of here," he said. With that, Jack walked back in the direction from which they'd come, and the Bering Group kept running forward. When the agents reached the president, they acted as if nothing was wrong. Harrison stood tall, frowned at all the agents, scoffed, and pointed back toward the vehicles. "I'm done running for today."

ACKNOWLEDGMENTS

I had no idea when I created my first novel, *Insertion*, I would have the support system that I did. My friends, family members, and people I've met during my book signings bring so much joy and excitement to me when I hear how much they loved reading my first novel.

When I write, although I don't know people in every field listed throughout the novel, I try and do as much research as possible to keep it as factual as it can be. Spending a month in Sri Lanka I had the pleasure of meeting and training with members of the Special Boat Squadron. They were some of the nicest and most professional people I've had the pleasure of working with.

Thank you to Kevin Ryan from New York Book Editors for finding time to edit my novel and giving me great feedback and constructive criticism. It was a long process but at the end of the day, everything was left on the table.